INSTINCT

Recent Titles by Nick Oldham from Severn House

BACKLASH
SUBSTANTIAL THREAT
DEAD HEAT
BIG CITY JACKS
PSYCHO ALLEY
CRITICAL THREAT
CRUNCH TIME
THE NOTHING JOB
SEIZURE
HIDDEN WITNESS
FACING JUSTICE
INSTINCT

INSTINCT

A Henry Christie Mystery

Nick Oldham

This first world edition published 2012
in Great Britain and in the USA by
SEVERN HOUSE PUBLISHERS LTD of
9–15 High Street, Sutton, Surrey, England, SM1 1DF.

British Library Cataloguing in Publication Data

Oldham, Nick, 1956–
  Instinct.
  1. Christie, Henry (Fictitious character) – Fiction.
  2. Police – England, North West – Fiction. 3. Detective and
  mystery stories.
  I. Title
  823.9'2-dc23

ISBN-13: 978-0-7278-8132-8 (cased)

All Severn House titles are printed on acid-free paper.

Severn House Publishers support The Forest Stewardship Council [FSC],
the leading international forest certification organisation. All our titles that
are printed on Greenpeace-approved FSC-certified paper carry the FSC logo.

Typeset by Palimpsest Book Production Ltd.,
Falkirk, Stirlingshire, Scotland.
Printed and bound in Great Britain by
MPG Books Ltd., Bodmin, Cornwall.

For Philip

ONE

Boone was sick of waiting. He took one last drag of his hand-rolled cigarette, inhaling the pungent smoke deep into his ravaged lungs, before exhaling with a death-watch beetle rasp, then flicked the minute butt over the side of the boat into the muddy river. It extinguished with a tiny '*phtt*'. A fish, believing it to be a fly on the surface, rose quickly and took it, but spat it out in disgust.

Boone hunched the collar of his battered flying jacket up around his ears and thumbed open the tobacco tin that contained another dozen or so pre-prepared filterless roll-ups. He selected one, closed the tin and tapped each end of the cigarette flat on the lid, and lit it with a disposable lighter. This was the fourth in the present chain.

As he blew out the smoke he tilted his head upwards and looked at the African sky which was becoming increasingly leaden. Thick black clouds moved ominously in from the west, laden with moisture, and the wind had started to build. Boone scowled as the first big spat of rain slapped on to his forehead.

He stepped under the cover provided by the cockpit of the sportfishing boat named *Shell* and turned to the man sitting uncomfortably on the bench seat. The man looked up at Boone through watery, yellow eyes.

'We need to get moving if we're going to make it,' Boone complained. 'I'll need to beat the weather out of the estuary.' He tapped his wristwatch to emphasize the point.

'He'll be here,' the man said. Set between his ankles was a briefcase that Boone glanced at, causing the man to react by sliding his feet closer together to trap the case more tightly.

'Don't worry,' Boone mocked, 'I won't nick it.' He checked the digital clock on the instrument panel and sighed impatiently. 'If we don't get out we could be trapped here for four days,' he warned the man. 'Big storm a-coming.'

'That cannot happen.'

Boone shrugged and sucked on his cigarette, already burned

down to his fingertips. His roll-ups didn't last long. 'I don't make the weather.' He paused. 'He knows where to come?'

'He knows,' said the man, who had introduced himself as Aleef.

Boone considered him and gave a 'whatever' shrug, then dropped down the tight steps into the galley where the kettle had started whistling on the single gas hob. He made himself a mug of strong tea, laced with a shot of Black Label. Now he could hear the rain hitting the boat's superstructure. Actually, the weather wasn't usually too much of a problem for Boone and his boat. At thirty-five feet long, *Shell* was a classic sportfishing craft, and although its length matched its age, it was still a formidable, trustworthy and well-designed boat, with a superbly balanced flying bridge, a functional galley and adequate sleeping accommodation. Rough seas and bad weather posed no problem for such a vessel.

Boone came back up into the cockpit bearing an extra mug of tea for Aleef, which was taken with gratitude, although he did sniff the brew suspiciously before taking a sip.

'No whiskey in it,' Boone confirmed. 'I know you lot don't like alcohol.'

'Very true.'

Boone nodded and walked to the outer cockpit door, leaning against the jamb to drink his coppery tasting brew. He watched the rain fall harder and looked down the road that ran by the creek where the boat was moored, near to Denton Bridge. It was eight p.m., still hot and humid, almost thirty degrees. Two other sportfishing boats were tied up on this creek just off the main Gambia River, but no one was aboard either vessel. They were owned by rich African businessmen, rarely seen in these parts. Boone was paid a retainer to keep an eye on them and see to their maintenance. Regular money, but not enough to keep him going.

He sighed, knowing he needed the money from this 'charter'. He took a sneaky glance at Aleef, the man who had approached him two weeks before in a seedy bar in Banjul, the country's capital, and put a proposition to him. Aleef had obviously done some homework on Boone prior to the meeting.

The approach and offer had been simple: two and a half thousand US dollars for a drop-off on Gran Canaria, then a pick-up three weeks later and a return to Banjul.

One package, no questions, simple return trip. Bread and butter.

Boone had swigged back the last of his drink, imported Dutch lager he'd become rather too fond of. Blinking at Aleef in the murky light of the riverside bar, he'd eased away a prostitute who'd been squirming around him most of the night, declaring her undying love for him, and had pushed his luck with Aleef by saying 'Four.'

It wasn't that he was flush and could manage without the money. Boone was constantly broke, always chasing the dollar or its sterling equivalent – but never the local currency that was as weak as water. He thought he could bargain with a man like Aleef – a man he had never met personally before that day, but someone he vaguely knew of as a shady entrepreneur. No doubt Aleef was acting on behalf of others – Boone had immediately pegged him as a middleman, a link in a complex chain just like Boone himself – and two-point-five G was simply the opening figure. If he couldn't get more out of him, then so be it, but he had to try. Business was business.

Boone didn't even ask the nature of the cargo, but knew it would obviously be a body, probably a crim, maybe a freedom fighter – someone else's terrorist – but Boone didn't care. It was the bottom line that interested him.

Aleef had shaken his head at Boone's preposterous response.

'Hey –' Boone had pointed at Aleef with the roll-up held between his nicotine-stained fingers – 'it means I go there and back, there and back. It's a long way and it costs, and even four big ones is a snip.'

'Mr Boone,' Aleef said patiently. 'I know what you do for a living. You deliver packages of all sorts up and down the coast. You purport to be a charter boat fisherman, but it's well known that your tourist business is, shall we say, virtually non-existent.'

'Not true.'

Aleef shrugged and gave Boone a withering look. A few beats of silence passed between the two men as they sized each other up. Boone, still over six feet tall, but his width now narrowing; Aleef, small and slim, of Asian origin, smart, dressed in a light summer suit, probably made by one of the tailors in Banjul; Boone, casually dressed in three-quarter length pants, tattered T-shirt and four days' growth on his face.

'Three-five,' Boone said, dropping the price. He knew he could actually make a decent profit on two and a half if he used the cut-price stolen fuel he had access to, but that wasn't the point. He had other jobs in the pipeline, even a few legitimate fishing charters, but he wasn't exactly rolling in it and needed every extra cent. This wasn't like the good old days of short crossings on a rigid inflatable and big bucks. They were long gone. Summer in the Gambia wasn't far away, the doldrum months – and he needed the cash to see him through. The cost of living was still pretty cheap out here, but booze and tobacco was rising all the time, as were the demands of his African wife to be.

Aleef considered this and said, 'Three. If you say no, I walk away and find someone else.'

'Yeah, but no one as honest and trustworthy as me,' Boone countered without a hint of irony, just complete sincerity. 'Three it is.'

And that was the deal made. Aleef dropped him five hundred dollars there and then, promised a thousand on the day, then the rest at the end of the final return – when 'the package' was brought back in one piece.

Boone disliked the terms, but the five hundred in Aleef's inner jacket pocket weakened him and made his eyes twinkle. He snatched the wad off him in mock disgust and quickly secreted it so none of the whores in the club would spot it and converge on him.

Aleef slid him a paper with a time and date scribbled on it and added, 'At your boat on Alligator Creek.' He slid off his barstool and seemed to disappear instantly into the crowd, while at the same moment the prostitute Boone had fended off earlier reappeared at his shoulder. Boone might have been quick to hide the wad of cash, but her eyes had been quicker in spotting it.

And now, here they were; at the appointed time, day, date and location, with the weather coming down fast. Boone wished he didn't have to go now, would have preferred to be in the bar flirting with the hookers before leaving at midnight to pick up his fiancée, Michelle, from the dancing club where she worked, sharing a late night curry, then curling up with her in the house-boat on the river.

But income had to be earned. Michelle's wages and tips were

nowhere near enough. His earnings were spasmodic and his capital was dwindling.

A pair of headlights turned on to the creek road, the car bouncing in the potholes.

Aleef rose quickly. 'He's here.'

'Only just in time,' Boone remarked.

Aleef crossed the gangplank to the wooden quayside as the vehicle arrived, splashing his white trousers as its wheels threw up a wave of muddy water from a puddle.

Boone leaned on the cockpit door, another roll-up dangling from the corner of his mouth, watching with interest.

The car was a big old Mercedes, fairly common in the Gambia. The driver and the front passenger got out – two tough looking black guys – and spoke hurriedly to Aleef who did plenty of nodding and displayed lots of submissive body language. Boone made out the dark profiles of two other men in the back seat of the Mercedes, catching the glint of their eyes in the light cast from the boat. Aleef pointed to Boone. The men glanced over, their faces expressionless. Then they shouldered their way past Aleef, stepped off the quay and boarded the boat, bringing mud from their shoes on to the pristine deck.

Boone, though annoyed by this, kept quiet, a condition encouraged by the handgun each of the men carried. They were heavy pistols, ugly, black and dangerous looking – rather like their owners, Boone thought.

The first man aboard said, 'We search.'

Boone shrugged, stepped aside. They went past him, down into the galley and stateroom, the toilet/shower, doing a sweeping and fairly cursory search. One lifted the engine cover, stuck his head down into the bowels of the boat, finding only a well-maintained Volvo diesel engine in there. Satisfied, they left the boat and went back to Aleef who was standing getting drenched in the rain as a heavy downpour came. His neat suit became misshapen and baggy. They exchanged a few more words, then one of them opened the rear door of the Mercedes and the two other men slid out.

Boone noticed that Aleef kept himself angled slightly away from these guys, eyes averted.

They came on board, the second one with an H&K machine pistol slung across his chest. The first man – who appeared to have Arabic features – walked straight past Boone, down into the stateroom, and closed the door behind him. The second man sat on the bench Aleef had been on a few moments earlier. He laid the H&K across his lap and regarded Boone stonily through creamy eyes.

Aleef stepped back on board.

Boone spun angrily at him. 'Two things here, Aleef,' he hissed. 'One – I don't allow guns on board, and, most importantly, two – the deal was for one passenger. *ONE.*' He reinforced the word by jerking his middle finger in front of Aleef's eyes. Truth was, the gun didn't bother him. Firearms were a fact of life in the way he made the bulk of his living – collecting and delivering packages dropped by ships from South America anchored in international waters just outside the Gambian national limits. But he did have an issue with numbers. Didn't like the change in odds.

The smaller man said, 'It's changed. Two will go and you'll bring him back.' Aleef indicated the lounging gunman.

Boone snorted. 'In that case the price has gone up. I'll do it, yeah, but it'll cost another grand.'

Aleef swung his briefcase on to the table next to the wheel, thumbed the combination and opened it slowly, slanting it away from Boone's inquisitive eyes. He handed over a stack of dollars. 'One thousand, as promised.' Then he gave him another stack, less heavy. 'Five hundred extra, and on the return pick-up run you'll receive another thousand.'

Boone snatched the money and tucked it under his jacket. Clearly these guys had dosh to spare, he thought, and said, 'You were expecting this, weren't you?' He sniggered.

'A man like you, Mr Boone, is very easy to second guess, something I factored into the equation. But you do need to know that you will not receive a penny more, nor,' Aleef added, 'should you even think about demanding more. That would be a very bad move on your part.'

'That suits.'

'May I also warn you not to engage in conversation with these men,' Aleef said. 'Speak only when spoken to. In fact, keep your distance, do your job and then forget the faces – am I clear?'

'Crystal.'

Aleef took a piece of paper out of the briefcase and unfolded it. 'You will be met at these coordinates just to the south of the Canary Islands and the package will be transferred. I take it you have the necessary electronic equipment on board to accomplish this.'

Boone took the paper and nodded.

'I shall see you when you return, then.' Aleef stepped off the boat and walked across to his own car on the quayside, a battered Citroën 2CV. The men who'd searched Boone's boat leaned impassively against the big Mercedes, guns hanging loosely by their sides.

Boone's mouth puckered unhappily as he turned to the wheel and pressed the starter, bringing the engines to life with a healthy burbling sound.

'Ready for off?' he asked the man on the bench. He got no response other than a half-lidded contemptuous look that brooked no conversation. Boone thought he would try anyway, despite Aleef's instructions to the contrary. He wasn't really someone who could not talk – unless he was banged up in a police cell – so he shrugged and turned his attention to the job at hand. Getting the human package from the Gambia to the Canary Islands, then bringing him back three weeks later. Straightforward and simple – with the exception of having an armed man on board, something difficult to explain should they run into the authorities. But that was something Boone was good at: slipping under the radar, keeping a low profile, so he wasn't too concerned on that count. Having a pretty nasty looking dude on board who looked as though he got a lot of pleasure drilling 9mm bullets into people was the bit he didn't like.

'Don't ask,' Boone said to himself. 'Just do it, keep your mouth shut, eyes closed, take the fucking money and run – and hope the bastard gets seasick and suffers.'

With that in mind, he released *Shell* from her moorings, gave the men ashore a cheery wave – got no response – and headed carefully out of the creek into the main river channel, hit the open sea, programmed his instruments and let the boat do the rest. Then he settled down for a long journey that promised to be rough.

TWO

The phone rang. It was two thirty in the morning. It continued to ring and even though the first ring didn't need to wake him, because he was already awake, Henry Christie did not reach across to the bedside cabinet to answer it. Then it stopped and the room returned to silence with just the faintest echo ebbing away. He lay there, the duvet halfway down his body, his upper half naked and chilled, eyes open, staring at the ceiling.

He knew it, or his mobile phone, would ring again. It had to because he was the only one available and they would keep trying until they contacted him, even if it meant sending someone round to knock him up. Part of him devilishly thought about taking it that far, but he knew he would answer next time. Henry did not like to keep people waiting, not where death was involved. Or as in this case, as he knew it would be, murder.

The call would be from the Force Incident Manager, the inspector based in the control room at police headquarters in Hutton, just to the south of Preston. All call-outs for Senior Investigating Officers – SIOs – were routed through the FIM, who held the rota for all disciplines, from public order to serious crime.

The bedroom was in darkness, a vague glow filtering in from the street light outside.

Henry's eyes were fixed open, staring upwards at the ceiling, his fingers interlaced across his sternum. He breathed shallowly, could feel the regular pumping of his heart and the occasional gurgle of his stomach as valves opened and closed and liquids gushed.

His mobile phone rang, as he had predicted. He had down-loaded the Rolling Stones' studio version of *Wild Horses* as his ringtone, a melancholy, emotional number that had fitted his mood at the time. Now, as brilliant as it was, it sounded stupid and needy, and he thought he might change it back to something more upbeat later. *Crazy Frog*, maybe. Something to make him smirk, not make his guts lurch. He *needed* to smirk.

His mobile lay next to his house phone and he fumbled for it with his right hand, the slight contortion and stretch hurting his mostly healed left shoulder, and answered it, mumbling something.

'Detective Superintendent Christie?' It was the voice of the FIM, a female inspector.

'Yuh.'

'Sorry to bother you, sir, but . . .'

Henry sat up stiffly, pushing the duvet back, taking the pad and pen from the cabinet top and jotting down the gist of what she was telling him: 'Murder . . . female . . . teenager . . . not yet identified . . . strangulation, maybe . . . Poulton-le-Fylde . . . near Carleton crematorium.' Henry wrote down the exact details of the location, the circumstances of the discovery of the body, asked if an arrest had been made – no – and if there was a suspect – not yet. Which detective was at the scene? After further questions, Henry ended the call with a time check – 2.38 a.m. – his thanks and an ETA.

He rubbed his eyes, making them squelch, then stood up and made his way to the en suite bathroom. There was a light knock on the bedroom door, which opened an inch.

'Dad? You OK?' It was his youngest daughter, Leanne, now twenty-three years old, so no longer young in that sense, and starting a career as a pharmacist. She had moved back home temporarily. To keep an eye on Henry had been the excuse, but the high cost of living and a bad on–off relationship made it seem to Henry that she was back for good. Whilst he loved her to bits, having her home again, mothering him, was not what he wanted or needed.

'Just a call-out.' He looked at her in her night things, still wearing jim-jams covered with bears cuddling each other. She was heartbreakingly beautiful, the spitting image of her mother. She moved into him and gave him a hug, asking if he wanted a brew doing.

He didn't, but she wanted to feel useful, so he said that would be great.

He had a very quick shower and a wet shave, timed to take only five minutes between them, and came out of the en suite with a towel wrapped around his waist. He was about to say something to Kate, his wife, purely out of conditioning. She often had some pithy remark about his turn-outs, something negative, usually funny. But Henry snapped his mouth shut. He hadn't got used to the fact she was no longer there and the sight of the empty bed made his chest jar sickeningly.

With anger he threw down the towel and entered the walk-in dressing room, shutting the door firmly behind him.

Henry actually enjoyed the mug of tea made for him by Leanne, even though he could only manage a few hasty mouthfuls before stepping out into the night, just before three. It was late spring, still chilly, making him shiver. He sniffed the air and smelled the sea two miles west of him. A good smell. If he found time he thought he would get down to the front and take a bracing stroll. It was a nice thought, but not very realistic. In his experience of turning out to murders at three in the morning, there was rarely any time for breaks in the day ahead. He would happily lay odds that he would be working till gone seven that night. Only sixteen hours away.

He had treated himself to a new car, thought he deserved it and the pleasure it gave him, even though its cost was crippling. A rare smile came to his face as he pointed the remote and unlocked it with a satisfying clunk. Then he climbed into his Mercedes E-Class coupé and reversed it carefully off the driveway.

There wasn't far to go. A few miles through the mainly bare streets of Blackpool, then out towards Poulton, cutting across the southern edge of that fairly affluent town to a small village called Carleton, making his way along narrow roads to the entrance to the crematorium, at which there was much police activity.

He purposely parked his car a couple of hundred metres away. Not just to ensure it didn't get scratched, but because he always liked to get the feel of a crime scene on foot. Too many detectives, he thought, rolled up and rolled out. If pressed he would probably struggle to provide concrete evidence that his considered approach ever proved fruitful, but he knew intuitively that good detectives liked to feel crime scenes. To inhale them. To taste them. It was maybe a way of getting somehow into the mind of a killer because crime locations often had some significance to either the killer or victim.

He hunched deep into his wind jammer, zipped it up, slotted his hands into the pockets, and approached slowly.

Henry had seen too many murder scenes like this one. The frail body discarded on a grass verge by the roadside. The tangle of thin limbs. The blood-soaked clothing. The battered face and head. Long hair splayed and matted with mud and blood. Eyes wide open. That last look of terror and disbelief on the face.

Henry had stepped into the zoot suit and paper shoes, the forensic overalls required of everyone attending the scene, logged in with the constable holding the clipboard down the road who was noting all comings and goings, then walked as directed on the chosen route that all officers had to take to the body and back.

He was standing perhaps six feet away from the body. His torch beam played over it from toe to head, then hovered on the girl's face.

She had been pretty and petite. Maybe sixteen, eighteen, he estimated. He glanced around at the location, the body next to the crematorium gates, trying to get his mind working.

The local detective inspector appeared at his shoulder. His name was Rik Dean, a man Henry knew well, not least because Rik was now living with Henry's feckless sister Lisa in a smart flat in Lytham. And because Henry had been instrumental in getting Rik on to CID years earlier as a detective constable. Henry had seen Rik's early potential to become a jack because as a PC in uniform Rik had been a superb thief-taker. Rik's subsequent rise through the ranks had been all his own doing – he was also a natural boss – and now Henry was trying to get Rik a place on FMIT – the Force Major Investigation Team – of which Henry was joint head with three other experienced detective superintendents.

'What've we got?' Henry asked.

'You probably know as much as me,' Rik replied. 'Body of a female teenager found by a uniformed PC on patrol. Thought it was fly-tipped rubbish, just a bundle of rags. On closer inspection turned out to be a body.'

'Which PC?'

Rik pointed him out, leaning on the bonnet of his unmarked patrol car. 'Paul Driver . . . a bit shaken by it.'

'What was he doing around here? A bit out of the way, isn't it?'

'Part of his normal route,' he said.

'Uh, huh,' Henry said. 'ID?'

'Not as yet, but there is a girl missing from Blackpool who fits the bill. A Natalie Philips, just turned eighteen, attends Shoreside College, doing a hairdressing NVQ. Reported missing by her mum last evening just gone, but had been missing a day before. I'm just waiting for the file to be brought up from Blackpool Comms, but . . .' Rik produced his BlackBerry, 'I got them to e-mail me a photo of her.' He pressed a few buttons and turned the screen around for Henry to see. A pretty young lady pouting at the photographer. 'Looks like her.'

Henry nodded, his face tightening. Something strange was churning inside him, making everything wrench up. His stomach was getting the cramps, and his chest seemed to be contracting around his heart, squeezing it. His legs felt abruptly weak.

A look must have come across his face.

Rik said, 'Henry, are you all right?'

The feelings dissipated as he breathed in and out slowly.

'Yeah, yeah.'

Rik laid a steadying hand on Henry's arm. 'You sure? You don't look it.'

'Hundred percent.'

'I know it's early days . . .'

'I said I'm sure,' Henry snapped. Rik, a hurt expression on his face, pulled his hand away. 'Sorry,' Henry said. 'Let me look at the body before the circus moves in, please.' He wondered just what the hell he'd felt inside him. Whatever it was, it was extremely unpleasant.

Then, as his torchlight played over the dead body, the sensations started again. His whole torso felt like it was in a vice, legs weak and rubbery; a deep bass pounded in his head as if a hand was inside his skull squeezing and releasing his brain; then dizziness and a roaring sound in his ears, and all he could hear was the rushing of the waves . . .

He had no recollection whatsoever of how he ended up in Rik Dean's office at Blackpool police station. Just a series of blurred images, a sensation of car travel, lamp posts hurtling by, his head spinning, someone else's hands firmly gripping him, while he tried to breathe normally, regulate his oxygen intake, steady his whole being.

The door opened. Rik Dean entered, holding two mugs of tea, one of which he handed to Henry, who was frowning.

'I know it sounds a stupid question – but what am I doing here?'

Rik sat down next to him on the small two-seater settee. 'In my office, you mean?'

'Uh – yeah.'

'I think you had a panic attack.'

'What!' Henry almost spilled his drink, which was halfway to his mouth.

'I might be wrong, but you sort of froze, then started gulping air and clutching your head, hyperventilating or something.'

'I what?'

'It was really weird. Then you said, "I don't know what to do".'

Henry's frown deepened. He recalled looking at the girl's body – then basically nothing. Other than the unpleasant sensation that felt like he was on a drug-induced trip, not that he'd ever been on one to make such a comparison. He guessed that was what they were like. 'It all went kinda strange,' he admitted.

'Panic attack,' Rik confirmed knowledgeably. 'People under stress, people who've suffered personal loss . . . it happens.'

'I don't have panic attacks,' Henry said, affronted.

Rik shrugged. 'Well, maybe not, but you weren't yourself. Something came over you and affected you, so I made the decision to get you away for your own good.'

'For my own good?' Henry blasted him. 'I'm not a child.' He stood up quickly, started pacing around the room. Still not right. As if he wasn't quite there. Rik studied him warily.

'I suggested taking you home, but you wouldn't have it – nor the hospital.'

Henry stopped abruptly. 'We had *that* conversation?' Rik nodded. 'I don't remember that at all.'

'Henry – it's only been two months.'

He stopped mid-prowl, glared at Rik, daring him to say more, to patronize him, but Henry's expression did not stop Rik from continuing.

'You've hardly taken time off, have kept going. This is the

third murder you've overseen in that time, plus dealing with all the shitty fallout from that nightmare up in Kendleton which still rumbles on. Maybe you need to stop, hop off the world and take a breather. Maybe it's all catching up with you now.' Rik blew out his cheeks. 'You just keep going . . . I know what you're doing – compartmentalizing, boxing things off. Perhaps the walls are starting to cave in, Henry.'

'You a shrink now?' Henry asked harshly.

'No – a mate,' Rik said gently. 'With all the things that go with that little word.'

Dawn came. Henry found himself on the promenade, not planning a long walk, just something to clear his head. The air tasted pure, a hint of sea salt in it, and he inhaled deeply, feeling it passing sweetly into his lungs as they expanded.

He had walked from the police station up to North Pier, then started to stroll south towards Central Pier, continually casting his eyes west across the silver shimmer of the Irish Sea, which seemed a mile away, the beach that lay between golden and pristine. No hint of the constant pollution that dogged the sands.

He stopped for a short while at the sea wall, gripping the rail. The sun was rising at his back and he could feel its warmth.

It should be raining, he said to himself. It shouldn't be a beautiful day.

He pushed himself away from the rail and continued his short walk south, able to see the snake-like metallic structure that was the 'Big One' a mile away on the pleasure beach, one of Europe's most terrifying roller-coaster rides. When he reached Central Pier he crossed over to the twenty-four-hour McDonald's and bought himself a filter coffee, taking it to a window seat in the otherwise empty restaurant, famous for once having been visited by Bill Clinton.

The coffee, he found, was actually excellent. He marvelled at how coffee had sustained him, kept him going, gave him energy over the years. His constant companion. That and Jack Daniel's Tennessee sour mash whiskey.

He was flicking his fingernails together, thinking about how ironic it was that he had ended up on the seafront after all, when he became aware of someone standing by his table. He hadn't seen the approach or noticed anyone come into the restaurant.

He looked slowly around, his eyes rising up the torso of a man who was grinning lopsidedly at him. A good-looking guy, very tall, built in proportion, with an all-American chiselled superhero face and a boyish innocent aura that fooled many people, because this man had a very dark side to him.

'What are you doing here?' Henry asked.

The man's name was Karl Donaldson. He had been Henry's good friend for over a dozen years now. He was an American, formerly an FBI field agent, now comfortably ensconced in the American Embassy in London working as an FBI legal attaché, though he still liked to think of himself as 'active'. They'd met way back when Donaldson had been investigating American mob activity in the north-west of England. They had subsequently become good friends as their paths continued to pass professionally and personally over the years. Donaldson had even ended up marrying a Lancashire policewoman, and he moved to the job in London, whilst she transferred to the Met.

'Could ask you the same.'

'I work and live in this town. You don't even live close.'

Donaldson said, 'I do now – for today, at least.' He checked his wristwatch, a chunky and horribly expensive Rolex Oyster Perpetual that his wife Karen had treated him to on the recent birth of their daughter, Katie – named after Henry's wife. 'I've got a half hour, then I need to get into a briefing . . . I'll explain in a moment. More coffee?'

Henry nodded and watched his friend go to the counter and order two coffees, returning with them and sliding in opposite Henry.

'Hey, good to see ya, buddy,' Donaldson said.

'You too.' Henry broke the hinged seal on the lid of his drink and took a sip. 'You must be here on some sort of hush-hush job?'

'Terrorism – following up some information with a house raid. Pretty low level stuff.'

Henry pouted. He hadn't heard anything was going on, but that wasn't unusual these days as his head often felt like it was in a bucket.

'Can't say more than that,' Donaldson added mysteriously.

Henry shrugged acceptance and found himself to be curiously uninterested. He knew Donaldson was deeply involved in the handling, sifting and grading of intelligence in connection with terrorism during the course of his work. From that he often got involved, as an observer, in the knocking down of doors, or surveillance of suspects and then, if arrests followed, the interviews of detainees to gather more intelligence. It was like doing a ten thousand piece jigsaw that was mostly blue sky, no corners and pieces missing. The ultimate aim was to disrupt 'events', as terrorist incidents were called, and maybe, just maybe, pick up that one vital clue that would lead the Americans to their ultimate goal – one Osama Bin Laden, the leader of al-Qaeda. In respect of today's operation, Henry did not have a clue about it, but assumed that the Intel must be pretty spot on to lure Donaldson out of his plush office.

'How did you know . . .?'

'That you were here? Bumped into Rik Dean . . . he told me where you'd sneaked off to and I watched you walk in. Last time we were in here was the day I found out Karen was "up the duff", as you Brits romantically refer to being knocked up.'

'I remember,' Henry grinned.

'Rik told me about . . . er . . .' Donaldson coughed with embarrassment.

'That I'd frozen at the scene of a murder?' Henry said sharply. 'Had a shed collapse?'

'Another quaint British phrase,' Donaldson said. 'But, yeah, something like that.'

Henry laughed sourly and shook his head at Donaldson's forthrightness, then looked sideways through the window to hide the bitter kink on his lips. Then he sighed in defeat, peeled the lid completely off his coffee and took a proper mouthful. 'So what's your advice?'

Donaldson had been very much alongside Henry over the last year or so as he crashed through an emotional roller-coaster ride, rather like being on the 'Big One' time and time again, so he knew what his friend had been through. Hope, despair, tragedy. It was only in the last few weeks that Donaldson, at Henry's insistence, had backed off and given him his own space.

'What's the job?' Donaldson asked.

Henry drew a breath. 'One likely to attract lots of attention and scrutiny. Minute fucking scrutiny. Female teenager murdered, something the press will love to bits . . . and I guess I'm not up to it.' He shrugged pitifully and swallowed something hard and sour tasting at the admission.

'Why do you say that?'

'Just feel I've lost all my drive, my rhyme and reason. I typed out my intention to retire report yesterday, you know? Three lines and a date. Just waiting to be printed off and submitted.'

'That what you want?' Donaldson lounged back and watched Henry grapple with the question.

'I have no idea what I want.'

'Let me ask you another question. What were you put on this earth to do?'

Henry knew the answer, but fought the response.

'But more importantly, H,' Donaldson said, 'let me tab back to the previous question and ask not what you want, but what would Kate have wanted you to do?'

Donaldson had gone. Henry was alone again, swirling the dregs of his coffee, watching the grains as though they might give him inspiration, like reading tea leaves. Nothing. He refitted the plastic lid and put the cup in the bin before leaving the restaurant and stepping back into the clear, warm morning.

He crossed the prom and retraced his earlier walk, not so quiet now as the day came to life and people and traffic began to move. He walked up to North Pier, Blackpool Tower on his right, but his gaze was drawn across to the north-west, where the hills of the Lake District were etched clearly on the horizon. It was a place Kate had loved and where Henry, following her wishes, had scattered her ashes.

Everything had happened so quickly, no preamble, no warning. Henry, emerging from a very bad situation in the village of Kendleton, having been shot in the left shoulder – not seriously, as it happened – then had to deal with the detritus that included police corruption and multiple murder, including the death of a policewoman. He had been overwhelmed with the paperwork and interviews and inquests and trials and the CPS and the forensics and the press. The list seemed endless. His mind was completely waterlogged with tasks and it had been a month later, during a breather from the mountain of statements he'd brought home to read that, seemingly, for the first time in weeks, he'd looked at Kate and thought, 'She looks as whacked as me.'

Her words in response to his enquiry had been simple and uncomplicated. 'Henry, I need to tell you something.'

He put down his highlighter pen, saw the tear emerge from her right eye and tumble down her face, and that night he held her tightly as they both cried in each other's arms.

It was a lump in her left breast. Though they acted quickly and decisively, the cancer could not be halted, spreading aggressively through her body. They fought, she fought, but then reached a point when she looked exhaustedly with half-blind watery eyes at Henry and he knew it was over. It had won. She had lost and her final weeks were a mixture of ecstasy, agony, happiness and hopelessness, but above all dignity and love.

The last month of her life was spent in a hospice where the speed of deterioration was terrifying.

And Henry held her as she died quietly.

Now, Henry looked out to the Lakes, his mind whirling with all of those images. He had immersed himself in work for the last two months, even though his heart was not in it. He had thought this was the best way to tackle things. But it always felt as though he was running ahead of something that was coming up from behind with the intention of smothering him. He always knew it would catch up and maybe that morning it had.

The opening chords of *Wild Horses* interrupted his reverie. He took his phone out and saw it was Rik Dean calling.

Henry had a quick thought. He knew exactly what Kate would want him to do. He also knew what he had to do. He had to stop running – and he also had to find a killer. Because that was what he had been put on this earth to do. And because there was a young girl lying dead on a grass verge and a family who needed him to do his job.

He thumbed the answer button and put the phone to his ear.

THREE

Henry threaded his way through the narrow corridors of Blackpool nick. They seemed fit to bursting with staff, unusual for such an early hour, but he could tell they had been brought in for whatever the operation was that Donaldson was part of. There were firearms officers, already tooled up, support unit officers, normal patrol officers, a dog handler – minus dog – and various ranks from sergeant to superintendent, as well as several plain clothes officers and some shady looking individuals Henry did not recognize. He assumed they were spooks from MI5, MI6, SIS and various other clandestine agencies.

There was a scramble for the lift as the briefing was being held on the fourth floor. Henry eased his way though the throng to get through to the CID office which was in the ground floor annexe.

As he stepped through to the large foyer that had once been the main entrance to the police station – the entrance having now been relocated more practically to street level on the other side of the building to allow easier public access – Henry came face to face with four men entering through the old front door. They had walked across from the police-owned level of the multi-storey car park adjacent to the station.

He recognized three of the men, the fourth he did not know at all.

One of the three was Robert Fanshaw-Bayley, Lancashire's chief constable – known as FB – someone Henry had grown to know all too well over the years; with him was PC Bill Robbins, a firearms trainer who also specialized in putting together any firearms aspects to operational orders. The third man he recognized was a guy called Martin Beckham, and seeing him confirmed Henry's suspicions that spooks were out and about. Beckham was a mysterious shadow of a man and Henry had encountered him a couple of times in the past. He was usually introduced as being from the Home Office. That may have been true, but Henry knew he was also a high ranking spymaster.

As the men came brusquely through the door, they were heads-down focused on some paperwork being shuffled between them, and they spoke in hushed, hurried tones, not even noticing Henry who, gallantly, held the door open for these clearly very important persons so they could get into the innards of the police station. He refrained from bowing.

Only Bill Robbins glanced up, surprised to see Henry, as they fell into single file to pass through, with Bill bringing up the rear.

'Henry,' he said, looking slightly guilty.

'Bill. How goes it?'

Bill stopped, but the other three went on and stopped at the lift, shouldering their way to the front of the queue.

Henry and Bill also went back a long way. In the recent past Henry had used the firearms officer on various investigations and tried to get him a role on FMIT, but the chief was having none of it. Bill did get a temporary role on the branch after his involvement in a shooting where it was quickly established that he had acted reasonably in the circumstances. He had then returned to firearms training, but had stayed in the classroom ever since, as well as advising on firearms operations.

'I'm good, Henry. You?'

'Poor to fair,' Henry said. He saw the lift doors opening and it was only then that FB came out of a deep confab with Beckham and the other man, and realized it was Henry who'd held the door open for them. FB mumbled something to the two men, who stepped into the lift and held the doors open, and came over to Henry, who noticed that the chief had become even porkier than usual.

'Henry – didn't see you there,' he said unapologetically. FB rarely acknowledged lackeys at the best of times, unless he was on a mission. 'Head down, concentrating,' he added. 'Anyway, how are you doing?'

He gave the chief the answer he wanted to hear. 'Brilliant.'

'I'm glad. Can't let a thing like that affect you too much. Anyway, got to go – big op this morning, all hush-hush. You know how it is.' He patted Henry's shoulder like he was a pet, jerked his head at Bill for him to get a move on, then joined his colleagues in the waiting lift.

Dumbfounded by the crass lack of anything – sympathy,

empathy, whatever – Henry silently mouthed a couple of choice swear words in the chief's direction which expanded the two letter acronym, FB. Shaking his head and laughing mirthlessly to himself, wondering why he had expected anything more from the guy who hadn't even sent a sympathy card after Kate's death, Henry allowed the door to close then walked across the foyer to the CID office.

Karl Donaldson took up a position at the rear of the briefing room, lounging against the wall and watching proceedings with a slight air of detachment. This was because he wasn't truly involved in the events planned for that day and was only here because he'd picked up a whisper and demanded to be allowed into the action.

In truth, he was extremely annoyed by the course of events, but at the same time he understood that occasionally there were lapses in communication between agencies. People, after all, were only human.

He spent much of his time filtering through intelligence, particularly concerning terrorism and following suspects, sometimes physically, but more often via bank and credit card databases and CCTV images from cameras in airports, ports and train stations. Or listening over and over to intercepted, crackly cell phone conversations between people who might be involved in terrorism. And much, much more besides. And then, if there was anything that might be of use to secret services or police forces in Europe, he would pass on what he had learned, after it had been sanitized. In return he expected the same consideration, but sometimes there were blips. Usually by mistake, but occasionally on purpose, because Donaldson knew that the sharing of information between agencies was still a relatively new concept and the old adage 'knowledge is power' still held sway in some quarters.

He would have very much liked to have been informed that Lancashire Constabulary were running a CT – counter terrorism – operation that morning when they expected to make arrests, rather than find out through a back door and have to get fractious with people. He hated discovering such things by mistake. He felt he should have been told days, maybe weeks ago that the cops were moving in on some suspected terrorists. Not found

out purely through an illicit conversation the day before with a
lady called Edina Marchmaine, who worked for a shady department in Whitehall. Donaldson had met her during a multi-agency
manhunt for a wanted terrorist a few years earlier, struck up a
rapport with her that had continued. She fed him occasional titbits
of information, none of it necessarily earth shattering, but just
the occasional juicy one that she thought he should know about
– without breaking the Official Secrets Act.

Donaldson knew the relationship had certain hazards – especially for her – but as an intelligence analyst he was reluctant to
cut out any source of useful information that might come his
way.

'Gentlemen . . . ladies . . . others,' the chief constable said,
bringing the briefing to order as he took to the slightly raised
stage at the end of the room. The hubbub settled quickly, a few
chairs scraped, some coffee slurping could be heard and the
munching of bacon sandwiches, the provision of which Donaldson
found somewhat ironic given the nature of today's targets. FB
went on, 'Thank you all for coming. I apologize about the short
notice of this, but as you'll understand, operations like this sometimes cannot be planned over long periods of time owing to their
very nature. So, without further ado, please let me introduce Mr
Martin Beckham from the Home Office, who will give you a
brief overview, then we'll get down to tactics and get you out
there.'

The very well turned out and groomed Martin Beckham stepped
on to the stage, adjusting his wire-framed spectacles, reminding
Donaldson of an SS torturer. He was a soft looking man, slightly
pudgy around the edges but with a core of ice.

He focused his attention on the briefing as surveillance shots
of two young Asian men were projected on to the screen behind
Beckham and the room lights were dimmed.

In the ground floor annexe, Henry was talking to Rik Dean about
the murder of a teenage girl who, it was almost certain, was
called Natalie Philips and who had been reported as missing
from home by her mother the night before. Rik had compared
the clothing the dead girl was wearing with the clothes Natalie's
mother had described her as wearing when she last saw her. It
matched. He also compared a photo he'd taken on his phone

with the actual Missing From Home file photo, the one that had been texted to him at the scene. They were identical.

'Based on what we know – that's her,' Rik told Henry. 'Without a formal ID, DNA and/or dental check, of course.'

'What's the full story?' Henry asked. He took the MFH report from Rik's fingers and skim read it whilst listening.

'Bust-up with mum over usual crap: boyfriends, home times, college work. Two nights ago she sneaks out during the soaps, it's believed, and she's not there at bedtime.'

'What did the mother do about it?'

'Nothing on that night. She's been out overnight plenty of times, so it wasn't really an issue. She is eighteen, so the mum only got anxious when she didn't come home after college next day. Then she called us.'

'Then what was done?'

Rik shifted slightly uncomfortably. 'Er . . . details taken but not circulated. As I said, she'd been out before.'

'Right,' Henry said, unimpressed.

'Mm – and it wasn't until she didn't land at college yesterday morning, then didn't come home for tea last night, or make contact with mum, that she was reported missing formally.'

'Circulated by us, you mean?'

Rik nodded. Henry counted back on his fingers. 'So we have a very wide window when Natalie's unaccounted for? When no one did anything.'

'Hindsight,' Rik said defensively.

Henry exhaled tiredly. 'Which never goes down as a brilliant argument in front of the media or a coroner or a Crown Court judge.'

He then realized he was being patronizing when Rik said, 'Thanks for that, boss.'

'Pleasure. Has the Home Office pathologist turned up yet?'

'At the scene,' Rik confirmed.

'Shall we head back there?'

Rik hesitated and looked uncertainly at Henry.

'What?' Henry said.

'Are you . . . er . . .'

'I'm OK, Rik. Just a minor blip on the recovery chart. Probably happen from time to time and I thank you for what you did.'

'Hey – it's OK. We could end up as family. We need to stick together and all that.'

'God forbid,' Henry muttered, causing Rik to jolt. 'Just kidding.' He shooed Rik out of the CID office ahead of him so he couldn't see the expression of alarm on his face. There was every chance Rik could become Henry's brother in law as, confounding all predictions, Rik and Henry's sister – two people who, historically, jumped into bed with virtually anyone of the opposite sex – seemed to be very settled. And now they had got engaged, much to Henry's shock, and happiness, of course.

Having been briefed the officers filed out to commence their allocated duties.

Karl Donaldson, seething, pushed himself off the back wall and weaved through the exiting bodies to the stage on which the taskmasters, FB, Beckham, a uniformed chief superintendent and another man, had clustered for a heads-together. Donaldson nodded at Bill Robbins, a man he'd known for some while now, who was leaving the room grim-faced.

Donaldson stood in front of the stage, folded his arms and waited for the gaggle of the high and mighty to break up. FB happened to spot him out of the corner of his eye. Beckham also glanced over and acknowledged him.

'I see you managed to get here,' Beckham remarked.

Donaldson nodded – an early hours' trip up the motorway had been how. Now he was tired and angry.

'You're more than welcome to accompany us to the dining room for some breakfast,' Beckham said. 'It's just a matter of waiting now to see what transpires.'

FB didn't look overkeen on Beckham's invitation. He and Donaldson went back a lot of years and they had never quite seen eye to eye, although they had forged a grudging respect for each other. But not enough for FB to want to sit down and break bread with the American.

'I'll pass,' Donaldson said. He saw the relief on FB's chubby face.

Beckham noticed Donaldson's troubled expression. 'Is there something else?'

'I'd like to speak to you.'

'Mm, not now. In due course.'

'Now.'

'OK – go ahead,' he relented easily.

'In private.'

'Oh, it's not about this intelligence sharing business, is it?' Beckham breathed with irritation.

'More fundamental than that.'

'What then? You can speak freely – there's no one else here but us.'

'OK, it's about basic officer safety.'

'What do you mean by that?'

'This – this briefing,' Donaldson said, his arms flying out in opposite directions, a gesture of exasperation.

'What about it?' Beckham said defensively.

'You haven't really told the officers everything, have you?'

FB shot a troubled look at Beckham, who said, 'They know what they need to know.'

'Oh?' Behind Beckham the screen still showed the two faces of the men who were that morning's targets. 'Don't you think a little more enlightenment would have been prudent?'

Beckham's eyes hooded over as though he was drawing a veil of secrecy. 'In what way?'

'Maybe you shoulda filled in the blanks for these guys and gals who're going out there this morning. One of the reasons I trailed up the motorway in the early hours was because I spent six hours yesterday afternoon digging—'

Beckham gave a short jerk of his right hand, an axe-chopping movement. 'That's enough, Mr Donaldson. Please do not interfere in operational matters that don't concern you,' he warned. 'I invited you up here as a courtesy due to an oversight, so please remain an observer.' He was clearly rattled.

FB picked up on it. 'What do you mean?' It was a question directed at both men.

Beckham took a step towards Donaldson, a steely glint in his eyes. The chief superintendent and FB exchanged worried looks. The other unknown man on the stage remained impassive.

'I advise you to keep your thoughts to yourself,' the Home Office man hissed threateningly.

Donaldson sneered, but he put up his hands in defeat. 'OK, look, I can see this is a glory bust and I don't have any problems with that. We all want to be hogs in shit and I'm not bitter about being left out of the loop. It happens,' he said philosophically. Then he leaned into Beckham's face. 'But not at the expense of innocent men and women who have to do your dirty work for you.'

FB stepped in. 'What does he mean, Martin?'

Beckham zoned-out Fanshaw-Bayley. 'They are well protected. They are armed and they have body armour, and they know what they're doing.'

'That may be the case – up to a point. What they don't know, what's not been fully explained, is who they're dealing with.' He jabbed his forefinger at the mug shots on the screen.

'What? Two low level extremists – no more than boys with possible delusions of greatness – who might possibly lead us on to real players.'

'Don't you mean two previously low level extremists who have just returned from training camps in Yemen? Who probably now have the ability to make sophisticated bombs and handle firearms, and who might just be brainwashed into believing that a whole bevy of belly dancing virgins awaits them on the other side? These guys could be suicide bombers – and you seem to have neglected to mention that fact.'

'That is only your speculation.'

Donaldson laughed harshly and he and Beckham glared at each other.

'There is nothing to support that view,' Beckham said.

'Maybe not, but if I was being asked to arrest them, I'd sure as hell like to know of the possibility, however distant.'

'We don't want to cause panic.'

Now Donaldson screwed up his face and shook his head.

FB made a snap decision. 'Get everyone back in here,' he said to the chief superintendent. 'They need to know exactly what they're up against.' He gave Beckham a look of contempt.

'B–but they've all gone out,' the chief superintendent said.

'Well fucking well get them back in again,' FB said. He glared at Beckham. 'And you think of something to say.'

The second briefing was much shorter. Beckham bluffed his way through it by saying that new information had just come to light literally in the last few minutes. Even then, he managed to gloss over the intelligence and basically reinforced the warning to any officers that might come face to face with either of the targets, whilst playing down the suicide bomber angle. Donaldson learned that Beckham was very much a man who understated everything.

They filed out a little more muted than previously. When the last one had gone, Beckham looked acidly across at Donaldson and said petulantly, 'That better?'

Donaldson shrugged.

Beckham said, 'Please refer to a previous conversation we had about your sources, incidentally. It's something I shall be actively pursuing on my return to London. Obviously we have a leak that needs to be plugged.'

Bill Robbins, the firearms PC, re-entered the briefing room to gather some paperwork he'd left behind. Donaldson spotted him and had an idea, then trotted out behind Bill, not giving Beckham any response to the threat.

'Bill – hi,' Donaldson said, catching up with Robbins.

'Karl, how's it going?' Bill was striding purposefully along the corridor.

'I'm good. You?'

'Well, back on firearms training, which is a step in the right direction,' he answered, turning into the stairwell.

'That's great news – but we still have the inquests to come?'

'Yes, but I'm not worried.' He started down the concrete steps, Donaldson at his heels. 'Henry's been fantastic and the force has been OK-ish. I was justified in what I did, so I'm not losing sleep, other than worrying about my aim.'

'You were superb actually – hey, what's your role today?'

'Do you mean on this half-baked operation?' he said, still talking over his shoulder as both men descended the stairs. 'Oops – hope I haven't said anything out of place?'

'Not as far as I'm concerned. You saw through it?'

'Always a cynic where the security services are concerned. They're crap and they never tell you the truth.'

'Amen to that,' Donaldson said, proud of his status as a law enforcement officer, which seemed so much higher a calling. 'So what is your role?'

'Just roving quality control, ensuring everyone knows their jobs, keeps on the plot. Welfare, that sort of thing.' They had reached the lower ground floor on which the custody office and garages were situated.

'Erm, any chance of tagging along with you today?'

'Not a problem as far as I'm concerned.'

'As I'm supposed to be here as an observer,' Donaldson said, 'I'll ride shotgun.'

FOUR

They returned to the murder scene in Henry's Mercedes, in which Rik had driven him to the police station in the course of the panic attack, or whatever it was that Henry had suffered. Rik coveted the coupé but Henry, a bit meanly, had always denied him the opportunity of driving it. Henry therefore suspected that Rik had seized on the chance when his brain had gone into free-fall.

Back at the crematorium, the mechanics of running a murder scene were well underway. The road past the cemetery was sealed off other than for essential traffic, and a diversion put in place. The scientific support vehicles were there, as were several paper-suited and booted individuals carrying out their tasks. Henry parked up in much the same place as on his first visit, this time drawing up behind a beautifully restored E-Type Jaguar that made him smile a little. He knew who owned it.

A little away, leaning on an unmarked police car, was PC Driver, the officer who had found the girl's body on his travels. He was drinking coffee, looking forlorn. Henry walked across to him.

'Are you OK?'

The officer, a man in his mid-forties, shook his head. 'No, boss, still can't get over it.' His left hand massaged his neck continually in a motion that Henry associated with shock.

'No – not your usual occurrence in Poulton.' Henry gave him a wan smile. 'Why don't you get yourself home? You've done a good job here, no need to stay on.'

'Thanks. I'll just get my statement done, first.'

'OK, do what suits.'

Henry and Rik were logged back on to the scene, clambered into new paper suits, ducked under the tape and approached the ten foot high screen that had been erected around the body to keep out prying eyes. A tent was due shortly.

During the journey Rik had batted about a few ideas about what might have happened to the girl. Henry had tried to concentrate on what he was saying because he didn't want another brain-freeze attack. He began planning his investigative strategy so as not to lose track. He'd stuck to the formula many times before so it was imprinted in his grey matter – under normal circumstances, that was.

Henry parted a gap in the screen like he was stepping through stage curtains, but in front of him was the scene of a real tragic death, not some country house murder with men in tennis shorts, ladies in twinsets and pearls, and dour mustachioed detectives solving the crime, often without evidence.

There was, however, the stereotypical comic character to lighten proceedings, who, at that moment, was on his haunches, down by the side of the girl's head, his back to Henry and Rik, instantly recognizable by the large ears sticking out at right angles from his narrow head. Henry walked up behind him and cleared his throat.

The man did not react. He was focused, his latex-gloved hands touching the side of the victim's head, talking softly into a microphone fastened to his head, the recording being made digitally on a machine in his shirt pocket. This was the owner of the E-Type Jaguar.

Henry coughed again.

Still the man did not turn round, but instead said patiently, 'Henry, I know it's you. If you don't mind, I'll just finish off what I'm doing, then I'll be right with you.'

Henry grinned at the admonishment, slid his hands into his pockets – by sliding them through the gaping holes in the sides of the zoot suit – and let his eyes wander around the scene.

Although the crematorium was on the outskirts of Poulton, it was rural and quite isolated, certainly not overlooked. The girl's body had obviously been dumped here from a car, and as there was nothing overlooking the gates, that deed could easily have been carried out unobserved. Making things much more difficult in terms of finding witnesses.

The man with the ears stood upright and turned slowly to Henry as though a huge wing nut was being twisted.

'Hello Doctor-Professor,' Henry smiled.

'Henry Christie! My God, feels like years since we met over a dead body.' Professor Baines, the Home Office pathologist, beamed at Henry. The two men had known each other for many years and developed a good relationship, often cemented by a trip to a local hostelry following a messy post-mortem in order to discuss the case informally. And, usually, to pass comments on ladies. Baines was the Home Office pathologist for the area, but over the last couple of years, because of other work, stand-ins had covered for him. Henry was relieved it was Baines today, though. Locums were OK, but they sometimes came with their own peculiar problems. Baines thrust out a bony hand to shake Henry's and Henry noticed, not for the first time, how narrow Baines's body was, accentuating the effect of the ears.

'Good to see you back at the sharp end,' Henry said, as they shook. 'I hear you've managed to wangle yourself an OBE. Services to teeth, or something.'

'Services to dental pathology,' Baines corrected him. He specialized in teeth and had built up a database over the years of all things connected to teeth, including the various methods dentists from all over the world used to carry out their work. This was all with a view to help identify dead people. He had been particularly busy in Central Africa as well as Bosnia, where mass graves were still being dug up to this day. It just wasn't news any more.

'Well, congratulations. Did you meet the Queen when you got your gong?'

'Nah, some royal lackey or other. Guy called Charles. Had ears like mine.'

'Ah, a minor royal.'

'And you,' Baines said, moving closer to Henry. 'I heard about Kate. I'm truly sorry.'

'Thank you.'

'However,' Baines said, standing back, 'it frees you to work the field again, eh?'

Henry blinked, then smiled. 'Y'know, I think I needed someone to say something like that to me.'

'Henry, if I can but help,' Baines said solemnly.

'Yeah – you're a great counsellor.' Baines had always been intrigued by Henry's often convoluted love life and had been severely disappointed when he'd remarried Kate and it had ground to a halt. 'However,' Henry said, 'back to more pressing matters.'

'Ah, yes, this young lady.'

'What can you tell me?'

Baines pursed his lips. 'Dumped here from a car. Beaten about the face, but looks like strangulation, could be with a scarf judging from the indentations in her skin. I'll have a clearer idea later, obviously. Female, sixteen to nineteen years, white, well nourished . . . sad.'

'Time of death?'

'Hmm, always a bit of a finger in the wind at the scene, but I'd say she's been here about six or seven hours. Could have been killed up to seven hours before that.'

Henry totted up the figures. 'So, maybe dumped here around midnight and murdered sometime between six p.m. and then?'

Baines shrugged. 'Best guess at the moment. More conclusive tests at the PM.'

'Fair enough. Are you available to carry that out today?'

'Yes.' Baines glanced around. 'Based on what I still have to do here . . . three o'clock this afternoon OK?'

'Splendid.' Henry turned to Rik, who had listened to the conversation and said, 'Mother?' Rik nodded. 'Then we pull a team together.'

'What was all that about?' Bill Robbins threw the unmarked Vauxhall Insignia around the streets of Blackpool north.

'All what?' Donaldson gripped the hinged handle above the passenger door.

'I half-heard something between you and that Beckham guy. I was lurking,' he explained.

'Interdepartmental rivalry, I guess. Which I don't mind in the least, but not at the expense of safety.'

'You mean the added-on bit.'

'Yep – but even then you weren't told everything.'

'Nature of the beast,' Robbins said. 'We accept it to a degree. It's the way spooks operate. Anyway, how come you've turned up for this charade? Us arresting a couple of would-be terrorists on what appears to be a purely speculative basis – uh, nothing new there – seems pretty low down the ladder for a guy like you.

I thought you went after the bigwigs? Like the man himself, old OBL, cave dweller.' He glanced sideways.

'Ahh, briefings,' Donaldson said fondly.

'What do you mean?'

'Like we said, they don't always reveal all.'

'As far as I can tell we're pulling in a couple of lads who are up to no good, then had an extra warning they could be dangerous.'

'More complex than that. Sometimes the little-wigs open up the path to the bigwigs.'

'Explain yourself.'

Donaldson regarded Bill. He had known him a while now, been involved in various investigations with him and found him sound and reliable. Dour, but likeable. 'If I do, and you blab, I'll have to kill you – you know that?'

'Only if you get in the double-tap first.'

'OK – for your ears only. The two men – lads really – that you've been told to pull in have just recently returned from an extended trip to Yemen. They've been on extensive training and indoctrination courses.'

'Brainwashing?'

'Fundamentalism . . . so, yeah, brainwashing. Also probably trained to use a variety of weapons and how to make bombs.'

Bill swerved at this revelation like a cat had just leapt in front of the car. 'They didn't quite tell us that.'

'No.' It was a wistful word.

'So really they've told us fuck all.'

'Because if it comes to nothing, it'll all be played down . . .'

'Which is why it has to look like a routine stop-check.'

'And if something is found, then they'll be whisked down to Paddington Green police station in London and interrogated.'

'Interviewed, you mean?' Bill said.

'Interrogated.'

'OK.' Bill got the less than subtle hint. 'So they've been trained – does that answer why you're here, Karl?'

'Do you recall the bombing of the American Embassy in Kenya in 1998?'

Bill scratched his balding dome. 'One of many, but I recall it.'

'A guy named Jamil Akram is one of the principal bomb-makers affiliated to certain terrorist organizations. First made his name making car bombs, more recently he's been mass producing body packs for suicide bombers. Also a weapons expert, particularly small arms.'

'And your interest is?'

'He had a major hand in that embassy bombing – with others, of course. I lost two good friends in that blast and I don't forget easily.' His voice became brittle.

'And somehow he's connected to these guys today?'

'In Yemen they were at a camp at which Akram is known to be a facilitator. The thinking is, I guess, although I can't be sure, that something will be uncovered by arresting these two today that will lead us closer to Akram. Nailing him, even with a missile fired from a drone, would be a major scalp, one which MI5 would like to claim for their own.'

The door opened as Henry and Rik walked up the pathway to the house. The woman standing there, maybe only in her late thirties, looked haggard and exhausted, a tatty dressing gown wrapped tightly around her, hair scraped and pinned carelessly back.

'I know you're the police,' she said shakily.

Henry flipped out his warrant card to confirm her suspicion. 'Mrs Philips, I'm Detective Superintendent Christie from the Force Major Investigation Team and this is Detective . . .'

Her face froze in an expression of horror. She had been able to recognize that two plain clothes cops were at her door, but when the first one introduced himself and stated his rank . . . that was when she knew, and it was as if an invisible weight had struck her. She sagged, swayed, her hand sliding down the door jamb. Henry lurched forwards to catch her before she hit the ground.

'You're going to be bored,' Bill said to Donaldson. They were parked up in a street about half a mile away from where the targets had their flat, the street on which their car was also parked. The purpose of the operation was to sit on that car, which was being observed by two cops in the back of a van, wait for the subjects to get in and drive off, then stop them in an appropriate place. Four other plain cars, each with two armed officers on board, a police dog van and a personnel carrier with six uniformed support unit officers were also placed in well thought out, discreet locations, ready to move and pounce once the target car was rolling.

There was nothing to say that the car would move that day. However, the operation would continue until it did.

Donaldson yawned, folded his arms and sank low in his seat, closed his eyes, felt his stomach rumble and said, 'Possibly.'

'How good do you think the Intel is?' Bill asked.

'Hard to say.'

'Who will have done all the legwork?'

Donaldson opened one eye and squinted through it at Bill. 'I always thought you were the laconic type, not loquacious.'

Bill frowned, decided it was a compliment and said, 'Thanks.'

'And in answer to your question, I don't know. MI5, MI6, SIS, Special Branch, Counter Terrorism . . .'

Bill was used to acting on intelligence received from unknown sources, usually crims with a grudge or a debt to repay. It was the way things were done these days, with many firewalls between informant and the officers who then acted on the information. It protected people and he guessed that in this case, the firewalls were pretty much impregnable. He yawned, too. Then said, 'Not much of an Asian population around here.'

'No, but plenty of white holiday-makers,' Donaldson replied and snapped open his eyes as a horrible thought struck him.

Clare Philips was a single mother and Natalie, as far as Henry knew from the information on the MFH file, was her only child. Henry didn't like to stereotype, but there was no doubt that Ms Philips was of a sort he had encountered many times during his service. Not that she was a bad woman, simply a victim of upbringing and circumstance. She lived alone in a tiny council house on Shoreside estate, one of Blackpool's most deprived areas. She was unemployed, survived on benefits, shoplifting, some part-time piece work – as evidenced by the hundreds of pairs of shoes stacked precariously in the living room that she was lacing up – and had had a succession of crappy boyfriends. The last characteristic was Henry's own guess, but he'd be happy to lay down money – 'a pound to a pinch of shit' – it was true. A series of feckless men who used her for one thing only, and he could see she was a good-looking lady behind the rather haggard face that she presented that morning.

But none of that mattered.

What was important was that it was almost certain she had lost a daughter. And no doubt it was a daughter she loved with all her heart.

'I'm truly, truly sorry,' Henry said gently.

Clare was sitting on the battered settee, staring blankly but disbelievingly at a photograph of Natalie. Rik Dean came in from the kitchen and handed her a mug of milky tea, laced with sugar. She took it absently.

'The thing is,' Henry went on, 'although the body we have found fits Natalie's description, we can only be certain after formal identification.' Clare nodded. 'That means you, Clare.'

'I know.' She swallowed. Her eyes were ringed with red. 'When?'

'Later today. We're not exactly sure when.'

She nodded again. Henry eased the photograph from her fingers and looked at it, a posed picture of Natalie, smiling up at the camera, wearing a grey and pink silk scarf.

Henry and Rik exchanged glances. Henry said, 'I know this is a terrible time, but we really need to ask you some questions about Natalie and her . . .' He was going to say 'life', but changed the word, realizing the girl hadn't really had one to speak of yet. Instead he said, 'Y'know, the things that were going on for her, who she knew, boyfriends if any, her mates, comings and goings. It's vital we build up a detailed picture of her.' Clare nodded numbly. 'Can I just ask a quick question, first?' Henry indicated the photograph. 'This scarf, was she wearing it when you last saw her? It's not mentioned in the clothing description on the Missing from Home forms.' He did not recall seeing it at the murder scene either.

'Yes – couldn't get it off her. She loved it. I thought I'd mentioned it, mustn't have done.'

'OK,' Henry said. 'Is there anyone we can contact for you? Anyone to be with you?'

This time she shook her head. 'No,' she said thinly.

Henry's chest was becoming heavy. He was on the settee alongside her, a couple of feet away, knees angled towards her, offering comforting body language. The tension in the room was incredible and he was being affected by it all. He had to breathe in, catch himself. He'd done this sort of thing dozens of times before, got through it, never let it affect him. But he found himself staring at Clare Philips, feeling her pain.

Not good. Empathy – OK. Sympathy – OK. Going to hell with the victim's mother – not OK.

He breathed out, rubbed his face.

'Henry?' Rik asked worriedly. He'd noticed Henry's change in demeanour.

Henry gave him a wave of dismissal. He was all right now. Had almost lost it, but had yanked himself back from the abyss.

'What I'm going to do is get someone up here for you now, OK? A family liaison officer . . .'

'What family?' she demanded. 'I have no family now. She was all I had. And now she's gone.'

Henry reached across to place a hand over her nicotine-stained fingers.

'I'm sorry,' he said, knowing the word was ineffective. 'But one thing I promise is that I will track down whoever did this and I will catch him. It's what I do, what I'm good at.' He spouted the claim confidently, but underneath he wasn't certain he truly believed it.

His eyes blinked sadly. Henry knew she was in shock. The news had hit her like a steam hammer even though she might have been expecting it, and may well have mentally tried to prepare herself for the worst. At the moment she was being scarily calm but Henry knew grief intimately and that this stage was unlikely to last. However, she did give him a nugget when she spoke.

'I know she had a big fall out with her ex-boyfriend,' she whispered. 'Had some horrible rows with him.' Henry remained silent, and despite how he was feeling emotionally – on edge, likely to crumble – the old ring piece did the dance of excitement, the bum twitch that meant he was on to something. 'It's that little shit, Mark Carter. You'll know him, I'll bet.'

As much as Henry would have liked to march out of Clare Philips's house and grab Mark Carter, who he did know, events in murder investigations rarely happened just like that. And in some respects Henry was glad he didn't rush out, because the nugget that was Mark Carter actually just became another coin in a handful of loose change as he and Rik Dean talked further to Clare.

Other names came into the frame and Henry realized that quite a few individuals needed to be interviewed very carefully, not just Mark.

Natalie's current boyfriend was one. A guy by the name of Lewis Kitchen (and at the mention of the name, Henry and Rik exchanged a knowing glance). They didn't delve at that point and they guessed that Clare possibly didn't know that Kitchen was known to the police as someone with a conviction for assaulting a female.

Next there was Natalie's real father, a lowlife called Scott Newton, again known by the detectives. He was someone who had reappeared recently in Clare's life after eighteen months inside for robbery. By Clare's own admission the 'family' had had some violent rows and Natalie had taken her mother's side and found herself taking a slapping from a pissed-up Newton, who threatened to kill them both. He needed to be tracked down and interviewed p.d.q.

Then there was a succession of previous boyfriends – a bit of a who's who of petty crims in Blackpool – that Natalie seemed to have succeeded in upsetting by ruthlessly dumping all of them. One had bombarded her with threatening texts and indecent Facebook entries and had been stalking her.

On top of that, one of the lecturers at Shoreside College, where she attended the hairdressing course, had shown an unhealthy interest in her. Clare suspected that Natalie and this guy had had sexual relations at some stage, but Natalie had been very secretive and Clare had only discovered him by accident – by looking in her diary which had disappeared after Natalie found this out. Diaries were always useful and Henry made a mental note to ensure it was searched for thoroughly.

As she spoke, Henry realized that unless there was a quick breakthrough, this could be a long slog of an investigation.

They left the house two hours later, with Clare being attended to by a female constable until a fully fledged FLO could be briefed. Both men were ravenously hungry and Rik suggested a KFC drive-thru, to which Henry agreed; then they could eat and drink on the move, which is what they guessed they would be doing for the next few days. Might as well get used to it.

The nearest Kentucky was on Preston New Road and Henry, at the wheel of his Mercedes – which he'd been dubious about driving into Shoreside in the first place – headed off the estate in relief. All four wheels were still on it and there were no key scratches down the sides.

'Opinions?' Henry asked.

'Lots to go at . . . Natalie sounds like a hot-headed promiscuous young lady who liked moving from lad to lad. We'll get a result sooner rather than later.'

Henry nodded. He did not want to get blinkered into thinking Natalie's death was definitely down to one of her circle of acquaintances, but the chances were it was. He knew he had to keep things wide open and there was still a possibility she could have been murdered by an opportunistic stranger. The fact her body was dumped out of town skewed things a little that way. However, it would all be part of his investigative strategy which he would have to work out in the next few hours. Already his mind was ticking over, relishing the prospect of concentrating on something other than self-pity.

He mulled over the things he would have to think about: location, victim, offender, scene forensics, post-mortem, and all the factors that could link them together. And the need to think logically as to what had happened, why it had happened, and who committed the crime. It was all pretty fundamental stuff for a murder investigation, but had to be done. Keep things logical, answer the questions, work the knowledge.

'But the most important thing,' Rik said thoughtfully, 'is whether I should have a boneless box or a two piece meal.'

'Some things,' Henry conceded, 'just take precedence. I'm on chicken burger and coffee.'

'Sounds good.'

Henry eased the Mercedes into the drive-thru lane at the KFC, three cars ahead of them. When it was his turn, he came alongside the speaker and placed the order, the tinny voice of the server then read it back to him, asking if any sauces were required – yes, mayo – quoted the cost and told Henry to drive up to the window.

He paid, took the bagged-up meals and drinks and passed them over to Rik. The KFC server did not once catch his eye, acting like he was on a *Brave New World* production line, which in essence was almost true.

Henry drove out and pulled into one of the grill bays on the car park by the side of the restaurant. Rik frowned. He'd been deeply engrossed in sending and receiving text messages – presumably to and from Lisa – and hadn't even raised his eyes at the drive-thru, even when he'd been given the food to hold. Now he had a quizzical look on his face.

'We're eating here?'

'How do you feel about striking while the iron's hot?'

Rik shook his head, no idea what Henry meant.

'Mark Carter – you didn't see him?' Rik shook his head again. 'He's the moron who served us.'

Rik pouted. 'Can't do any harm, I suppose. Let's play it by ear, see what he says about Natalie. We don't have to mention she's dead, do we? It's not common knowledge yet.'

'My thoughts exactly.'

'Let's eat first. I hate cold KFC.'

'Er – no,' Henry said, as much as he wanted to devour his food. If Mark was linked to Natalie's death and he *had* clocked Henry in the drive-thru, he could well be spooked and ready to run. Rik emitted a sound of great disappointment.

Henry knew Mark for a few reasons, none of them good. Firstly, Henry had dealt with the death of Mark's sister from an overdose of a lethal drug concoction and Mark had helped Henry track down the supplier. Secondly, Mark had witnessed a murder and this had resulted in Mark's mother becoming a target for killers who'd actually been trying to track down and silence Mark.

Henry had always thought Mark was a fundamentally decent lad, struggling against a crap upbringing. His father had disappeared many years before and he'd been raised by a mother more concerned with a fraught love life than giving Mark the attention he deserved.

Henry also had a bit of his own baggage with Mark. Truth was that Henry had used Mark for his own ends when tracking down the aforementioned dealer, making fake promises before cutting him loose. And Mark still bore that grudge, rightly, even though Henry had been instrumental in keeping Mark out of the hands of social workers after his mother's brutal death.

Henry hadn't had contact with Mark for months now. And here he was again, turning up like a bad penny, half-suspecting that Mark might have committed a murder without any supporting evidence.

Inside the restaurant there were two vague queues up to the counter and Henry spotted Mark, capped and uniformed, at the drive-thru window, taking orders via a headset, collecting money and dispensing food. He did not once look up at anyone in the cars.

Henry and Rik walked to the gap at the right of the counter and waited to catch Mark's eye. But it was as if the lad was on autopilot, everything blanked out bar his task.

Another server, bearing a manager's badge, stepped up. He was nothing more than a mega-spotty lad.

'Help you guys?' he asked. 'Queue's there,' he said authoritatively.

Henry saw his name was Marlon. 'Need to speak to that lad.' He pointed a finger at the still oblivious Mark.

'I'm afraid he's a bit busy. May I ask what it's about?' Marlon asked, doing well to string the words together. Henry showed his warrant card and Marlon squinted at it.

'Mm, OK.' The manager turned to Mark who was handing a bagged-up meal through the serving window to a passing motorist. He tapped him on the shoulder and spoke into his ear. It was quite noisy in the restaurant with piped music, voices, cooking sounds, traffic. Mark leaned sideways slightly, his eyes came into focus and he recognized Henry, who gave him a little wave. Mark's face wilted. In his short life – he was now seventeen – the appearance of Henry Christie had always spelled trouble.

Mark muttered something to Marlon, who nodded and returned to Henry.

'I'll let you have five with him, pal,' Marlon said. 'He just needs to fulfil these orders and I need to deploy someone to stand in for him. That'll be me, I guess. So if you want to grab a seat.'

'OK, no probs, Marlon,' Henry said. The detectives backed off and found an empty table.

Henry did not sit, though. 'You hang on here,' he told Rik. 'I'll just mooch out back.'

'Think he'll do a runner?'

'He's programmed for it.' Henry glanced over the counter. Marlon had already stepped in for Mark who was nowhere to be seen. Henry walked quickly out, made his way to the rear of the restaurant, and leaned casually on the wall next to a fire exit. He started to count, and as he reached five, the fire door opened outwards and Mark Carter stepped through, zipping up his jacket. Although he glanced both ways, Henry, flat against the wall, was just outside his field of vision for a moment – until the detective pivoted, grabbed Mark by the jacket and slammed him against the wall.

'Shit,' Mark uttered, taken completely by surprise.

'Naughty boy,' Henry said, pinning him back with one hand, his elbow locked straight. Mark struggled for a few seconds, realized the futility of it and then sagged in acceptance of the situation.

'What do you want, Henry?'

'Hey – didn't realize you'd got a job as a chef.'

Mark eyed him. 'I'm at college. It just about keeps me afloat. Like I said, what do you want?'

'Natalie Philips.'

'What about her?'

'When did you last see her?'

Mark shrugged, pulled a face. 'Dunno. Couple of days ago – why?'

'Been reported missing. Her mum's worried.'

Mark snorted derisively.

'What's that supposed to mean?'

'About as worried as my mum used to be about me. Look,' Mark was still stuck to the wall, 'let me go, eh? Won't run. Promise.'

'How can I believe that? You've already tried.'

'Only cos I don't like you. You bring fuckin' trouble all the time.'

Henry released his grip. 'When did you last see Natalie and under what circumstances?'

Mark shrugged again. 'Like I said, couple of days ago.'

'Where?'

'College. She does hairdressing there.' Mark's eyes played over Henry's face, trying to read him. 'Why do you want to know anyway? I know what you do . . .' Mark faltered. 'You investigate murders,' he said slowly. His lips pursed into an unspoken question as his mind tried to pull the fragments of his knowledge together. And he hit the jackpot. 'You don't investigate missing persons.'

'I hear you were her boyfriend,' Henry probed, ignoring Mark's conclusions. Mark suddenly withdrew into himself. Henry sensed that the promise about not running was about to be broken. His hand shot out again.

'Were you?' he demanded.

'I . . . I might've been,' he stuttered.

Suddenly Rik Dean skidded around the corner of the KFC, a harried look on his face, his personal radio gripped in his right hand. Henry looked at him, annoyed, his face saying, 'What?'

'We need to go – now.' Rik waved the PR, from which could be heard shouts and general noises of mayhem.

'Why?' Henry released his grip on Mark's jacket. Mark didn't hesitate. He saw the opportunity and fled, ducking sideways, vaulting over a low fence and away, leaving Henry faffing in thin air. He turned on Rik, almost apoplectic. 'Why?'

'Officer down,' Rik said.

FIVE

There had been times in the lives of both men when they'd had to endure tedious hours, sometimes days, of just sitting, watching and waiting for someone to move, or show up – or as in today's case, simply get into a car and drive off. It was part of the job, but no one could argue that it was anything less than soul destroying. Like most aspects of law enforcement, boredom ruled ninety-eight percent of the time. But most law enforcement officers thrived on the two percent, when it all came together and the adrenaline flowed like champagne.

Today was nothing, particularly for these two men. At least Bill had a roving commission of sorts, whereas the others on the stake-out were tied to their observation points come hell or shine.

They reminisced for a while, each trying to outdo the other with tales of boredom. Donaldson got the gold medal. A four-week long surveillance of a gang of suspected armed robbers operating out of a factory unit in Miami. Donaldson, then a true field agent – a role he recalled with fond whimsy – had endured the month cooped up in a ship's container with no air-con and very basic sanitation. He and his partner, Joe Kovaks, were determined to see it through, despite the contempt of their colleagues. The gang of four were supposed to set out from the unit, commit their crimes, then return and destroy every fibre of clothing in a blast furnace and wash themselves thoroughly, before stepping back into society.

The intelligence was partly correct.

They did return to the warehouse having committed four cross-state armed robberies in quick succession, killing one man in the process, but where they had set out from was never established.

Donaldson and Kovaks rounded them up without a shot being fired and recovered close to four million dollars in cash.

'Good days,' he said dreamily, recalling how shit-scared he'd been.

'Never had anything quite like that,' Robbins admitted, 'but I was part of a team that arrested four armed robbers doing a bank in Preston a couple of years back. Real scary stuff, but I think they were more scared of us, really.'

'I got that impression too.'

'You worked Miami, then?'

'Yep – and New York for a while.'

'And what happened to your partner, Joe, was it?'

Donaldson gulped. 'Dead. Hit by a mobster in Miami.'

'Sorry.'

'Yeah, sometimes part of the territory,' Donaldson said. 'But, reality is, these things are usually damp squibs, even when the bad guys turn up.' He checked his watch and wondered why he'd really decided to hop in with Bill. Mainly to avoid spending time with FB and Beckham, he supposed. But he'd had enough now and there was no need for him to be out and about. 'How's about dropping me off at the police station, bud?'

'No stamina?'

'Agreed – no stamina.'

'Not a problem.' Bill started up the Vauxhall, weaved his way to the promenade and drove south, past the Hilton and Imperial Hotels on his left, reaching the huge Metropole building on the right, then to the traffic lights at Talbot Square. Donaldson, slumped low in his seat, absent-mindedly watched pedestrians on the pavement to his left. Lots of them. As the lights changed, Bill set off slowly, past Talbot Square, with Blackpool Tower on the nearside stretching towards the clear blue sky. Across to the right, the tide had crept in and the sea was still and silvery, the horizon clearly pencilled in.

Donaldson thought briefly about his earlier meeting with Henry Christie, who was obviously still reeling from Kate's death. It was early days and Henry, though often brittle at the best of times, was pretty resilient. He'd come out the other side, Donaldson guessed. Hoped.

They hit another set of lights at New Bonny Street. At the next set, Chapel Street, Bill would turn left and loop around to the lower ground floor of the police station to drop Donaldson off at the public enquiry desk. Then Bill would head back to the stake-out area and hope something would happen.

Donaldson yawned and stretched. The lights seemed to stay red for ages. He turned his head lazily to the left, rolling his neck muscles, and he looked slightly back over his shoulder.

As the lights turned green and Bill, who happened to be at the front of the line of traffic, moved the Vauxhall forwards, Donaldson suddenly shot upright.

'That's one of them,' the American uttered, craning his neck as he tried to keep track of the youth.

'What?' Bill said.

'One of the two we're after.'

'You certain?'

Donaldson shot him a withering look. 'Pull in here, let me out – and get on your radio. Let everybody know we somehow missed them leaving the flat.'

Bill swerved, mounted the kerb. 'I'm coming too. We need to keep in touch somehow.'

Donaldson was already out, walking briskly back to the lights about fifty metres away, his senses, his instincts, whirring. Bill scuttled behind him, abandoning the car with three wheels on the pavement, causing a slight blockage on the prom.

Donaldson weaved through a sea of day trippers and holiday-makers, all of whom seemed to be walking in the opposite direction to him. All of a sudden he had a flashback. Just for an instant he was transported back a few years, to that time when, on foot in Barcelona, he was chasing a terrorist. Although

Blackpool was no Barcelona, then as now, the streets had been crammed with people. On that occasion he'd been pushing against the tide of bodies washing up Las Ramblas like a human tsunami and today he was on Blackpool promenade. A culture away – but still the same fear stalking the streets.

He paused briefly on the kerb at New Bonny Street, remembering to check right before stepping out. His conditioning, even after more than a dozen years of UK living, was to glance left for vehicles first.

He rushed across to the central reservation, then diagonally across from there, striding purposefully towards the town centre, a large amusement arcade on his left. Bill was a few paces behind, gabbling into his PR to alert people to the change of events. He had no details as yet.

Bill was shocked when Donaldson stopped, turned quickly and dragged him up to the building line, hissing, 'No radios now – unless it's covert.' Meaning hidden, able to be used without anyone realizing. Which Bill's wasn't. He was holding the PR up to his mouth as he transmitted and it was as large as a house phone, so no discretion there. 'If we catch up and he spots us and we spook him, it's game over. Could be game over anyway,' Donaldson said bleakly.

'What game?'

'Suicide bomber game.'

It had been a fleeting glimpse, seconds only, but long enough for Donaldson to do two things. First, to ID the young man. Second, to take in all the points that suggested – nay, screamed – he was a suicide bomber.

First the ID. Donaldson had spent over twenty years looking at faces, memorizing them, remembering names. One of his pastimes, if you could call it that, was to peruse the Wanted Persons files and put names to faces. It was a basic skill of being an FBI agent, learned and constantly updated. Even on quick reveals Donaldson was one hundred percent certain he could identify someone in a crowd.

As in the case of Zahid Sadiq, one of the two faces he'd seen only for the first time that morning at Beckham's iffy briefing. Donaldson had taken in the face, the eyes, the ears, the nose, the forehead of a young good-looking Asian boy.

And he was sure he'd seen that same lad walking along the promenade. Even though he was now clean-shaven, Donaldson recognized him. Which led to point two.

Suicide bomber.

Only that brief glimpse as he passed in the car had told Donaldson that.

First the beard – or lack of it. The boy, who was only nineteen and who had a pretty crappy beard anyway, as shown on the photograph at the briefing, had shaved it off, a procedure that had the effect of lightening the skin in the shaved area, under the nose, on the chin, on the side of the face. He had also shaved his head to the bone. Although he was wearing a skullcap, Donaldson had clearly seen that the head was devoid of hair. That was just one of the many things that Donaldson took in and processed.

Next was the three-quarter length coat, bulky and inappropriate for a day that was getter hotter by the minute. Everyone else on the prom had shed their coats and was down to shirtsleeves and light clothing. The lad's hands were thrust deep into his pockets and Donaldson also caught sight of a white wire coming out of the right-hand pocket and up the sleeve. He saw only a half-inch of it. But he saw it. Initial thought: was this hand gripping a detonator, thumb on button? Why was the coat extra bulky? Were explosives strapped to the boy's torso? The lad was also staring dead ahead as he walked, as though he was walking down a tunnel, another classic sign of a suicide bomber. And he was mumbling to himself, lips moving . . . praying?

The thought that he might be completely wrong was in his mind, too. Perhaps the lad was chilly. Had a few pullovers packed on and was simply listening to his iPod. Donaldson hadn't seen an earpiece, though.

But he also did not care if he was wrong. Better that than the other.

Bill fumbled in his own earpiece, connected it to his PR and shoved the radio in his pocket. 'I need to tell 'em something,' he said, pointing to the PR, meaning he'd alerted comms and they now needed more information.

'Tell them Zahid Sadiq is walking into the town centre and he could be carrying a bomb.' Donaldson said it matter-of-factly, then spun away from Bill and started walking quickly, turning the corner into Central Drive hoping he hadn't lost Sadiq, but spotted him immediately. It helped being a few inches taller than most of the people around him. Sadiq was about seventy metres ahead, walking straight on to Adelaide Street, the big McDonald's on the corner to the right, then into Bank Hey Street, which ran along the back of the Tower, where the main entrance to that attraction was situated.

Donaldson rushed forwards, wondering how best to deal with the situation. Sadiq was entering an area chock-full with people, but was that the target? A suicide bomb on a shopping street? Just by standing there and detonating it outside WHSmith he would probably kill over fifty people, wound another fifty and cause a huge amount of damage. Easy. But as a target, a statement? Donaldson doubted that would be the case.

Perhaps the Tower itself?

Getting inside and detonating a bomb. Now that would be something. A real statement of intent that would show how vulnerable British society was. Blowing up the heart of a traditional holiday resort. Working class people from all over the country murdered. Not politicians, not cops or the army. A strike to the heart. Everybody at risk.

Donaldson powered on. Bill scuttled behind him, talking into his PR via the microphone attached to the earpiece.

Resources were moving quickly as all patrols dropped everything and converged on the town centre, controlled by a comms operator who was becoming increasingly hysterical.

Sadiq was forty metres ahead now. On Bank Hey Street, slowing right down near to the Tower entrance. A queue was already snaking out of the door as people waited to get in. Sadiq stopped and was looking around.

Donaldson swore. He knew he was right. This was the target.

Then another thought struck home.

Where the hell was the other guy, the other target for the day? Suicide bombers were often accompanied by another who often also had a trigger device, such as a mobile phone which could remotely detonate the bomb for those times when the bomb carrier's courage failed and the enormity of what they were doing struck home: not just blowing others to smithereens, but themselves also. Even the most fanatical could find that a tough step to take, or a hard button to press, and they often needed help from a remote source. Many suicide bombs in the Middle East were detonated by a third party.

Donaldson stopped, as did Bill, who had also focused in on Sadiq, a young man who now looked confused, uncertain and afraid.

'He's got to have a partner,' Donaldson said.

'What do we do?' Bill asked.

Donaldson shrugged. He knew the blood had drained from his own face and that he was feeling scared now.

Sadiq moved, joined the end of the queue into the Tower. His eyes moved continuously, he mumbled to himself – trying to refocus, Donaldson thought. Prayers, incantations, mantras.

Sadiq wasn't really looking at anyone in particular, even though his eyes seemed to be searching. Donaldson used this to his advantage and said, 'Let's just stroll along together,' to Bill who glared at him, horrified. 'You know you want to.'

'Actually I don't.'

Donaldson swung a big arm around Bill's shoulders and looked at him grinning. 'Do you see any other way?' Bill shook his head. 'The first six virgins are mine,' Donaldson quipped and they started to walk along like two mates, chatting innocently.

'The next eighteen are mine.'

The pair were perhaps ten metres from Sadiq, who now had people behind him in the queue and was getting closer to the Tower entrance. Donaldson noticed a sign saying there was a lunchtime performance in the Tower circus, and this was obviously attracting lots of families with young kids.

Sadiq's head started to rock back and forwards, his lips continued to mumble their prayers.

Five metres.

Bill was saying something into his radio.

Then a police car with blue flashing lights turned on to the pedestrianized street.

'Shit,' Donaldson said.

Four metres.

Sadiq spun, saw the cop car.

Then another police car screamed up from the opposite direction.

Sadiq saw that one, too. Panic seared across his features. Suddenly trapped, he reacted in a way that gave Donaldson a chance of survival. Sadiq's knees sagged slightly and his hands came out of his jacket pockets in a response to being caught, like an escaping prisoner in a spotlight, but holding nothing.

Donaldson bowled sideways at him. Hard and low, enveloping him with a bear hug, pinning his arms to his side and smashing him down on to the ground. As the American connected, he felt the hard outline of packed explosives strapped to Sadiq's body underneath his coat and knew his call had been justified.

Donaldson worked quickly and expertly. Sadiq was nothing more than a thin, skin and bone youth, with hardly anything to him, whereas Donaldson was big, fit, strong, agile, a man with years of physical training and operational experience behind him.

Within moments Sadiq was face down, hands trapped behind his back, his wrists cuffed by Bill who had moved in to assist.

There had been no fight in the lad. He'd just succumbed to the assault.

Bill leaned into his ear and called him the worst name in the English language, but just through relief rather than anything else. The last couple of minutes had seemed like hours of stress.

Bill held him down as Donaldson stood up and looked around. Cops on foot and in cars were converging. The public were shocked, confused and excited, but it would only take moments for the police to take control, push them back and form a sterile ring around Sadiq. But Donaldson knew this was no time to relax because there might be a back-up plan in place. The number two guy with the mobile phone on speed dial, ready to press send. Donaldson didn't know enough about bombs and electronic pulses even to think of trying to dismantle whatever concoction was underneath Sadiq's coat, but he knew everyone needed to be on full alert and the lad had to be neutralized as soon as possible.

He guessed that if there was a support bomber in place, that person would either have to have a line of sight on Sadiq to keep a check on progress, or be waiting nearby for a particular time. Such as giving Sadiq half an hour to do his stuff, and if a blast hadn't been heard by then, press send-and-boom remotely.

Obviously Donaldson did not know for certain, but he did know that these were critical moments.

A bomb disposal expert was needed on scene quickly to disable Sadiq's body pack.

The public had to be herded away a serious distance. A

perimeter had to be established of at least two hundred metres and everyone had to be out of line of sight.

One hell of a job, he thought, as he looked desperately around. Some cops had arrived and, acting on Bill's shouted instructions, as he held Sadiq down, were moving people away now. But more officers were needed.

Donaldson spun around. Mobile phones were at people's ears, in their hands, folk were making calls, some were doing their best to take photos as they were pushed back. Panic surged into his gut. He twisted and knelt down by Sadiq's head. 'Who's with you?' he demanded. Sadiq's cheek was crushed into the paving and he looked up at Donaldson with one eye, like a flatfish. Spittle dribbled out of his mouth. He sucked it back in. 'Who's with you?' Donaldson repeated.

Sadiq's half-face laughed. 'Allah,' he said.

Donaldson suppressed a serious urge to slam a fist into his head and smash his jaw to pieces, but he fought it, then rose again, his sharp eyes taking in everything that was happening around. The cops working urgently, Joe Public now getting the message, more police arriving.

Bill gripped the rigid bar of the handcuffs, angling them slightly so that they dug into the nerve endings in Sadiq's wrists, and kept the lad down. 'Next move?' he asked.

Donaldson didn't have an answer. His eyes were constantly roving up and down the street, desperately searching for the accomplice.

Then he saw him. A man moving against the tide of people. The support act.

Curiosity had drawn him out. If he hadn't been dark-skinned, Donaldson probably wouldn't have zeroed in. But he did, and he recognized the face instantly. But it wasn't the face of the other youth from the briefing, the one who was Sadiq's friend.

This was Jamil Akram, the man Donaldson had been hunting for over a dozen years.

Realization hit Donaldson hard as their eyes locked. Akram immediately saw that he had been recognized and began to fumble through his pockets as Donaldson surged into a run.

There was another roar from Donaldson's throat. People spun round to see what was approaching and a path opened in front of him. Akram pulled out his phone but it seemed to dance through his fingers as if it was burning hot, or had a life of its own, and it fell to the ground, splitting into several pieces on impact, the battery and the back panel going in separate directions.

Akram turned and ran into the crowd.

Donaldson was only metres behind him, his arms punching like huge pistons. But Akram moved with the agility of a deer. His head went down and he weaved and cornered around people like a skier hurtling down a slalom.

Donaldson had no finesse in his speed, no grace, and he shoved individuals roughly aside. He was taking the direct route and everyone had better get out of his way.

Akram, though, was getting further away. Keeping low, he entered Hounds Hill shopping centre and disappeared into the covered mall. Donaldson cursed as he ran in and found himself faced with a dilemma. The mall was a large, curving semicircle, which split to the left and right. There was no sign of Akram, who could have gone either way and ducked into a shop, then used another exit, or a fire escape.

Donaldson spun on the spot.

Bill Robbins came up behind him.

'Lost him,' Donaldson gasped. 'Is Sadiq still pinned down?'

'Yes,' Bill assured him.

'And has the phone been seized?'

'Yes,' Bill repeated.

Two more cops rushed in behind, armed and in uniform, wearing peaked caps with chequered bands, and brandishing H&K machine pistols.

'Who's the guy you chased?' Bill asked.

'Akram – the guy I was telling you about.'

'Jamil Akram? Shit,' Bill blurted.

'Yeah – and he's gone to ground here – but he won't be hiding long. He'll break cover.'

'I'll get more people, get the exits sealed.'

'Make sure you tell 'em to take care. He'll be armed,' Donaldson said. 'And dangerous,' he added, not caring if it sounded clichéd.

'Description?'

Donaldson gave him a glance. 'I know this sounds racist, but any Asian male, thirty to fifty, in this vicinity needs pulling and slamming down. But he is wearing a black zip-up wind jammer, blue jeans, grey trainers and he's got a black moustache.'

'Understood,' Bill said, and he transmitted this through to comms.

Donaldson indicated to Bill that he was going to start looking and moved into the mall.

He prowled slowly, like a predator, but felt that Akram was now likely to be on the other side of the shopping centre or maybe in a car – at which moment Donaldson spotted a sign pointing to the Hounds Hill multi-storey car park, adjacent to the mall. It was only a guess, but Akram had appeared at the scene having come from the direction of the shopping centre, so maybe he was simply retracing his steps to get back to his escape vehicle.

Donaldson looked back at Bill and the two firearms officers. Bill was still talking urgently into his PR but Donaldson managed to get his attention, pointed at one of the firearms officers and then placed the flat of his hand on the crown of his skull in the old military signal. *Come to me.*

Bill nodded and shoved one of the officers in Donaldson's direction, yelling something in his ear. He ran up to the American, who said, 'I want to check the parking lot.'

The two men headed towards the double doors leading to the car park steps. 'I'm Karl,' Donaldson said quickly.

'Steve. And what are you?'

'FBI.'

'And who are we after?'

'Jamil Akram.'

'He's a bad guy, is he?'

'Ultra bad.'

Steve, the firearms officer, pushed through the double doors and the two men stepped into a concrete stairwell.

'Where from here?'

Donaldson thought quickly. 'First level, then up through the parking lot, one level at a time.'

The firearms officer was kitted out in overalls, boots, a Kevlar vest, a utility belt holding handcuffs and a holster (in which was a Glock 17), the MP5 across his chest. He was weighted down like a storm trooper but he went quickly up the first two flights of stairs to level one. As they stepped out on to the concrete a

Ford Fiesta shot out from a parking space, tyres screeching on the shiny floor. It accelerated towards the exit, and therefore in the direction of Donaldson and the firearms officer.

In spite of the reflection on the windscreen, Donaldson saw it was Akram at the wheel. 'That's him,' he shouted.

The car gained speed, the engine revving.

The two men separated and Donaldson saw that Steve was already having doubts. What had this man actually done? What are his intentions? Is my life at risk? Are others in immediate peril? What happens if I shoot and kill? Am I out of a job? Goodbye pension. All questions that needed answers.

Donaldson had no such qualms. Problem was, he wasn't armed.

The car sped between them, Akram's head low over the wheel. As he passed Steve, he dinked the car purposely at him and caught his right leg with a glancing blow, sending him spinning away. But at the moment of impact, the officer had managed to smack the stock of the MP5 into the windscreen, cracking it like a spider's web across its width. The weapon, though, flew out of his grasp and clattered away.

Akram sped on.

Donaldson rushed across to Steve, who was on the floor, gripping his injured leg. Without hesitation, Donaldson expertly flicked the restraining loop on the officer's holster and released the Glock. Donaldson was familiar with the weapon, had used one many times in the range. He pivoted on his haunches and fired two shots at the back of the Ford as the car veered down the exit ramp.

Certain he'd put at least one bullet into Akram, Donaldson turned back to Steve who writhed in pain on the concrete floor, gripping his leg tightly with blood-soaked hands. Donaldson prised the hands away, wincing when he saw the misshapen thigh bone. He grabbed the officer's PR and spoke coolly into it.

SIX

That transmission was the one picked up by Rik Dean, sitting alone in the KFC whilst Henry had gone to check whether Mark Carter had done a runner out back. Up to that point in the day, neither detective had his PR on and Rik had only switched his on for . . . well, boredom, really. He was instantly transported into a foot chase in Blackpool town centre, consisting of various hurried and worried transmissions, others more measured and calming, and he recognized the gruff but controlled tones of Bill Robbins in amongst them. There were many exchanges between mobile and foot patrols descending on an incident – one which Rik did not immediately understand – and then came the '*Officer down*' message, at which point he had rushed out to Henry, thinking he would want to know about this.

He found him around the back of the KFC talking to Mark – who had, as Rik guessed, tried to slip out and disappear. Henry was holding Mark's sleeve and it looked as though the pair were having a few moments of tension. But Rik knew what was important and that he and Henry might be needed elsewhere p.d.q. Mark Carter could be picked up as and when, so it didn't concern Rik too much when Mark saw his chance and fled.

The two detectives raced to Henry's car and jumped in. Henry reversed out of the space and screeched on to the road, turning up to the traffic lights on Preston New Road. From there, a left turn would take them towards Blackpool, right to the motorway roundabout at Marton Circle, the M55. The lights were on red.

'What's the situation?' Henry demanded.

'Not entirely sure,' Rik admitted, looking at his PR which was alive with traffic and some pretty panicked voices.

'Find out,' Henry said.

Rik hesitated slightly, waiting for an appropriate gap in transmissions into which he could dive. Impatient, Henry snatched the PR and said, 'Superintendent Christie interrupting.' From what little he had heard he could tell it was very confusing and, for a short time, no one seemed to be taking proper control. Part of the problem was that patrols were on radio talk-thru, meaning everyone could hear everything being said and could interrupt without permission. On big incidents, this wasn't always a good thing and sometimes the radio operator needed to take a firm grip, switch off talk-thru and assume total control. Which is exactly what Henry ordered the comms operator, who sounded out of his depth, to do. Maybe it was a new guy. At Henry's instigation the man took a deep breath, became more authoritative, and cancelled talk-thru. Henry asked him then to recirculate brief details of the incident, offender and vehicle.

The lights changed to green.

Henry stuffed the PR back into Rik's hands, considered his position, zipped across a lane, cutting up another driver, and headed towards the motorway junction. His feeling was that enough people were already at the scene, so he thought that a few minutes sat at the motorway junction could be fruitful. Maybe. A traffic car was en route to do just that, but was ten minutes away at least, so Henry decided to plug that gap for a while. Patrols covering checkpoints such as motorway junctions was pretty standard procedure anyway, basic coppering that sometimes got overlooked in the heat of an exciting incident. Escape routes had to be covered and sometimes it paid off.

All this was in Henry's mind when Rik said, 'We're not going to the scene, then?'

Henry gunned the Mercedes, feeling the smooth surge of power at his light touch. God, it felt good. 'No.'

'But . . .?'

'I know there's no guarantee, but a Ford Fiesta with a cracked windscreen might just come sailing past.'

'And pigs might fly.'

Henry grunted like one. But he knew that being a lucky cop was often about diligence and doing routine things . . . and patience. He said, 'Sometimes it happens, especially if an offender is panicking leaving a scene because they haven't worked out an escape route properly, one that avoids main roads. Sounds like the guy in the Ford was surprised and maybe he didn't even think he'd need an escape plan.'

'Mm, whatever.' Rik would most definitely have preferred to be charging to the scene. Those emotive words '*Officer down*' drew in cops automatically. They always felt the need to be there, even if they ended up acting like headless chickens. Henry, too, felt the urge to be at the scene, but he knew a wider perspective was needed – which is why he was a superintendent. That was his argument, anyway.

His mobile phone rang and he answered it by pressing a button on the dash which linked to the handset via Bluetooth and also switched the call to speakerphone. Henry grinned, amazed at how he had embraced the technology.

'Henry Christie.'

'Henry – it's Karl. I heard your voice on the radio, barking orders like some sort of mini Hitler.'

'Karl – you at the scene?' Henry asked, ignoring the remark.

'Right at it,' Donaldson confirmed.

'Tell me,' Henry said. Donaldson did so, succinctly.

He ended by saying 'The cop he clipped looks pretty bad – big thigh injury. He did well to crack the windshield with his gun, though.'

'Are things being controlled now?'

'Yeah. There's a uniformed cop with a lot of bird shit on his collar at the scene, ambulance just arriving, bomb squad, too. I think we're OK. The initial scene down by the Tower entrance is sealed, I think, and that guy's been neutralized. But Akram's on the loose. Hell, if we could take him, that would be . . .' Donaldson was lost for words.

'OK, pal. I'll have to leave you with it. Unfortunately it's not my job, but I'll sit on the motorway checkpoint until the traffic car deigns to turn up, then I'll have to resume my day job.'

'Gotcha.'

'Oh, Karl – you planning on staying up here tonight, or going home?'

'Hadn't given it a thought.'

'Spare room at the Christie household if necessary,' Henry invited him. 'Just turn up if you need it. Cheaper than a Premier Inn.'

'Roger that.'

Henry drew the Mercedes on to the forecourt of the petrol station situated just five hundred metres before the motorway junction and parked up close to the exit ramp. An ideal position from which to view passing traffic. The two officers picked up their just-warm meals.

'I knew Karl would be involved somewhere,' Henry smirked, then sat back in the comfortable leather seat, watching traffic, not hopeful for a result. 'Suicide bomber in Blackpool,' he murmured, taking a bite from his chicken burger.

'Why bloody Blackpool?' Rik said, disgusted.

Henry shrugged. 'Terrorists terrorize. Hitting a target like Blackpool makes the whole country feel unsafe. Up to now, if you don't live in London you feel pretty secure strolling around your own town. Remember the IRA?'

'Mm.' It was a bitter murmur from Rik's throat.

'Surprised they don't do it all the time – make everybody feel threatened all the time. Provincial towns . . . middle England . . . low-class places . . .'

'I get your point,' Rik said uncomfortably.

'I'm sure they have the resources and the willing bodies,' Henry pressed on relentlessly.

Rik raised his hands in defeat. 'I get you.'

Henry grinned.

'So, come on then,' Rik demanded, making his point with a chicken leg. 'Have you ever actually sat at a checkpoint after a job and *actually* seen the offending vehicle drive by?'

'*Twice*, actually.'

'Yeah, sure.'

'True. Once, when I was on the crime car and a taxi driver got robbed at gunpoint, the offenders stole his cab and came sailing past ten minutes later. That was a good lock-up,' Henry remembered with pride. 'Other time was after a post office robbery . . . that got a bit messy, but it was a good result.'

'OK – so twice in thirty years?'

'You've got to cover all avenues.' And to confirm it, the comms operator informed all patrols that all checkpoints in the division were now covered by static patrols and adjoining divisions were doing the same.

'So if he tries to get out of Blackpool by main road, we might get lucky,' Rik said cynically. 'There's loads of other ways out.'

Henry looked at him and shook his head sadly, then returned his attention to the traffic flowing by. He could not help but feel a pulse of excitement in his veins. A murder and a suicide bomber in one day. He thought about his 'Intention to Retire' report sitting on his computer's hard drive, waiting to be printed off.

Days like this meant it could wait a little longer. Kate's illness and death had certainly taken the sheen off police work for Henry, but that had been the fault of the circumstances as much as anything. A loved one dying took the shine off everything. However, there was no doubt about it, he still got a serious buzz from coppering, even if he'd had a mental hiccup earlier at the murder scene. But that was something he'd occasionally witnessed in other colleagues when they'd been affected by personal trauma. He just never thought it would get to him on the job, thought he was immune to it.

'So Carter did a runner?' Rik said. 'Think he's guilty?'

Henry screwed up his nose. 'Famous last words, but no, I don't think he did it. He's a decent lad, really.'

'You go all soft around him,' Rik said.

'He's had a tough life.'

'He's a little shit and I wouldn't put it past him.' Rik was very unforgiving, never able to accept that an individual's upbringing or situation was any excuse for criminal behaviour. It was a point of view Henry knew well.

'Take your freakin' blinkers off,' Henry whined – a slightly ironic statement as at that exact moment a Ford Fiesta with a cracked windscreen drove past them on the main road in the direction of the motorway, one Asian male on board.

Henry's adrenaline spurted into his already fast-pumping blood flow as he bagged his food and clicked the Mercedes into drive. He moved smoothly off the forecourt, slotting in three cars behind the Fiesta which was in the nearside lane.

'See,' Henry said. 'You get lucky if you do the work.'

Rik glowered, stuffed his uneaten meal back into its package then picked up his PR.

The Fiesta peeled left on to the M55, picking up speed but not excessively so. This made Henry frown slightly. He hung back as cars in front of him moved out to overtake the Fiesta leaving a sixty metre gap between himself and the Ford. The speed edged slowly upwards to the seventy mark as Rik relayed the position to comms. The force control room at headquarters then muscled in and took over the running of the 'follow', diverting and deploying traffic and motorway patrols. The FIM made the decision that if the Fiesta stayed on the motorway, a rolling road block would be instigated to box it in and bring it to a halt on an appropriate stretch of hard shoulder when enough patrols were there, together with armed officers.

Henry was instructed to keep his distance, simply report progress, and not to get involved directly.

First to join was a big Volvo traffic car, overtaking Henry and dropping into the space between his Merc and the Fiesta. The speed was still around the seventy mark.

'Doesn't really give the impression of a desperate man,' Henry commented dryly.

'The Fiesta isn't a fast car, especially a shit heap like that one,' Rik said.

'Granted . . . but . . .'

'Yeah, I know . . . I've been in a car chase with a Reliant Robin three-wheeler going faster than that.'

Another traffic car tore up alongside Henry, then moved ahead so that it was abreast with the first one in the nearside and middle lanes of the motorway, both still hanging back from the Ford. Control room said that other traffic cars were a few miles ahead of them on the motorway, waiting.

Henry's mobile rang.

'Henry – it's Karl.'

'Yeah – we're with the Fiesta,' Henry said. 'Something odd, though.' Henry explained the lack of urgency in the demeanour of the supposedly fleeing felon who'd knocked over a cop and been back-up for a suicide bomber. 'He's just trolling along at seventy, no evasive tactics, dangerous driving, attempts to force cop cars off the road or anything.'

'Did you get a look at the driver?'

'Not a good one,' Henry admitted, and arched his eyebrows at Rik, who shook his head: he didn't get a good look either. 'Just enough to see an Asian male.'

'Tell them all to take care,' Donaldson said. 'Could be a set-up – oh, and by the way, I shot the driver.'

'You what?' Henry blurted, but Donaldson ended the call on that note. 'Shit,' Henry said.

Another traffic car joined the chase as the convoy reached the exit for Kirkham, but the Fiesta stayed on the motorway, which meant that the next exit was at Broughton, north of Preston, about eight miles distant and eight minutes at the current speed. That was enough time and distance to pull the car if they could get their act together. This was already being discussed over the airwaves and Henry could see this would be the preferred option, rather than allowing the Fiesta to get on to the M6 where life would become much more complicated and far busier.

Henry picked up the PR and put that point across to the FIM, his only reservation being that there were no armed officers present at the moment. That problem was negated when a plain Volvo sports saloon roared up behind with two AFOs on board. Added to that there was another traffic car further ahead, waiting on the hard shoulder. That gave three liveried traffic cars and an armed response vehicle . . . *game on.*

Two miles had shot by while that short discussion was taking place, so they had to move now.

Henry dropped further back in the Merc. The firearms vehicle slotted into his vacated space. As if on cue, all the traffic cars switched on their blue lights. One then took up a position behind the Fiesta, another drew alongside it in the middle lane, and then they tightened up their positions. Further ahead, the traffic car that had been waiting on the hard shoulder accelerated into the nearside lane.

The Fiesta now had a police car alongside it, one behind and one in front, with nothing on the nearside except for the hard shoulder.

Then, like jet fighters escorting another plane down to earth, they edged the Fiesta across on to the hard shoulder without touching it, slowing the car down bit by bit.

Henry watched the operation being executed with precision from his position at the back of it all.

It wasn't far now to the Broughton exit, maybe two miles.

The police cars continued to slow down.

The Fiesta made no effort to avoid what was going on, seeming to accept the inevitable, slowing down as indicated.

'Far too easy,' Henry remarked. He could feel the tension increasing as if a band were tightening across his chest.

Then they were at a crawl.

Then at a virtual standstill.

Then stopped.

For a few seconds nothing happened. Then the two AFOs in reflective jackets got out of the ARV – which was parked ahead of Henry on the hard shoulder – handguns drawn, and stood behind the open doors of their car, using the V-shape for support and protection. One had a loudhailer. Then the doors of the traffic car in front of them opened, the officer jumped out and ran back, whilst the AFOs ran forwards at a crouch, each taking up a position behind the open doors of the traffic car, directly behind the Fiesta.

Meanwhile, normal traffic continued to roll past and, without exception, every vehicle slowed down and the occupants gawked at the incident unfolding in front of their eyes. Traffic may have been light, but it was a problem, and it needed to be completely stopped behind them somehow.

Henry and Rik climbed out of the Mercedes which was parked about fifty metres behind the ARV on the hard shoulder, hazard lights on.

A gust of wind buffeted Henry, causing him to stagger. Then he was almost spun full circle by the slipstream of a passing lorry. He felt extremely vulnerable and suddenly realized what a very dangerous place a motorway was, even at the best of times. He went to the boot of his car and fished out a couple of reflective jackets that he always carried, handing one to Rik. Then, keeping to the side of the motorway, he strode up to the traffic officers, the wind in his face, amazed by how strong it was on such a nice day. The fact that the motorway was exposed and slightly raised made it cold and forbidding.

The man in the Fiesta had not moved. Henry could see his outline in the driver's seat.

Henry mentioned the passing traffic to one of the officers who shouted back at him, raising his voice because that was the only way to be heard against the combined thunder of passing vehicles and swirling wind. He told Henry that the gantries had been activated further back down the motorway and blocks had been set up on the slip roads to keep anyone from coming on. The overhead signs were telling drivers to stop because of a police incident. The officer added, 'No one ever does, though.'

Henry patted the guy's shoulder and, crouching low with Rik just behind him, he jogged up to the armed officer using the passenger door of the traffic car as a shield. This was the one with a loudhailer.

Henry assessed the whole scenario, very unhappy about it.

'We need to get him out from the nearside door and up to the Armco barrier,' he shouted.

The officer nodded.

Then the driver's door of the Fiesta opened, the guy swung out his legs, stood up and faced Henry's direction. Henry saw a young, skin-headed Asian youth, maybe nineteen years old, dressed in trainers, jeans and a big anorak. This was not the man that Donaldson had described to him, the one he'd chased through the streets, who had driven this car at a cop, the one he'd shot. Not the man called Akram.

'Stand still,' the AFO with the loudhailer shouted. 'Do not move.'

The lad had a blank expression. He seemed to be saying something to himself, mumbling. His hands were down at his sides, fists clenched. He walked between the Fiesta and the traffic car and stopped by the rear offside wing of the Ford as though he hadn't heard the shouted instruction.

Henry's eyes took in everything – including the other firearms officer crouching behind the driver's door of the traffic car, armed with a Glock pistol, held down in front of him in the classic two-handed grip. This officer had a clear, unobstructed view of the lad.

Henry thought he saw the twitch of a smile in the corner of the Asian's mouth. His head rose slightly and he looked at Henry across the gap that separated them.

Several cars hurtled past in the fast lane.

Henry spotted something in the young man's right fist. It looked like the top of a pen. Henry knew exactly what it was. A button. A detonator. Attached to a bomb that was strapped to his chest.

Henry had been here once before, face to face with a suicide bomber. Last time, in the backstreets of Accrington, he'd been lucky. A mis-connection meant the device failed to explode. Since that moment, Henry knew he never wanted to be in that position again. He knew he would not be so lucky next time. This time.

The young man raised his right hand.

Several things happened.

Henry screamed, 'TAKE HIM DOWN!' to the firearms officers.

The young man shouted something, words that were blocked by the wind, but Henry knew he was saying that Allah was great.

The firearms officer on the other side of the car stepped sideways, raised and aimed the Glock, bringing it up into the point of an isosceles triangle formed with his locked arms.

The young man lifted his thumb in a gesture designed to show that he was now going to press the detonator in his hand, blow himself up and whoever else he could take with him.

Henry cringed and cowered away, as though turning his back to the situation would protect him from a bomb blast.

SEVEN

Steve Flynn was looking at one of the most beautiful women he had ever seen in his life. He adjusted the peak of his tatty baseball cap to reduce the relentless glare of the African sun in his eyes, squinted and did a dreamy double-take just to make sure. But there was no doubt about it, even from this distance. The young woman was something special.

Flynn was in the cockpit of the sportfishing boat *Faye2*, carefully manoeuvring her backwards into the tight mooring space alongside Ray Boone's boat, *Shell*, when the woman appeared on the shaky wooden quayside, walking from the direction of Boone's houseboat tethered in the next creek. Just for a moment Flynn lost concentration and almost scraped Boone's older boat, a mistake that would have left him more red-faced than he already was. Flynn was proud of the way he handled boats.

Boone himself emerged from the galley and glanced sideways at Flynn as he passed him at the wheel. Boone winked smugly and said, 'Spotted her, huh?' and continued out on to the rear deck. Flynn's eyebrows arched. He reversed the last few inches into position and Boone stepped ashore with the mooring ropes, looping them over two wooden stanchions. He then walked towards the beautiful woman, said a couple of words into her ear and embraced her gently. Her face widened into a wonderful smile, and she then gazed lovingly at the old hound dog that was Ray Boone. She said something softly to him, her green eyes sparkling shyly.

Flynn killed *Faye2*'s Volvo engines and the boat he'd come to love over the past eighteen months became silent, rocking gently in the river current. He slid off the pilot's seat, walked out on to the deck and rolled the narrow gangplank across to the quayside. He then stood there with his hands on his hips waiting for Boone to tear his attention away from this stunning woman and remember he had a guest to attend to.

Finally Boone looked at Flynn, a broad, proud smile across his weather-ravaged features, an expression that knocked about ten years off his grizzled face.

'Hey, pal – permission to come ashore,' he called, and gestured to Flynn.

Flynn shot across eagerly to meet Boone's lady, the one he'd had an earful about over the last six hours. He had started to believe she was actually either a figment of Boone's tropical-sunshine-addled imagination or something far worse – a wizened old hag who Flynn would have to pretend was as beautiful as described.

But no. Boone, the old time crim, had come up trumps and was not fantasizing, as evidenced by the slender female who now stood alongside him with one arm draped intimately around the older man's thickening waist.

Boone beamed and announced, 'Flynn – meet Michelle, love of my sordid life and saviour of my soul, after whom my boat is named and who is also a great sportfisher and sailor.'

Flynn's right hand extended and she shook it with a soft hand of her own, blessing Flynn with a magical welcoming smile that gripped his heart then slam-dunked it right down through the hoop.

'Welcome to the Gambia, Steve,' she said in a lilting West African accent, the words almost singing from her lips. 'Boone has told me all about you. He called you a complete bastard,' she said innocently. Boone's crooked smile stayed firm as Flynn gave him a sardonic glance. 'But,' she laughed and added, 'as honest as the day, fair and firm. At least that's what he wanted me to say.'

Flynn chuckled. 'He's been too generous in his praise.'

Michelle extracted her long fingers from Flynn's over-tight grip and said, 'I'm pleased to meet you.'

'Likewise,' Flynn said. 'Ray's told me all about you – but being a man who can't string too many words together, he has completely and inadequately failed to describe how lovely you are.'

'Thank you.' Michelle lowered her eyes demurely at the compliment and looked slightly discomfited by it. Flynn also felt a bit awkward. He was actually a man of few words, most of them usually short and to the point. Complimenting did not come naturally to him – unless he was trying his seduction techniques – but somehow Michelle's radiant ambience had made him gibber like a jerk, he realized.

He smiled simply at her and gave a shrug. He certainly wasn't trying to seduce this woman, not just because she and Boone were an item, and Boone was an old foe-turned-friend, but because Boone would probably have killed him outright for chancing his arm. That kind of thought always made Flynn hesitate.

Boone coughed. 'OK guys, end of the BS.'

'I have a wonderful spicy chicken casserole for the evening meal,' Michelle announced. 'All breast,' she added cheekily, 'with sweet potatoes and ice-cold local beer.'

'Jul-Brew?' Flynn asked. She nodded and his mouth watered at the prospect. He loved its taste. His stomach gurgled hungrily at the thought of a decent meal. He and Boone had grazed on sandwiches, crisps, cola and strong coffee all day on the boat and he was famished, his body yearning for proper food.

But the rub was that however hungry you might be, or ill, or whatever, the boat came first. Flynn said, 'I'm really hungry, but I'll clean her and the equipment first if that's OK?' He jerked a thumb at *Faye2*. 'Then I'll clean myself, too.' He said to Boone, 'Ray, you get on and I'll do it. Be about an hour if that's OK?'

'You sure, pal?'

Flynn had spotted the exchange of lustful looks between Boone and Michelle. From Boone's boasting, Flynn was fully aware of the full-on sexual nature of this relationship and Flynn guessed it would be a good move on his part to let the two of them get it out of their system before the evening meal.

'Certain.'

Boone gave him that smug wink again. Flynn watched as the two lovers sloped away, draped around each other like teenagers, Boone with a hand firmly gripping one of Michelle's buttocks. Flynn readjusted his cap again, smiled slightly enviously, then took the three strides back across on to *Faye*'s deck.

There was the accumulated debris of a long sea journey and then a six hour fishing trip for tarpon to clear up. Flynn liked to keep the boat spotless and was intensely proud of the way he cared for *Faye2* and the fishing tackle, so he got to work.

He hosed down the decks, vacuumed and dusted the small galley, lounge and stateroom. He cleaned the rods of any salt and fish debris, all of which took longer than an hour, by which time the sun had dropped in the sky, then dramatically hovered hugely over the horizon before disappearing. A hot, sultry night had fallen over the Gambia River.

Flynn, sweating heavily, was desperate for that beer. Still, he took the time to grab a quick shower and shampoo, applied a manly underarm spray, then mosquito repellent, a wicked combination that he hoped would defeat even the most determined insect invader. He changed into his beloved Keith Richards T-shirt, a pair of three-quarter length pants and flip-flops. From the fridge he grabbed the box of chocolates he'd been keeping there. Then he ensured the gas bottles were tightly closed and the engine cut-off that he'd wired to a secret compartment under the tackle station was definitely in the 'off' position. As he extracted his hand from this hidden compartment, his fingers brushed against the Bushmaster .223 AR-15 Predator rifle also secreted in there. An additional piece of kit only he knew about, kept for purely defensive purposes, he would argue. Pirates and desperate refugees were a growing menace.

Next he secured the boat and rechecked everything, because he knew theft was endemic around these parts. Lastly he set the alarm which, if breached, would scream loudly and deafeningly for twenty minutes. He stepped ashore clutching the chilled chocolates, gave his babe one last all-over glance and set off, hoping to reach his destination before his gift melted in the oppressive evening heat.

Boone's houseboat was moored in the next inlet alongside another poorly constructed quayside, affixed to shore by various ropes and chains that allowed it to rise and fall with what little tide there was, while flexible power cables and sewage pipes ran into the riverbank.

It was not a houseboat in the way most people might visualize one. Usually they would imagine a square, wooden structure afloat in a marina or along a canal bank, or perhaps a refurbished narrow boat, but Boone's was completely different. Flynn knew exactly what it was and from where it had originated.

It was actually a huge concrete barge, consisting of two levels – upper and lower deck. It had been built probably sixty years before by British Waterways for use on the canals of northern England, but it had spent only a short time performing that function.

Flynn smiled at the memories it brought back to him, as for most of its life this fairly ugly looking two-storey barge, well over sixty feet long and twenty wide, had been moored at the edge of the marina at Glasson Dock, the tiny port on the Lune estuary on the north Lancashire coast. It had been converted into a cafe and fish and chip shop. Flynn knew it from his youth and adulthood. As a kid he had been taken there occasionally by his parents for a treat. He recalled wonderful fish and chips and mugs of tea. He had never known the barge, which was called the *Ba-Ba-Gee*, to serve any function other than a floating, but permanently moored, refreshment stop.

Over the last few years the restaurant business had failed and the boat, one of Glasson Dock's best known sights, had fallen into disrepair and been put up for sale for one pound, it was rumoured, conditions attached.

Then it had disappeared and Flynn now knew where it had ended up. Luxuriously refurbished, lashed to a muddy river creek off the Gambia River, a home for one of north-west England's biggest drug dealers – as was – who had a bit of a soft spot for the place in which he'd almost died.

The upper deck accommodation was fitted out as a large covered sitting and dining area, whilst below decks there was a lounge, a large bathroom and two double bedrooms, the master having an en suite shower and toilet. On deck it was spacious and open plan with floor to roof sliding windows. The whole boat was air-conditioned, vital in the heat of this tropical country. The living area was surrounded by a wide, walk-around deck constructed of teak, which opened to an outdoor, rattan-covered sitting area at the stern, the roof of which could be extended or folded away as required.

Boone and Michelle were relaxing on cane chairs on the open deck area, each with a beer in hand, chatting softly. The deck was illuminated by fluorescent lights that were less attractive to bugs, but even so Flynn could see huge numbers of massive moths and other insects flitting through the light. Fortunately a fine mesh curtain surrounded the seating area and did a reasonable job in keeping out the unwanted guests.

He coughed to attract attention.

'Flynn, old pal, come on, come on,' Boone greeted him effusively. He got to his feet and drew back the curtain to allow him to step through. Michelle had also risen to her feet. She gave Flynn a double-cheeked kiss and he caught a sexy, musty scent on her.

'Sorry I was a bit longer than anticipated,' Flynn said.

'No problems,' Boone said. 'Have you battened everything down? They're a thieving bunch of bastards hereabouts,' he warned.

Flynn nodded, then handed Michelle the chocolates. 'For you.'

Her bottom lip tightened with surprise and pleasure. 'Thank you.'

'Probably need to get them into the fridge,' Flynn advised.

'I will.' She batted her long eyelashes at him. 'I'll get you a beer at the same time.'

'That would be fantastic.'

She went to the steps in the centre of the boat that led below decks. Both men watched her until Boone raised his eyes slowly at Flynn, caught him looking and said, 'Kill you if you even think about it.'

'I was just concerned about the chocolates.' Flynn grinned, and the men laughed.

'Take a seat,' Boone gestured.

Flynn dropped into a cane armchair. 'This is a great job,' he commented, his hands indicating the barge.

Boone's head bobbed with the compliment. 'Yeah, thanks. It is, even if I say so myself.'

'Surprising what you can achieve with drug money,' Flynn said, mischievously straight-faced.

Detective Sergeant Steve Flynn from the Drugs Branch of Lancashire Constabulary's Serious and Organized Crime Unit had been hunting Ray Boone for two years solid.

Back then, Flynn's job was to bring about the downfall of some of the north-west region's top level drugs traffickers, Boone being one of them.

The frustration for Flynn was that although he knew Boone used an RIB – a rigid inflatable boat – to bring drugs ashore, usually from Ireland on to the Lancashire coast, he always managed to fox him as to his pick-up and landing locations. On the face of it, it should have been easy to capture someone like Boone, but it wasn't. RIBs were fast, could easily outrun and outmanoeuvre customs boats, could come ashore at almost any point (once he had even run on to Blackpool beach), could navigate shallow, treacherous waters and were easy to hide. But Flynn knew Boone was active and he should have been able to catch the sneaky bastard.

But so far he'd been unsuccessful.

This was partly due to having to follow other targets, often selected at whim by the powers-that-be, and Boone was not always the top of that heap.

But one night it all came together. Using information from a snout and other intelligence, Flynn and his team ambushed Boone bringing a consignment into Glasson Dock on his RIB. The operation went well until Boone – heavy smoker that he was, coupled with the excitement of the bust – had a heart attack as he was being put into the back of a police van.

Flynn saved his life, all his first aid training clicking in – cardiac massage, mouth-to-mouth, the full hit.

Flynn's mouth twitched at the memory. Boone must also have been sharing the flashback as he raised the bottle of Jul-Brew.

'Thanks for saving my life – in so many ways,' Boone said gratefully.

'Could have gone either way,' Flynn admitted, recalling the mad ambulance journey to Lancaster Royal Infirmary. It took ten minutes but felt like a lifetime.

Flynn visited him often and saw a change in the man who had been so close to death. A heart attack can soften even the toughest men.

'I know you'll be on me like a hawk on a sparrow as soon as I'm fit to walk out of here,' Boone had whispered hoarsely to Flynn during one of his visits. His throat was like sandpaper from the number of tubes that had been inserted and removed from it. 'Anything I say after that will be on record and I'll say what you expect me to say – fuck all.' Flynn had grinned. 'But I've had time to reflect, and when this is all over and I've paid my dues, I'm off out of here. Going to live in the sun. Get a new life. You did that for me – gave me that chance, and I thank you.'

'Plans?' Flynn had asked.

'Big ones,' Boone answered. 'A life in the sun, sea fishing and maybe a few bits 'n' bats if necessary. If you know what I mean.'

Flynn knew. 'Bits and bats' meant things that were not above board, but what caught Flynn's attention more than anything was the mention of sea fishing. He was well into the sport and when Boone revealed his plans to up sticks, head for the tropics, buy a boat, he was hooked and despite their positions on opposite sides of the legal fence, they became tentative friends.

And Boone kept his word.

At Crown Court he received a ten year prison sentence and was out in 2007. By using a stash of money the police had failed to find (and to be honest, Flynn hadn't tried *that* hard to find it), he headed south never to be heard of again, paying for the *Ba-Ba-Gee* to be shipped down with him.

Flynn got a phone call from him a couple of years later. Boone had heard about Flynn's inauspicious departure from the police, suspected – but never proved – to have stolen a million pounds worth of drug money from Felix Deakin, another big time drug dealer, RIP. By that time, Flynn had also gone south, tail between his legs, skippering a sportfishing boat out of Puerto Rico on Gran Canaria. The men had met up a couple of times and Boone insisted on Flynn coming down to the Gambia, where he had relocated, to spend a few days tarpon fishing in the river estuary.

Flynn had persuaded his boss, the actual owner of *Faye2,* to allow him to use the boat, take a holiday and visit Boone so he could check out the commercial viability of fishing in the Gambia.

It had been utterly fantastic.

He and Boone had spent the day of Flynn's arrival fighting huge tarpon and Flynn could see the possibility of running some sort of operation down here, although the weather was always hot and sticky, more so than the Canaries.

'Do you know how much this place cost?' Boone said, handing Flynn another chilled beer. Flynn pouted and shook his head.

'One.'

'What? One thousand?'

'No – one. One pound.'

Flynn blinked. So the rumours had been true.

'Yep – condition being that I took it away from the mooring

in Glasson. Cost one hell of a lot to get it transported down here, and refurbished, but it's bloody great. And the superstructure is still in fantastic condition, easily last another thirty years.'

'Why though?'

'Nostalgia. Used to get my fish 'n' chips on it when I was a biker. Bikers used to congregate at weekends in Glasson and I loved it. Didn't want to see it broken up, which is what would have happened.'

'So how much did you have stashed?' Flynn asked cheekily.

Boone's lips twitched a smirk. 'I could ask you what you did with Felix Deakin's million quid,' he retorted playfully, but realized he'd touched a raw nerve when a cloud passed over Flynn's face. The allegation was one that was destined to haunt him. Sometimes Flynn wished he'd been the one who had taken the damned money. It was his partner, Jack Hoyle, who had – whilst also having a torrid affair with Flynn's wife behind his back.

'Oops,' Boone said.

'No probs.' Flynn coughed and shook it off. As a cop he'd been tough, often violent, but definitely honest. He forced a smile and took a long draft of the beer. 'So . . . how do you keep the wolf from the door around here?'

'Oh,' Boone shrugged, 'bits 'n' bats, you know . . .' At which point Michelle reappeared from below decks and cooed that dinner was ready, and that she needed a hand to carry the pots upstairs.

The food was remarkably good. Flynn ate ravenously, drank the excellent wine and enjoyed the nice small talk, mostly about fishing and lifestyle. Boone seemed to have it good and was very content with his lot. He took a few tourists fishing on the coast and upriver. He also did a few other moneymaking tasks and, reading between the lines, Flynn reckoned that an old dog like Boone certainly hadn't learned any new tricks. Flynn guessed he was still dabbling, just in a new environment. The Gambia, as he knew, was just one link in a worldwide drug and people smuggling chain and Boone was probably getting his cut, using his boat as a means of transport. But Flynn was past caring what others got up to. He wasn't a cop any more and certainly felt no obligation to get involved in preventing or detecting crime. Those days were long gone.

As the meal finished Boone's mobile phone rang. He excused himself and wandered down to the front of the houseboat where a muttered conversation took place, leaving Michelle and Flynn at the table, sipping wine. She produced the chocolates Flynn had bought for her.

'Do you have a wife?' she asked him directly.

'Er . . .' He was slightly taken aback by the question out of the blue. 'Did have . . . went *very* wrong.'

'But you must have someone,' she insisted politely. 'A man like you.'

'Did have. That went wrong, too.'

At the far end of the boat, Boone said in a loud voice, 'What, now?' into his mobile. Flynn and Michelle glanced down at him, then looked at each other.

'Is there someone – at all?' she asked, still probing.

His face screwed up. 'Nah. I think I might be past settling down now anyway. Not many women would put up with me. Too selfish.'

'It's good to share your life with someone. I really love Boone. We'll get married I expect and live on the *Ba-Ba-Gee*.' She spoke with heart-warming simplicity.

'I truly hope so,' Flynn said. He didn't wish to dash her hopes but he thought Boone had a wife back in the UK. He smiled warmly at Michelle and selected a Turkish delight from the chocolates.

Boone returned, clearly agitated, phone conversation over. He shook the phone. 'Pal, I'm really sorry about this. Bit of urgent business needing attention.'

'Bits 'n' bats?' Flynn ventured.

EIGHT

At eleven p.m. that night, Henry Christie was in a bleak mood as he walked into his kitchen and went through each cupboard for the fourth time since arriving home. Once again, there was nothing in them, certainly nothing that appealed to him.

He still hadn't changed, was still wearing the same clothes he'd been in since two thirty that morning when he'd been turned out to the murder of Natalie Philips. Many, many hours ago. A day which had seen him freeze at the scene of that murder (like a 'numb twat', he kept castigating himself), then get his act together, only to find himself on a wind-battered motorway dealing with a serious incident that had no connection whatsoever with the earlier murder.

He bent over to open the fridge door, then went light-headed as he stood upright again, stepping back a pace to keep his balance. He needed food. Behind the knife rack, the unofficial pending tray for letters delivered to his house, was also a menu for a local Chinese restaurant, one that he and Kate ordered takeouts from regularly. He hadn't used it since she had died and unfolded it slowly whilst walking back into the lounge. He sat down and looked at the third-filled tumbler of Jack Daniel's, still untouched, but tempting. He picked up the phone as he flicked through the menu and settled on his old favourite. Nothing fancy, just a chicken curry. They both liked the same and would order two, one with boiled rice, the other with chips and a bag of prawn crackers. They'd split the rice and chips and scoff the lot in front of the TV.

Henry looked around the lounge. It was deathly quiet. Leanne was out, so he was alone in the house. He could hear the wind outside. He looked through the menu again and decided to plump for something he'd never tried before, otherwise he'd just end up wallowing in the self-pity of what had once been. He placed the order by phone and was told it would be twenty minutes before it was ready. In that case, he thought, I'll have a drive round in my new car.

As he opened the front door, Leanne was coming up the driveway with her boyfriend. She halted abruptly, surprised by Henry's appearance. She and the man were obviously sneaking up to the house.

'Dad! I thought you'd be in bed.'

'Well I'm not.' Henry's cold eyes turned to the man. 'What's he doing here?'

'We . . . we . . . uh, made up,' Leanne stuttered.

'This man has caused you endless grief,' he said, his eyes still locked on to his prey. 'And if you think he's coming under my roof, you're one off.' He now moved his gaze to his daughter.

'Your relationships aren't my business, but I know a shitbag
when I see one.'

'Oi,' the young man said warningly.

Henry's head jerked back to him. 'I'm not going to argue
about it, but he isn't coming in here – end of. I'm going for a
takeout. I'll be back very soon and he'd better not be here.'
Henry walked towards the pair, stopping shoulder to shoulder
with the young man, who was fit and broad, but had no real
scare factor about him. 'And,' Henry said, 'no one "Oi's" me
at my house.' He bustled past and got into his car, feeling a bit
of a shitbag himself at his outburst. But also unrepentant. He
didn't like the guy and whilst Leanne was old enough to make
her own mistakes, he still felt a certain parental responsibility
towards her. It was odd, though, that she could not see what an
out-and-out bastard the boyfriend was, yet he could. Why was
life like that?

He reversed the Mercedes off the driveway and burned a bit
of rubber to emphasize his disapproval. As he hit the roads of
Blackpool, he exhaled, took a mental chill-pill and concluded
that a ten minute tootle up the prom might give him chance for
reflection on what had been, in Henry's own words, 'One hell
of a fucking day.'

In complete contrast to the way in which his brain had imploded
at the scene of Natalie Philips's murder, Henry had remained
clinical and professional on the motorway.

From the moment the young man from the Ford Fiesta
had raised his right hand with the detonator in it, shouted words
to his God that were scooped away in the wind, Henry had gone
into Superintendent mode, shouting instructions to the firearms
officers – which, incidentally, had not been heard by anyone
else.

The AFO did everything that was expected of him in assessing
the threat posed by the youth. That said, there was no time to
shout a warning.

And even though the officer was only armed with the Glock
self-loading pistol, and the distance between him and his target
was at least ten metres – which is a long way to shoot a pistol
accurately, even on a blustery motorway – his shooting was
superb.

The two 9mm bullets he fired ripped the top portion from the lad's skull and also destroyed his facial features.

Henry, although pirouetting away defensively, was still looking at the youth. He saw the lad's face disintegrate as the bullets passed through and completely stopped all bodily function – which was the intent. It had to be an instantly fatal shot, otherwise there might have been a chance for the boy to either deliberately press the plunger – one last act of hatred – or to do so because of a twitch of the thumb. The latter chance still existed but was lessened by the complete and utter destruction of the brain.

It was technically brilliant shooting.

The lad jolted backwards as though yanked by a cable and landed on the carriageway between the Fiesta and the traffic car. His fist opened with a spasm and the detonator lay across his palm, looking for all the world like a ballpoint pen.

Then Henry took control – a calm, cool, efficient, effective presence. And he was pretty proud of himself.

Lots of things had to be concurrently and consecutively considered. A series of parallel and intercrossing thoughts tumbled through his head, like a four-lane Scalextric track with side by side racing, crossovers, chicanes, bridges and no excuses for collisions.

He had to secure and preserve the scene and save life. All traffic had to be stopped – properly this time, and from both directions. The motorway had to be closed immediately. The shooting officer had to be seated in his car, his gun seized. Extra resources had to be called in, such as more cops, the ambulance service, forensic and crime scene teams. Everyone had to be informed – but above all, Henry had to keep a firm grip, which he did, and focus on the task.

On autopilot he drove to the Chinese takeaway, a journey he'd made a hundred times or more over the years, and picked up the trial new dish. Spicy Ku Bo King Prawn, with boiled rice and an appetizer of Salt and Chilli spare ribs. The place was also licensed, so he added three large bottles of chilled Chinese beer. The aroma of the food filled his car and he became ravenous.

Then his mind wandered back to the day he'd just experienced.

He had had spent six bone-chilling hours on the motorway and as the day dragged on, even though the weather was good, it got colder and colder. Even as he was dealing with the shooting, he was also thinking about Natalie Philips and feeling guilty because he'd become involved in something that wasn't really his business. In the end, he realized he wouldn't be able to get away from the motorway scene, so he sent Rik Dean back to Blackpool to carry on with the investigation.

It was seven p.m. by the time that Henry made it to the public mortuary at Blackpool Victoria Hospital. He stood alongside a stainless steel slab, looking across the stripped body of Natalie Philips at the pathologist, who was ready to carry out a post-mortem that had already been delayed for four hours. She had been formally identified by her distraught mother some hours earlier, accompanied by Rik Dean and the Family Liaison Officer.

In the reception area outside, preparations were also underway for the arrival of the Asian youth, whose body, with explosives strapped to it, had eventually been scooped off the motorway tarmac and was next in line for the pathologist's scalpel. That was a post-mortem Henry would not be attending because that incident had been taken over by a detective chief superintendent, much to Henry's relief. He'd done his job at the scene and that was plenty.

Not long ago Henry would have fought hard for the opportunity to lead such a job but now, although he'd done well at the scene, it would have been too much for him. One murder at this delicate moment in his life was enough, thank you.

Professor Baines looked at Henry over the top of his surgical mask, which moved comically when he talked.

'Been a busy day,' he said, voice muffled by the mask.

'I assume you're going to do the PM on the boy?' Henry knew the question was superfluous because Baines had been out at the scene to carry out his preliminary tasks. His second killing of the day, too.

'I am.'

'Best of luck.'

Natalie's post-mortem lasted three hours. Baines concluded that she had been sexually assaulted, beaten about the head, most likely with fists and a blunt instrument of sorts, and then strangled, probably with something like a scarf. The pattern of the indentations in the skin around her neck, he believed, could possibly be matched to the item if it was ever recovered. He took all necessary samples from her.

Afterwards, Henry had a brief chat with Rik Dean to go over arrangements for the next day, then he'd gone home and started riffling unsuccessfully through his kitchen cupboards.

And by 11.30 p.m., Chinese takeaway propped up carefully in the front passenger footwell, he was returning home, relishing a midnight feast, maybe with an old Clint Eastwood film for company.

His phone rang. He answered without taking his hands from the steering wheel, still quite amazed by Bluetooth. 'Henry Christie,' he said, trying to sound brusque and businesslike. There was silence on the line. Henry repeated his name.

'It's me, Mark Carter,' came the feeble sounding voice of the teenager who'd done a runner on Henry and Rik at the KFC. Mark had Henry's mobile number from previous encounters, none of which had been pleasant.

'Go on,' Henry said coolly.

'I've heard.'

'Heard what?'

'About Natalie.'

'What about her?'

'I didn't do it . . . kill her.'

'Well, we need to talk about that, don't we? Blackpool nick, nine tomorrow morning. Be there,' Henry said.

'What about now?'

'You heard – and don't make me come looking for you.' Henry ended the call. Instantly another one came in. 'Henry Christie.'

Again, there was silence on the line. Henry wondered how Mark could have rung back so quickly. With irritation, he said, 'Tomorrow morning, nine o'clock.'

'Henry, it's me.'

The voice was female, slightly breathless, hesitant and sweet. Henry recognized it immediately and he swerved to the side of the road, heart pounding.

'Alison?' he said.

'Oh God, I'm sorry . . . I'll hang up . . . this is ridiculous.'

'No! No, it's fine.'

'It's just . . . I've been dialling your number, then hanging up, or just pressing delete . . . a million times . . . a billion.'

Henry gasped. 'How are you?'

'Good. Question is, how are you? I was so sorry to hear about your wife. Kate?'

'That's OK. These things happen, but thanks.'

'Such a tragedy.'

A tear formed on the lip of Henry's right eyelid. 'Yes.'

He had met Alison Marsh well over a year before when he had stumbled into her pub in the village of Kendleton in North Lancashire and found himself involved in some violent shenanigans with ruthless gangsters and corrupt cops. There had been an instant attraction, but at that time Henry had been happily married to a live and kicking Kate. Why would he have married her twice if he was going to be unfaithful, he'd thought. So he had kept Alison at arms' length and following the events that took place in the village – during which Henry strongly suspected Alison may have killed a very bad man who was about to murder someone else – it was probably a wise thing to do. Part of him didn't want to find the evidence that she'd pulled the trigger because it would have complicated an already confusing scenario. And she would have had to face a legal situation that she didn't deserve. Fortunately there was another legitimate suspect who might have shot the man and the inquiry into the death veered away from Alison.

'I didn't know if . . . if I should ever phone you.'

'I'm glad you did, Alison.'

'Really?' She sounded relieved.

'Yeah, really . . . but so late?'

She laughed. It was a nice sound.

'Hey, look. How does a coffee sound?'

'Sounds brilliant,' she said.

'I'll call you tomorrow, when I know what's happening. I've got – er – some hot investigations ongoing.' He almost chuckled at the way it sounded so self-important. 'I'll have more idea tomorrow afternoon, so it might be the day after . . .'

Henry breathed out at the end of the conversation; an amazed smile broke on his face. As he was about to set off the phone rang again. This time he didn't get a chance to introduce himself as an American voice came strongly on the line. 'Henry, where the hell are you?' Karl Donaldson demanded. 'That Chinese better be a massive portion because I'm starving and there's nothing in your cupboards.'

Boone returned an hour later, fairly breathless and flustered, but businesslike. Flynn had spent the intervening time in Michelle's laid back company, which, as she smoked a couple of spliffs, got even more relaxed. Flynn declined the offer of sharing one with her. Taking a drug other than alcohol – which he acknowledged was just as destructive as any other drug – did not appeal, not after all those years on the drugs branch, seeing the effects they had on people. He stuck with the Johnny Walker Black Label she produced. They'd chatted about their lives and she had gradually become very dreamy and sexy, her pupils expanding as they talked and she inhaled.

When Boone came back on to the houseboat, he was full of apologies. Flynn thought he was going to settle down for the night, but he went down to the main bedroom and stuffed clothing into a rucksack, with Michelle watching him in her haze.

He came back on to deck and said to Flynn, 'Sorry mate, I need to get going.' He rubbed his first finger and thumb together, meaning money. 'Had an offer I can't refuse, but I need to go now.'

Flynn said, 'It's midnight, near as dammit.'

'I know. Needs must.' He turned to Michelle who seemed to be floating on air. 'Babe, sorry, but you know.'

She smiled wonkily, which was very alluring, Flynn thought. 'It's OK,' she said.

Then to Flynn, Boone said, 'Look, pal, hang on here if you can, will you? I should be four days at most, y'know, there and back. Easy in *Shell* and the weather'll be kind.'

'Want company?' Flynn offered.

'No,' Boone snapped. 'No,' he said more softly. 'Solo job – y'know how it is.' He clicked his tongue. 'Can you wait? Michelle will look after you – in a motherly way, that is.'

'I can wait,' Flynn said.

'Look – go down the coast, do some shore fishing like we talked about. You know what you're doing. Use my truck, no probs. But stay if you can. We still have a lot of fishing to do.'

*   *   *

As Henry stepped through the front door of his house, Leanne skulked out of the living room, gave him a heart-chilling stare and grunted, 'Your friend is in there.'

'And your friend?' Henry said pointedly.

'Gone,' she said furiously. 'Dad, you have no right—'

Henry's right hand shot up, palm out: the classic police 'stop' signal. 'I have every right to decide who comes into my house. We'll talk about this later.'

'Mum would've—'

Once again his hand shot up, this time his fingers spread apart to reiterate the body language. 'That is not something you may ever – *ever* – throw back at me.'

She scowled, turning a lovely face into a harsh one, then stalked upstairs. Henry shook his head and entered the living room. He looked down the length of the open plan lounge/dining room to the conservatory beyond in which he could see Donaldson's bulky figure slouched on the cane-backed sofa. He and Donaldson had had many serious discussions, and some not so serious, whilst sitting in the large conservatory that overlooked the rear garden and the flat farmland beyond. Henry had always liked the conservatory. It was a good place for relaxation, reflection and occasional nature watching. There was rumour that a housing estate was to be built on the back fields at some stage and if it ever happened, Henry would be devastated.

He walked through and called, 'Hey' to his friend, who turned and gave him a friendly wave. Henry raised the takeaway and said, 'Enough for two, easily.'

'Great – I helped myself to a beer, hope that's OK.' He held up a bottle of San Miguel.

'No probs, bought some more anyway.'

Henry picked up his untouched JD from the coffee table as he walked past and downed it in one, then went into the kitchen where he plonked the food on a worktop and rooted out a couple of bowls and forks. As he opened the tin foil dishes, Donaldson joined him. The big American lounged on the door frame and sipped his beer. 'Leanne's pretty pissed at you.'

Henry tilted his head and looked at Donaldson, halfway through tipping boiled rice into a bowl. 'I'm saving her from herself – and the git that was, or is, her boyfriend.'

Donaldson watched Henry divvy up the meal, finished his beer and took the bottle of Chinese beer that Henry gave him. Both then retired to the conservatory, perching their dishes on their laps and starting to eat.

The new dish was good, but there was something pleasant and familiar about a chicken curry that Henry missed slightly.

After they had each shovelled a few hot mouthfuls down, drunk some of the beer – which was exquisite – and the combination was having the desired effect, Henry looked at his friend.

Since their early morning conversation on Blackpool seafront – it seemed almost a lifetime ago – Henry had only seen Donaldson once. That had been when he had turned up in a police car at the scene of the shooting on the motorway. By then, all traffic had been stopped in both directions, diversions were in place, and Henry was waiting for the circus to turn up.

In the meantime, he had ensured that the body of the young Asian man had been covered by plastic sheeting and kept everyone away from it – once they were certain he was dead and nothing could be done to save him. The missing quadrant of his head and punched in face pretty much confirmed that. Once the scene protection was done, Henry had sat down with the AFO who had pulled the trigger.

Henry didn't know him personally. He turned out to be a thirty-one-year-old constable by the name of Jeff Clarke, who had four years' experience on firearms, and was also a police sniper – hence the accurate shooting. Until that moment, other than in training scenarios, Clarke had never pointed a weapon in anger at anyone.

Clarke had been ushered into the rear seat of the Volvo he'd arrived in – after his gun had been taken from him by Henry and sealed in the boot of his own car. Henry had done what was necessary with the scene, then had slid in alongside Clarke.

The officer was silent, stone-faced. He glanced suspiciously at Henry.

'How're you doing?'

Clarke's cheeks blew out, he shook his head, shrugged, his hands jittered and he obviously couldn't think of what to say.

'You did well,' Henry said.

'I killed a man. A boy.'

'Lawfully. I've checked him as much as I dare without

contaminating or setting anything off, and he's definitely got explosives strapped to his body and a detonator in his hand.'

Clarke nodded numbly, taking this in.

'You did your job when it counted.'

'Yeah, sure.' He wiped some spittle from the corner of his mouth.

'No – you were superb and I'll back you up one hundred percent.'

Clarke angled his face at Henry, a cynical expression on it. 'You're a superintendent, aren't you?' Henry nodded. 'Then forgive me for saying it, sir, but I'll believe that when I see it. If I know this force, I'll be strung out like wet keks.'

Henry realized this wasn't a point of view he would be able to change sitting in the back of an ARV, on a motorway, fifty metres from a very dead body, so he didn't try. Clarke would have to see that Henry meant his words in the fullness of time. His actions would speak for themselves.

Other cops and specialists – the circus – were rolling up to the scene, including Donaldson who arrived in a car with the FB and Martin Beckham, the MI5 man.

Henry laid a hand on Clarke's shoulder, could not think of anything reassuring to say, so he got out and was instantly buffeted by the wind again.

He had stretched crime scene tape around the area, using police cars as temporary points to attach it from, and Donaldson immediately ducked under it and almost ran to the body, squatting on his haunches and lifting back the plastic sheet, great hope on his face.

Henry watched his head shake and a very pissed-off expression come on to his face. He lay the sheet back carefully and slouched dejectedly back to where Henry, FB and Beckham were standing behind the tape. Donaldson was still shaking his head.

'Not Jamil Akram,' Donaldson announced. 'I thought it wasn't from the description.'

'Are you sure it was Akram you chased in the first place?' Beckham said.

'Totally.'

'And you're sure Akram is the one who knocked over a policeman?'

'Totally. That guy,' Donaldson jerked his thumb in the

direction of the body on the carriageway, 'is Rashid Rahman, the second of the two guys you briefed the cops on so well earlier. You know, the ones who were supposed to be holed up in a flat the cops were watching and who, somehow, got out without being seen? Shit like that happens, I know.'

'And you're sure you took a pot shot at Jamil Akram?'

'As eggs is eggs – and somehow he changed places with that poor sucker, which means that Jamil Akram is still out there in the wide world, free as a bird.'

'But you shot him – well, at least you say you did?' Beckham sneered.

'Oh, I shot him – obviously not well enough.'

'Maybe you got it wrong in the heat of the moment. Maybe you didn't chase Akram and maybe you didn't put a bullet into him – maybe the male in the car was this one.' Beckham gestured towards the body.

Donaldson and Beckham glared at each other and continued to bicker on the hard shoulder. Henry just walked away, stunned by the childishness of it all.

'Are you and Mr Beckham friends yet?' Henry asked Donaldson. They had finished their meal, the Chinese beers, and Henry had rooted out some more San Miguel, which was cooling them down.

'Uh, wouldn't say that,' Donaldson muttered. 'Reached an impasse, which is probably as good as it gets.'

'So where is everything up to?'

'Well, as you know, Rahman was rigged up to explode, so the death call by your man, PC Clarke, was right on the money. He did the right thing.'

'Let's hope he hears that from all the right places,' Henry said. 'Including the justice system.'

'He will.' Donaldson sipped his beer. 'The guy I wrestled down near to the Tower, Zahid Sadiq, will now be at Paddington Green police station in London for questioning. Usual procedure with a terrorist. Hopefully I'll get to have words with him at some point – if your security people will allow me. Both he and Rahman were wearing the same explosives rig, and the guy behind that, the bomb-maker and brain-washer Mr Jamil Akram, is still free and no doubt already out of the country.'

'So quickly?' Henry said in surprise.

'Yup – organized to run, these guys.'

'But you're sure you shot him?'

Donaldson nodded and Henry believed him. 'Winged the bastard, that's all. I know exactly where I shot him.' Donaldson pointed to a spot at the back of his own right bicep. He sighed. 'Sadly it wasn't through the head. They'll find his blood in the car once they examine it.'

The plane touched down twenty minutes ahead of schedule. The tailwind had assisted passage, but the flight itself had been beset by turbulence and the seat belt signs had been lit for most of the journey. Most of the passengers were mute and a little afraid, despite attempts by the cabin crew to keep up spirits.

The small, ill-looking man in row 39, seat E – the window seat – hardly moved throughout the flight. He'd positioned himself at an unusual angle against the side of the plane, tucked in tightly, facing the window. He smiled wanly at the couple in the seats next to him, then closed his eyes and slept.

On landing he waited for most of the other passengers to leave the plane before tugging out the small piece of hand luggage he'd stored under the seat in front of him. Then he rose slowly and stiffly, and tried to disembark without drawing attention to himself.

It worked. No one had taken much notice of him. No one would really remember him, which was as it should be. He walked out unchallenged through the terminal building after showing his British passport to a bored and tired looking customs official.

Normally the interior of the plane would not have been so thoroughly cleaned. If it had been a straight turn around, the cabin crew would have done a quick once-through and without much care.

As it was, the plane had reached its resting place for the night and therefore a proper cleaning crew entered and worked their way methodically through it.

When a cleaner reached seat 39E, she stopped suddenly, puzzled at first by the dark stain on the seat and seat back. It was big, not the normal food or drink stain she usually came across. She beckoned over a colleague and both women inspected the stain closely, then looked knowingly at each other.

In unison, they said, '*Si, la sangre.*'

Blood.

NINE

A sour-faced, very exhausted Mark Carter sat defiantly in an interview room at Blackpool police station. His arms were folded and he glared up at the camera positioned high in one corner that recorded his movements. Having attended the station voluntarily he had not been arrested, but he knew it was probably only a matter of time.

Not that it worried him. He'd done nothing wrong, but there was always a problem demonstrating innocence to cops. They always worked on the assumption that you were guilty and worked backwards from there, making the jigsaw fit around that. At least that is what Mark Carter believed they did. Fit you up because it was easier than unearthing the truth.

He jerked his middle finger up at the camera lens and mouthed a word that didn't need a lip reader to translate.

Henry's morning had been hectic. Up at six thirty after a fitful night's sleep exacerbated by severe indigestion: note – order chicken curry in future because that never made him feel bad. He had showered speedily and was walking into the station just after seven, trying to focus his mind on the day ahead.

He met Rik Dean in Rik's office just off the main CID office, where they sat down over a strong filter coffee and bacon sandwiches to organize the hours that lay ahead. They worked on to-do lists, wanting to miss nothing, and get the inquiry into Natalie Philips's murder kick-started. Henry was aware that some of the momentum had been lost already because he'd got involved in yesterday's motorway mayhem. He wanted to pick up speed and get a well-briefed team out there knocking on doors, making people who knew Natalie feel very uncomfortable. He knew how crucial the first seventy-two hours of a murder investigation were – and that had now been whittled down to forty-eight hours.

By nine he had screamed and bawled at too many people. Not something the 'old' Henry had been prone to do, but since Kate died he'd discovered he was far less patient with people who dragged their feet. Anyway, it seemed to work that morning and something resembling a murder inquiry was coming together. Search and forensic teams were at the scene outside the crematorium, six pairs of detectives were responding to various 'actions' that had been generated and house-to-house enquiries were underway in the area around the crematorium.

There was a slight problem in that the location of the murder was actually just over the border in another division, but Henry wasn't too concerned about it. Natalie was a Blackpool girl and it was more than likely her death was associated with people she knew in Blackpool, so Henry had decided to run the job from the resort.

He was desperate to find the last person to see Natalie alive and his early theory was that it was probably somebody in Blackpool. At the back of his mind, he hoped it wasn't Mark Carter.

Henry sat back and stretched. Everything ached. Joints cracked and creaked. He felt his age and he scoffed contemptuously at whoever said the fifties were the new thirties.

Next task was to get the Murder Incident Room – MIR – up and running with the necessary staff in it and to get the murder book up to date.

The phone on Rik's desk rang. The DI scooped it up. 'Right, thanks, yeah . . . in an interview room . . . if he tries to leg it, arrest him . . . uh-huh . . . murder . . . be down, say five minutes. Cheers.' Rik hung up and looked across the desk at Henry. 'Well would you credit it?'

'Mark Carter?' Henry guessed as though he could read Rik's mind. He hadn't mentioned the phone call he'd got from Mark.

Rik nodded. 'You a mind reader or something?'

The boy was almost eighteen now, old enough to be interviewed without any parent or other responsible adult being present. Not that he had a parent or anyone else that was interested in his welfare. No father, dead mother, jailed older brother, dead sister; Mark was pretty much alone in the world.

'Good of you to come in willingly, Mark,' Henry said.

'There was a choice?'

'Ultimately, no.'

Mark shrugged. 'So here I am.'

'We want to talk about you and Natalie, as you know.'

'So you said yesterday.'

'Why did you run?'

'Because, Henry, you always bring me bad news. You always fuck with my mind and it's always best to avoid you.'

'Yet you rang me?'

Rik gave Henry a puzzled sideways glance.

'Only because you'd have nicked me if I hadn't – and because I have nothing to hide.'

'You and Natalie went out together?' Henry asked.

'A bit.'

'Tell me about it.'

'Nowt to tell. We went out for while, then we split.'

'Mutual decision?'

'Are they ever?'

'I thought you were smitten with Katie Bretherton.'

Mark screwed up his face. 'Not now. It's all over.'

Henry studied Mark, seeing a much older, time-scarred lad than the one he'd first met. He was spotty now, had acne, was sprouting hair all over, looked unwashed and frankly a bit of a mess.

'What do you do other than work at KFC?'

'College.'

'Doing what?'

'Astrophysics,' he laughed bitterly. Henry waited, then Mark relented. 'A course in motor vehicle technology.'

'Oh, good lad.'

'Yeah, right. I'm going to be a grease monkey. Ho-di-hey!' He set his face hard at Henry. 'What about Natalie?'

'You tell me.'

'We went out, we split up.'

'Did she dump you?'

Mark blinked and Henry thought, yes . . . another person either leaving or dumping him. Not one person has stayed with him, poor sod. Mark nodded.

'Why?'

'Duh – because I wanted a steady relationship and she didn't. She was a bike and liked being ridden – or didn't you know that?'

'A bike as in . . .?'

'Shagged left right and centre,' he said crossly, his body language leaking a touch of rage.

'So you screwed her too?' Rik Dean piped up at this point, leaning forward on the table. Up to then he'd sat silent, just shot Henry the occasional quizzical look.

Mark's mouth snapped shut. His head rotated slowly to Rik, his eyes dead.

'We need to know,' Henry said. And they did, because the results of the post-mortem had also shown that Natalie had had sexual intercourse sometime leading up to her death. Samples had been taken, and, together with other samples taken from her skin, underneath her fingernails, and from other orifices, were now with the Forensic Science lab for analysis. But that process would take some time. Even if Henry could sweet talk an official fast-track, it would be at least two weeks before any results came back, even with a tailwind. Henry thought for a moment, then made his decision. 'This interview needs to be taped, Mark. We'll need to take various samples from you and at this point the best thing for you would be to get the duty solicitor. Costs nothing.'

'You're locking me up?'

'Tell me when you last saw Natalie.'

'Yesterday, just before lunch.'

'When did you last have sex with her?'

'Yesterday, just before lunch.'

'Shit,' Henry sighed. 'Did you kill her?'

Mark shook his head and Henry believed him, but this was only based on his previous knowledge and opinion of Mark, like a 'halo effect'. But Henry did not want to miss the chance of nailing a killer just because he thought he was too nice to do it. He had to deal with Mark straight down the line and give him no favours. This was the best thing for Mark, too, although Henry doubted if he would see it that way.

'Mark, you're under arrest on suspicion of murdering Natalie Philips.' Henry then cautioned him.

Mark's blood drained from his face. He shook his head in disbelief, then said, 'Now you know why I ran. I fuckin' hate you, Henry. You've done nothing but screw me over since we met.'

Henry took a step back at that point. He did what he should have done in the first place and let Rik Dean appoint two detective constables to interview Mark. He briefed them on what he knew so far, then let them loose on Mark, who had become unresponsive – to him, anyway. He knew their shared history would be a bar to any meaningful interview, so Henry did what any good superintendent was skilled at doing: delegated the job.

This gave him time to ensure the investigation as a whole was moving forwards. If he'd been tied up in interview he could easily have lost the bigger picture and then would have been criticized from on high.

It was all looking good. There was a semi-suspect in the traps, other jacks were out following leads, the scientific people were on top of things, doors were being knocked on, the MIR was almost up and running. Henry was reasonably confident with progress. Now he just had to find out what Mark Carter had to say.

That was when his mobile phone rang. He answered it absently as he skimmed through the first few pages of the murder book.

For a moment, there was silence, then came the hesitant voice.

'I . . . I was wondering about that coffee . . . really, I'm not being pushy . . . it's just, I'm in town for the day.' The voice rushed on a little now. 'Sorry.'

'It's fine,' Henry said, reshuffling everything in his mind, trying to work out if he had time.

'I know you said you were busy and you'd phone me this afternoon . . . and I know all the other personal stuff must be hell . . .'

'I'm really glad you called, Alison,' he said. 'I'm not sure if I would've had the nerve to call back to be honest . . . so, where are you right now?' She said the name of a town centre street. Henry said, 'You'll find a Starbucks on that street, yeah?'

'Yes, I can see it.'

'Go in, grab a table and give me ten minutes to get there.'

His thumb was dithering so much he could hardly press it down on to the end-call button. He took a few breaths to ward off hyperventilation, then gave Rik Dean a quick call as he trotted through the police station. It went to voicemail and Henry left a message to say he'd be otherwise engaged for an hour.

*   *   *

For some miles, the car in which Karl Donaldson, Martin Beckham and Robert Fanshaw-Bayley were sitting – a powerful Jaguar being driven by a brilliant driver from the Road Policing Unit – had reached speeds of over one hundred and thirty miles per hour. That meant the journey from Blackpool to Liverpool John Lennon Airport took somewhere in the region of thirty-five minutes. The slowest part of the journey was actually the last five miles of dual carriageway on which ninety was about the safest maximum.

The driver pulled in directly at the front of the terminal building and was told to stay in the car and wait. The three passengers hurried into the airport where they were met by a DCI from Merseyside Police, who led them quickly through to the security and customs and immigration services offices behind the line of check-in desks. The DCI ushered them into an office with nothing on the door; inside was a sparsely furnished room – table, four plastic chairs – and a wall-mounted large screen TV and what looked like a DVD player.

'Gents, if you'd like to take a seat,' the DCI said. His name was McMullen and he was emitting nervousness.

Silently the three visitors did as bid.

Then Donaldson, who was bursting, said, 'What've you got?'

'Your man, I think.'

The three men were only at Liverpool Airport because of a tired, but sharp-witted and well-informed, Spanish cop who had been dragged against his will by a worried airline official out of his cosy office – just to have a look at a bloodstain on an airplane seat.

The cop actually hadn't seemed sharp-witted at all when the official had knocked on his door at three that morning. Detective Luis Delgado was working the night shift, six p.m. to six a.m. After the last plane had landed at one a.m. without any problems and the passengers had filed wearily through the almost farcical customs check, observed by Delgado through a two-way mirror, he'd settled himself down for the night with the intention of getting in some serious sleep before the next flight landed at five thirty, just before he finished. He had a comfy chair, footstool and pillow, and if those bastards wanted him to work at Las Palmas Airport, then he would, but only on his terms. Because he didn't want to be here.

His eyes had only half-opened when the sharp, urgent knock came on his office door. His arms were folded tightly across his chest, feet were up on the stool, and he was snug, certainly did not want to move.

'*Si?*' he grunted in an off-putting way. The door opened a fraction. '*Que?*' Delgado said, his mouth turned down underneath his heavy moustache.

'Detective Delgado,' the man said. His name was Ceuta, and Delgado knew him as a representative of one of the budget airlines that provided a service to Gran Canaria. 'Please, I apologize. I know you are busy, but could I ask you to come and have a look at something the cleaning crew have found on one of my planes?'

Delgado's tongue smacked the top of his mouth. He shook his head at the thought of the loss of sleep. '*Vale*,' he said, meaning OK. He rolled himself reluctantly to his feet, expecting to be told they'd found a stash of drugs or money, which was fairly common.

But blood?

Delgado bent over and looked closely at the stain on seat 39E. He was as sure as he could be that it was blood – quite a lot of it. Working out the position of whoever had been on the seat it looked as though the injury, or source, was from either the back of the right arm or the right side of the chest.

'Leave it,' Delgado ordered.

'But *Señor*, the cleaning staff need to do their work and this plane will be back in the air in four hours, on its return journey,' Ceuta pointed out.

'To where?'

'Liverpool.'

'As I said – leave it until I say anything different. For the moment, this area is a crime scene,' he declared. 'You may clean the rest of the plane.' Delgado was nothing if not a realist. 'But leave these three seats.' He leaned over and touched the stain with the tip of his little finger. It was still wet.

His next step was to return to the security offices and access the computer hard drives that stored the CCTV footage of passengers who had disembarked this flight as they went through passport control. He also had access to the passenger manifest. He had been well in the background as the passengers from the flight had filtered through and, as is usual, they had all entered the island quickly, without challenge, their passports only cursorily examined by gritty-eyed customs officials. No record was even taken; the passports were just fleetingly shown and individuals waved through. Delgado printed off the passenger list and then watched a recording of the passengers with a mug of strong coffee at his lips, his eyes narrowing as he tried to recall them. Truth was he hadn't been taking too much notice. There were two hundred and sixty people going through and none of them had seemed suspicious, out of place or injured.

Maybe the blood meant nothing anyway, and for a moment he felt a little foolish declaring the seat a crime scene.

The passenger list was nothing special, and nothing struck him as odd. And there was no way of telling which passenger sat in which seat because seats on this flight were not allocated to individuals. Boarding was a free for all, where everyone scrambled for seats.

He sat back and pondered. Blood on a seat. So what?

Then his heavily lidded eyes glanced up at the TV monitor affixed high in one corner of the room, permanently tuned into a twenty-four-hour Spanish news channel. Headlines scrolled across the bottom of the screen as newscasters relayed stories above. The sound was muted . . . but Delgado jumped off his chair, crossed to the TV and stood right in front of it, willing the news loop to come round again. For once, news of a Real Madrid signing was of no interest to him.

It came and suddenly Delgado realized he might have something to throw into the pot in the hunt for a major terrorist. Even if he was wrong, he knew he had a duty to reveal what he had. First he would check all international police bulletins on the computer in his own office. Then, even if there was nothing on them, he would still make the phone call.

The image on the TV screen behind DCI McMullen was paused. He said, 'This is security footage of the passengers going through Liverpool passport control. As you know in this day and age, with on-line booking and check-in, travellers carrying only hand luggage don't have to queue at check-in desks any more, not on these budget airlines, anyway. They just take their self-printed boarding passes and passports to immigration, which get scanned into the system, and then they're through into the departure lounge after security checks.' He paused and surveyed the faces of the three men, got little response, so carried on. 'Obviously I knew a bit about what happened at Blackpool, but there wasn't a full APB out, so there was nothing about border controls at the time of this flight out.' He sounded guilty, but didn't have to. Proper circulations took time. 'When the Spanish detective got through to me, that was only when I really had a proper delve into anything. The thing is, with on-line check-in, it means that passengers can leave it to the last minute to arrive, or turn up hours before. They're not obliged to turn up just within the two or three hour pre-flight time any more. And, of course, there are lots of flights leaving, so people coming through passport control could be there for any one of a dozen flights.'

FB waved his hand. 'We get the picture.'

'OK,' McMullen said '– anyway, what I've done is got the passenger list from the airline, then cross-checked with the boarding card and passport database and I now know the exact time every passenger on last night's flight to Las Palmas went through security here in Liverpool. I've gone through CCTV footage and watched every person go through, all two hundred and fifty-eight of them, to be exact. Quite a task, I might add.'

Freakin' hero, Donaldson thought.

'So, I've got this . . . this guy, wearing a peaked cap which more or less hid his face from the cameras without it being too obvious he was hiding it, is the only Asian on the flight. All the rest are the great unwashed out for a lager-fuelled holiday. He seems to be travelling alone, one piece of hand luggage – and that's it.'

He pressed a switch on the TV remote and the screen came to life, showing a baseball-cap-wearing man approaching the desk at which boarding cards were scanned. He had a small bag over his left shoulder and his travel documents in his left hand. His right arm was held tightly up to his ribcage and hardly moved. He passed his self-generated boarding card over, that being a barcode printed on a piece of A4 paper, which was scanned by the official and handed back to the man, who then walked on, the whole interchange lasting about twenty seconds at most.

The efficiency of modern travel, Donaldson thought. Ripe for terrorists, despite all the crap about heightened security.

The screen then chopped to the next shot: the man passing through security. Placing his bag on the conveyor belt that ran through the X-ray machine, then walking through the body scanner without setting it off. He collected his bag then walked out of shot into the departure area. All the time, his right arm was held against his body, but not in a way that would have brought any attention to him. It was only watching it now that it looked odd, and each man watching the screen knew the reason why.

McMullen flicked off the screen.

Donaldson's mouth was dry, every pulse beating.

'He boarded the Las Palmas flight fifteen minutes later, then made it through their customs at the other end unchallenged – then gone!'

Donaldson said, 'Passport?'

McMullen picked up a piece of paper. 'Seems to be a genuine British passport in the name of Ali Karim. I have the details here. I'm getting it checked now. Question is – is that your man?'

'It is. That's Jamil Akram,' Donaldson said.

'Can you be sure?' Beckham said. 'Those images are not completely clear.'

'It is,' Donaldson said dully. 'We need to check the booking,' he said, thinking out loud, 'see where it originated from, how long it had been made for, whose computer it was made from. And the passport.'

'We wouldn't be here if it wasn't for the cop in Las Palmas. He did well,' McMullen said. 'Followed his instinct.'

'Did his job, you mean?' Donaldson said.

'Whatever,' McMullen said, seeing he wasn't going to get much praise or anything from these three. Fact was, a top-class terrorist had escaped right under their noses by simply walking into an airport and jumping on to a flight. No one was feeling good about that.

'He must have started to bleed again on the plane,' FB said. 'He must be in real pain.'

'And now he's made it to the Canary Islands – but he won't be there for long,' Donaldson said. 'I'll lay odds he's already gone.' His lips pursed and he felt a dark shadow in his brain as his mind juggled all the angles. Some had already been mentioned, such as the origin of the passport and backtracking the on-line booking. Everything would have been in place for Akram to get out of the UK quickly, the only complication was that he – hopefully – still had a bullet in him. It was therefore vital to discover who helped Akram in the hours between him escaping from the car park, getting Rashid Rahman to take over the car, and walking into Liverpool Airport. It was a window of over eight hours.

'Guys,' McMullen said. 'The plane he was on is due to land back here any time now. The seat he sat in and the two next to it have been kept free . . . would you be interested in having a look?'

'Can we also get CSI to have a look?' Donaldson asked. 'Get a sample from the blood, check for prints . . . if anything it could help us get Akram's DNA – which would be good.'

'Grande latte, wet, extra hot, skinny, decaff,' Henry said to the barista at Starbucks, 'and a normal, small latte, too, and a couple of those iced buns,' he added. He was in the short queue in the coffee shop, his eyes constantly checking out the woman he'd arranged to meet.

He paid for and collected the drinks and the buns on a tray and ferried them across to Alison at the small circular table she had managed to snaffle by the window. He slid the mugs and food off the tray, then propped it up next to the window.

'Sorry about the food,' he said. 'Major peckish.'

'Me too. Shopping's hell. I heard your order, by the way,' she grinned. 'You obviously spend too much time in coffee houses.'

'It's become a habit I don't seem capable of breaking. Costing me a small fortune.' He took a sip of his extra hot coffee, which wasn't that hot, but tasted good. He had always subsisted on the kick of coffee, it had sustained him through many a long inquiry, but now he was a little bit addicted to it and lurking around cafes, alone. It felt a bit shameful, like frequenting brothels, but less fun.

Alison sipped hers, her eyes shining across the rim of her mug. 'Well, here we are.'

'Mm.' Henry wiped his lips. 'Yep – here we are.'

He had literally no idea what to say to this lady.

'You never called or came to see me,' she said. It wasn't spoken in a belligerent way, just factual.

'I thought it better not to. For personal and professional reasons.'

Her brow furrowed.

'The personal reasons may have skewed professional judge-
ment, so I thought it better to delegate and let others reach
conclusions, maybe with a few nudges from me.'

So he knows, she thought wildly.

Henry drank more coffee. It wasn't hot at all any more.

'I'm so sorry about your wife,' Alison said.

Henry opened his mouth to say something but no words came
out. Instead, he heated up from the neck and felt slightly nauseous.
In the end, he half-shrugged and drank more coffee, the flow of
which took away the sickly sensation. She reached across and
laid her cool fingertips on the back of his hand, genuine tender-
ness in her eyes.

Henry knew that Alison had lost her husband a few years
earlier in Afghanistan where they had both been serving in the
armed forces, she as a medic. On leaving the forces she had
bought the Tawny Owl pub in Kendleton, where she lived with
her husband's daughter from a previous marriage, and they ran
the place between them.

Hesitantly his hand covered hers. He puffed out a long sigh
that ended with a chuckle. 'What a pair,' he said. 'Us, I mean
. . . not . . .'

'Henry,' she said solemnly, 'talk to me. Say what you need to
say about you and Kate. Unload – because I get the feeling that
so far it's all still bottled up inside.' She paused, her eyes searching
for acknowledgement of this truth – which she got when his eyes
refused to meet hers. 'I won't judge you,' she promised. 'I'll
listen, nod, ask questions and then, when you've finished, maybe
we can possibly think about us. What do you say?'

He squinted, then said weakly, 'I'm not sure where to begin.'

'We'll find a place,' she said, but was cut short by Henry's mobile,
the ringtone of which he'd changed for another Rolling Stones'
intro: *Miss You*. He almost rolled his eyes at the corny pathos.

'Sorry,' he said and answered it, stating his name. He listened
and grunted, then said, 'Fifteen minutes,' and hung up. 'Really
sorry, Alison, got to go. I'm investigating a murder. Got a suspect
in custody.'

'OK,' she said sadly. They looked at each other for a few
lingering seconds before she found the courage to say, 'I'm
booked into the Hilton for the night . . .'

*   *   *

Donaldson leaned over and looked at the bloodstain on the aircraft seat, then turned to the air stewardess who had been on the flight out and who recalled the quiet passenger wedged into the seat. She seemed to quake slightly as Donaldson's eyes took her in and she gasped as she responded to his question.

'Yes, I remember him. This was my section of the plane.' Donaldson watched her mouth and eyes as she spoke and also saw redness creeping up her neck. 'He . . . he . . . er . . . actually didn't move once. He didn't buy anything, no, he did, sorry, a bottle of water. Otherwise just pulled his cap down and slept . . . now I see why.'

'You've been a great help. Thank y'all, ma'am.' He purposely switched on the Yankee twang and the OTT politeness. He had only just learned, maybe in the last eighteen months or so, the effect he had on women, many of whom virtually swooned in his presence. 'Can you tell me anything more about him?'

'No, not really. It was a fairly late flight and quite a few passengers just tucked in and slept.'

'OK, that's great.' He treated her to his best lopsided grin, which made her pupils expand with a blood rush and sent a tremor all the way through her. She turned and walked unsteadily down the centre of the plane, wafting herself with her hands.

Shuffled behind Donaldson, FB and Beckham were both looking at the blood. Donaldson's winning smile morphed into a bitter line as he looked at them. 'What is it now?' he pondered. 'Well over twenty-four hours gone? He walked straight on to a plane at an airport not fifty miles from where he'd been operating, unchallenged, wounded, using a false passport f'Christ's sake. Disembarks four hours later and two thousand miles south, and he's vanished. Fuck!' He looked squarely at Beckham. 'This operation could have gone so much better.'

'I'll let you into a secret,' Beckham retorted, 'this was one of half a dozen anti-terror operations that happened in the UK yesterday, one of over three hundred each year . . . you can't expect—'

Donaldson cut him off. 'But this was the real deal. We ended up with two real live suicide bombers. One dead, one in custody. *Real deal.*'

FB stepped in. 'We still have things. The flat, for one, which might reveal something, and a body to sweat. There's every hope he'll talk.'

'Oh, he'll talk,' Donaldson said. 'I'll make certain of that.'

What Donaldson didn't see was the expression on Beckham's face as he turned away from the American, an expression that said, 'Oh no you won't.'

'What's so urgent it couldn't wait? I said I'd be back, or didn't you pick up your messages?' Henry demanded of Rik Dean, who looked hurt by Henry's sharpness.

'Uh, sorry, boss . . . it's Mark Carter.'

'And?'

'He won't speak to Martin or Ray . . . say's he'll only speak to you.'

'Look, I didn't kill her,' Mark said, voice stressed.

'Right,' said Henry, unimpressed.

'But, like I said, we did, y'know, screw . . . you're going to find my stuff inside her, can't deny that.'

'Can't deny how bad it will look for you, either.'

They were in an interview room within the boundaries of the custody suite. Mark had been processed and had opted for the services of a duty solicitor, who sat alongside him, facing Henry and Rik across the table. The tape and video recorders were running.

'Why do you want to talk to me?' Henry asked.

Mark shrugged helplessly. 'Cos I know you, I suppose. Not that I like you; I don't.'

'Fine. Get talking. The tape's running.'

Mark glanced at the solicitor, one of Blackpool nick's regulars. He nodded encouragement to his client. Mark took a breath. 'I suppose I've been stalking her, really,' he revealed. Henry groaned inwardly. 'She dumped me and I couldn't hack it. Like I said, it was just someone else fucking me off. And I kept, y'know, following her and harassing her and generally pissing her off. But I didn't threaten her or hurt her or anything like that. Just kept annoying her, I suppose.'

'You stalked her,' Henry stated flatly. Mark's body language was desperate, like he was trapped in a well. 'Did you rape her? Is this what it's all about?'

'No – NO! Did I hell. Henry, you know me. I wouldn't hurt

a fly. I was just so . . .' He threw his hands up, lost for words. 'Angry . . . pathetic . . . all alone. Y'know, we'd had a good time, had lots of sex. She was on the pill – but her mum didn't know. Then she dumped me. I could kinda see it coming, bit by bit. She liked lads, lots of 'em.'

'How do you mean?'

'Putting it around. Lewis Kitchen was shagging her too.'

'Just hold on a second. How come you had sex with her a couple of days ago if she'd dumped you?'

'She caved in to my . . . persistence.'

'Stalking, you mean?' Rik interjected.

'OK, yeah,' Mark admitted. 'I knew her mum was out because I'd seen her go. I was, like, watching the house. Then Natalie snuck back, I think, and spotted me lurking. We talked through the window and she let me in. Felt sorry for me, I suppose. She said she was getting ready to go out but I begged her to let me in so we could talk. One thing led to another, next thing we're banging each other's heads off. One for old times' sake. We did it in the front room. Then she kicked me out, said it was over and she had people to see.'

'Did she say who?' Henry asked.

'No.'

'Lewis?'

'Nah, he was well dumped, too.'

'Who, then?'

Mark shrugged

'And that was the last time you saw Natalie Philips? After you'd screwed her on her mum's front carpet.'

'Yes.'

'Was she alive?'

'Yes, she fuckin' was.'

'You sure about that?' Rik swung in. 'You killed her, didn't you? You killed her at her mum's house, I'll bet.'

'Fuck you. I'm saying nothing else.'

TEN

S ailing into Nouadhibou always gave Boone a feeling of desolation – and the creeps.

The final resting place for over three hundred rotting hulks of ships made it the world's largest ship graveyard. Boone shuddered, not just at the sight, which was awesome and ominous in its own way – some ships were almost intact, run up on to sandbanks and abandoned, others just husks, lying on beaches like huge animal carcasses – but also at the thought that each ship had had a life, a meaning, a journey, a crew, and had been brought here to die by way of bribes paid by shady shipping companies to corrupt officials, who then turned a blind eye to the dumping. It was an incredibly sad journey up into the port for any seafarer.

Boone had pushed himself and *Shell* hard northwards along the African coast to Nouadhibou, formerly Port-Étienne, which was Mauritania's second largest city, with about 75,000 inhabitants. Stuck on a forty mile headland, the city had the dubious accolade of being the most popular departure point for African migrants hoping to reach the Canary Islands, thence the EU. It was a very dangerous sea crossing in substandard boats and many thousands were drowned en route every year. About nine thousand actually made it, many landing on the shores of Gran Canaria.

Boone was familiar with the sun-battered port. He'd often called there, either to drop off or pick up cargo – goods or human beings. It was part of the way he maintained his income, for although he had eschewed his completely bad ways, he still had a living to make. Being a small cog in a bigger and very complex wheel of illegal smuggling kept the cash flowing. Ideally, he would have liked to make his living from tourists fishing off the Gambia but that was never going to happen, especially as cash was tighter than ever for everyone.

Not that he was going to let Steve Flynn know exactly what he was up to; once a cop, always a cop, Boone thought, even if Flynn had quit under a cloud. Whatever had been said about the guy, Boone never doubted Flynn's basic honesty – which is why he thought it better not to tell him the details of his bits 'n' bats. That said, he realized Flynn was astute enough to guess, but that was his problem, not Boone's.

And keeping his hand in also gave Boone a bit of a thrill, though occasionally he did worry about his heart. It fluttered a little too much and sometimes he had to pray to keep it beating.

He manoeuvred *Shell* into port, mooring in a convenient gap between some gaudily painted fishing boats, waving at the African faces that watched him idly. Boone had not expected to be here at all. The deal was that he would pick up the man in three weeks' time from another vessel at the same location he'd dropped him off, to the south of Gran Canaria, and then ferry him back to the Gambia; a mirror image of the initial journey. Drop him in Banjul, then bye-bye. Something had obviously gone awry, judging from the frantic phone call Boone had received from Aleef, summoning him immediately to his office in Banjul. That was when Boone had left Flynn in the company of the slightly stoned Michelle – with the hope she didn't pounce on him and screw his brains out whilst Boone was gone. Under the influence of weed and alcohol, she became almost predatory in her needs.

Aleef, the small man, the fixer, had been in a real tizz. He needed Boone to drop everything and get his boat up to Nouadhibou and collect the guy he'd dropped off only a few days earlier.

'Nouadhibou?' Boone exclaimed. 'That lawless shithole? What the hell's he doing there?'

'You don't need to know the whys and wherefores,' Aleef said. He was sweating profusely. 'Just that he's there and needs to be picked up urgently and brought back.'

'Now?'

'Yes. You've been paid to do it, so please do it.'

'No. I've been paid – well, only part-paid actually – to pick this guy up in three weeks. As such I can't just drop everything. I have plans, commitments . . .'

'You can and you will.'

'Fuck you,' Boone said, and made to go.

'How much?' Aleef said hurriedly. 'How much extra?'

Boone paused in mid-turn. Hearing the hint of desperation and recognizing the glint of weakness, he said, 'I want the rest of my money up front for a start – and an extra four thousand. Dollars. I'll have to cancel the charters I've got booked.' He didn't have any charters, but Aleef didn't need to know that. The little man did not even blanch. He spun his desk chair around and leaned towards the big old safe behind him. Edging himself in front of the digital keypad so Boone couldn't see, he tapped in a five-digit code and opened the heavy steel door.

Boone did not see the combination, but did manage to get a glimpse of the contents over Aleef's shoulder and saw it was stashed with blocks of cash. Nothing but. Big blocks of it. And his heart fluttered.

As Aleef spun back and closed the safe, a wad of notes in hand, Boone pretended he had not seen a thing. Aleef tossed the notes on to his desk. 'That should see you.'

Boone snatched the money. 'It'll take me two long days to get up there if I set off now.'

'Then set off.'

'Am I being accompanied?'

Aleef squinted at him, not understanding for a moment. Then it dawned. 'No, you go alone. You get there and he'll find you . . . oh, and you'll need this.' Aleef handed him a green plastic box, the size of a small attaché case, with a red cross emblazoned on it. A comprehensive first aid kit.

Boone didn't ask, just grabbed it and left. Two days later he was in the stinking African port, waiting as instructed. It had been a punishing voyage even though the seas had been kind. After connecting up to the electricity supply, dropping the harbour master fifty dollars, Boone stretched out in the air-conditioned cabin and fell into a much needed sleep.

'At least he was telling the truth,' Henry Christie said, scanning the results of the DNA tests carried out on the sperm found inside Natalie Philips's body, samples having been taken from her uterus and stomach. Henry had pushed hard for the results which often took six weeks to come through, even with a following wind. The sheer volume of work stacked up in the forensic labs was incredible. Only the fact that he knew one of the scientists personally had enable Henry to cajole him into doing a one-off favour – to ascertain if any of the sperm samples matched Mark Carter's DNA profile. A perfect match was made.

He was discussing the results with Rik Dean as they sat at desks in the MIR at Blackpool police station.

'He remains our prime suspect then,' Rik stated. He had not seen the results that had been e-mailed directly to Henry, forwarded ahead of the official report.

'He does . . . but I still don't think he did it.'

'You're just soft on him,' Rik said.

'Over the short time I've known him, I've actually been bloody hard on him.'

'Yeah – and he plays on it. He knows you feel guilty about him. I reckon we pull him back in and sweat the little shit – obviously within the bounds of the Police and Criminal Evidence Act.'

'No. He's on police bail, let's leave it at that for the moment. We need to look at all the other lines. Y'know -- the other ex, Lewis Kitchen, the school teacher who's been paying her too much attention, the missing stepdad. We should have some updates on these, shouldn't we?' There was a debrief due to take place at nine that evening, and the inquiry teams would be reporting their findings. It was now seven.

'Pointless,' Rik said. He jabbed his finger at the printed out e-mail in front of Henry containing the result of the DNA comparison. 'He's our man – boy – whatever. I'm convinced. He admits stalking her – and the way he clammed up when I put it to him. Says a lot, that.'

'Baby love, that's all,' said Henry.

'I vote we bring him back in.'

Henry shook his head. Then he glanced up past Rik's shoulder and saw the figure of Karl Donaldson enter the MIR. Henry pushed the e-mail print out over to Rik and said, 'Read this.'

'Hi pal,' Donaldson said to Henry. He nodded at Rik who'd taken the e-mail and plonked himself down nearby. Donaldson looked exhausted. Henry had hardly seen him in the last couple of days. He'd given him a key to his house with instructions to use the facilities when necessary, but Henry knew he'd been down to London and back again, then back down to keep track on the progress being made in interviews with Zahid Sadiq, the failed suicide bomber. Henry had no idea how that was going. Another high ranking detective had taken over the police shooting on the motorway and apart from being interviewed himself and making a statement, that was as far as his involvement went. He knew it wouldn't go away, though, because the Independent Police Complaints Commission was now in the mix and Henry would be speaking to them shortly. And what a jumble it was, he'd thought: cops, Counter Terrorism, Special Branch, the FBI, MI5, IPCC. He hoped to keep as far away from it as possible. It was like torrid porridge.

'Karl – how goes it?'

'Can we get a coffee somewhere?'

'Sure – Rik's office has a machine on the go. Rik, that OK?'

Rik's eyes rose from the e-mail, wide and astonished. 'Yeah, yeah . . .' he said absently, then, 'fucking hell, Henry. Now I see your point of view about Carter.' He stabbed his finger at the piece of paper. 'According to this she had sex with at least three other men before her death – and oral sex with one of them. She's got four lots of sperm in her.'

'Yep – and we don't know who they are.'

Donaldson took the coffee gratefully, then sat in one of the comfortable chairs in Rik's office. Henry, also coffee in hand, perched on the corner of the desk.

'You look jaded.'

Donaldson held up his mug in a 'cheers' gesture. 'Love you too.'

'Been a slog?'

'Feel like I'm hitting my head against a shithouse wall.'

'I thought you Yanks called them restrooms?'

'Getting too English for my own good. I even queue without complaining these days. Even skipped complaining altogether about anything.'

'Jamil Akram,' Henry guessed.

'Mm.' Donaldson looked despondent. He sighed, 'Part of the problem I have is that I foisted – *foisted*? – myself on Beckham, the spookmeister, and he don't want me around because I annoy him. I know more than he does, but they – your security service – seem content with what they've got.'

'Two suicide bombers, one in custody, one dead?'

'Hey – a victory in the war on terror.'

'A good victory, Karl,' Henry assured him. 'And you played a major part in it.'

'Hell, yeah . . . but it could be so much better . . . and not only that, this goes real deep, Henry. Feel it in my bones.'

'Feel what?'

'Instinct, Henry, instinct. You know what the hell that is?'

'The dictionary definition or the gut-wrenching feeling you have when you just . . . just *know*? That can't be defined.'

'That's the one.' Donaldson stifled a yawn. 'We missed him by a gnat's todger. I picked that up from one of your Met guys.'

'A midge's dick.'

'Same difference.' He sipped his coffee. It was good, slightly bitter and with a subtle kick to it. 'Jamil Akram is a fanatical terrorist,' he said forcefully. 'He runs training camps that teach stupid kids how to make bombs, shoot guns, stick knives into people and he has the ability to brainwash people, too. Simple kids who are disaffected and want something . . . his bombs have been planted in war zones and shopping malls. People he's brainwashed have walked up to military checkpoints, superstores, and blown themselves and hundreds of others to pieces. His bombs were used in the American Embassy blast in Kenya in 1998 where I lost a good pal. Mostly, though, he doesn't come out of hiding. But when he does, it precedes something major.'

'Do you have evidence of that?'

'Intelligence over the years, yes. Which is why I have a very bad feeling.'

'As to why he put in an appearance here?'

Donaldson nodded.

'What does Zahid Sadiq have to say on the subject?' Henry asked, naming the young man entombed in the depths of Paddington Green police station.

'Not a lot . . . I haven't been allowed in to torture him yet. Haven't been allowed near him, come to that,' he said wistfully.

A deep tremor zinged through Henry's veins. Donaldson – FBI agent, husband, father of three incredible kids – gave the impression of being a simple, straightforward bloke, good at his job and a bit naïve in the ways of the world. But if this veneer was peeled away, Henry knew there was much, much more to this man. He could be a violent operator, in a controlled way, and had no qualms in making bad guys suffer. Over the years, Henry had pieced bits together and was fairly certain that his friend carried out clandestine jobs for the US government and certainly wasn't averse to torture if he thought it necessary. Henry had witnessed some of Donaldson's interview techniques first-hand and they had shocked him, even though he understood the purpose behind them. And his little offhand remark, Henry knew, was more than a joke or a flight of fancy. If he could have Sadiq to himself, Henry had no doubt that the misguided youth would soon be begging to confess all.

A text message landed on Donaldson's phone. He shuffled it out of his chinos pocket, read it, then said, 'You got Internet access here?' Henry pointed to the computer on Rik's desk. Donaldson handed his phone to Henry and said, 'Can we have a look at this?'

The knocking woke Boone. He jerked awake, almost falling off the bench in the cockpit. Rubbing his eyes and making a dry clacking noise with his tongue on the roof of his mouth, he stood sleepily and took in the figure standing at the cockpit door.

It was a hunched, desperate looking, grey-faced man, gaunt and wild, and for a moment Boone did not recognize him. Then he did, just in the moment before he said, 'What the fuck're you doing on my boat?' But the words, though formed, did not come out because he realized this frail individual was the man he'd taken to Gran Canaria a few days earlier, and transferred to another boat. Boone also recognized there was something very wrong with him now, hence the appearance.

'I'm here,' the man said. He stepped forwards and then, seemingly for no reason, he stumbled. His eyes rolled up in their sockets, so that they now resembled yellow billiard balls, and he fell. Boone's tired mind clicked into place and he caught the guy before he, literally, hit the deck.

Boone dragged him roughly through the cockpit into the state-room and heaved him on to the bed. As his hands came away, they were wet and, when he looked, covered in blood. Boone swore.

The man opened his eyes, gasped.

'Jesus, man,' Boone said. He removed the man's zip-up jacket and saw that the area around the top of his right arm and chest was soaked in blood. The man moaned. Boone gagged slightly, tossed the jacket to one side and peeled the man's shirt off, blowing out his cheeks as he saw the equally blood-sodden bandages around the man's bicep.

'What the hell happened?'

'You do not need to know,' the man whispered.

'OK. Nor do I know what's underneath those bandages, but I do know you need medical attention.'

'I've had some. You must take me back to the Gambia.'

'After you've seen a doctor.'

'No. Just take me back. That is what you have been paid for.'

'I haven't been paid to take a dead man on my boat.'

The man's eyes were cold and he meant it when he said, 'If I die, then throw me to the sharks.'

Boone and he regarded each other. Boone ground his teeth noisily. The man exhaled and winced. Boone weighed up the odds – and saw the blood starting to stain the duvet cover.

'I want extra money. I'm not a fucking paramedic.'

'OK. There's money in my wallet. Sterling. But I need the wound re-dressing, I think. The bullet has been removed, so you don't have to worry about that.'

Boone sneered and knew that there and then he should have set sail and hoisted the man into the Atlantic, dead or alive. But the money lured him and he was also proud that – up to a point – he was a man of his word. He had been contracted to do a job and he would do it to the best of his abilities.

He nodded and realized why Aleef had given him the first aid kit, in which he'd found half a dozen morphine ampoules amongst everything else. He knelt down and peeled the blood-soaked bandages from the arm, revealing a truly ugly wound underneath, most likely caused by a gunshot that had entered the back of the bicep. He looked into the man's eyes; his head was angled down as he watched Boone.

'Jesus,' Boone said again.

'Your prophet, not mine,' the man said. 'Although I doubt you have a religious bone in your body.'

'Strictly an unbeliever.'

'Then why blaspheme?'

Boone shrugged and dropped the bandages into a plastic waste bin, where they landed with an unedifying splat. With distaste on his face, Boone inspected the wound closely. Under normal circumstances it looked like a pretty treatable wound, if getting shot could be considered to be normal. Something any half-competent ER doctor would have eaten up. But it was blatantly obvious that this man did not wish to turn up at a casualty department.

'Who took out the bullet?' Boone asked.

'A friend.'

A friend who hadn't really cleaned up after the mess. It needed disinfecting, though the blood oozing from it appeared to be nice and clean at the moment. But wounds like this had to have proper treatment in Africa because it was a continent of disease. At least it didn't whiff just yet.

So far the guy had been lucky.

Boone wiped around the hole with antiseptic pads, then squeezed a tube of antiseptic cream into it, before covering it with a clean plaster and a bandage. He broke one of the morphine ampoules, filled a syringe and jabbed it into the man's thigh through his trousers, then thumbed the plunger down slowly.

'I'll get you a mug of tea and a bottle of water. You need to keep yourself hydrated. Then we'll be on our way.'

The man nodded. 'Thank you.' His eyes became dreamy as the morphine took effect. He laid himself out on the bed and closed his eyes.

Ten minutes later they were underway and Boone was easing *Shell* carefully out of port, past the ships in the graveyard, and heading out to open sea, sailing south. He had slipped the man's passport and wallet out of his jacket without him noticing and had them both resting on the angled console in front of him.

By the dimmed cockpit light, he inspected both documents.

The passport, in the name of Ali Karim, meant nothing to him, other than it was British and looked genuine enough. The leather wallet, soaked in blood, was much more interesting. It contained five hundred pounds sterling and three hundred and fifty euros. Boone flicked through the wads, thinking, these guys certainly have money behind them. He visualized the cash he'd peeked at, stashed up in Aleef's safe. He eased three hundred pounds and two hundred euros out of the wallet and slid the notes into his back pocket, wondering what the wounded Ali Karim had been up to, if that was his real name – Boone doubted that – and who might be after him.

*   *   *

They watched the computer screen in silence, Rik Dean joining them and standing quietly behind, still holding the e-mail.

A bearded young man sat cross-legged in front of a draped Islamic flag with a green crescent moon and five-pointed star, wearing a turban, a grubby white *galabiyya* and rubber slippers, telling the world in a regional English accent just why he was prepared to give his life for Islam, why he hated Western infidels and why his death was easy in the fight against the oppressors. Laid across his lap was a Kalashnikov rifle and unfolded in front of him was a waistcoat packed with blocks of explosives.

Henry's nostrils flared as he watched the rant. A chill came over him to see such alienation coupled with brainwashing. But much worse, the thing that made it all the more chilling, was the English accent. Pure Lancashire.

This was the video posted on-line, made by Rashid Rahman, the young would-be suicide bomber who had been shot dead on the motorway. The fact he hadn't had a chance to detonate the bomb that had been strapped around his middle was not the point. That he hadn't taken fifty other innocent people with him, as he clearly stated was his intention – 'so they may go to hell and I to heaven' – did not matter. He was to have died an Islamic hero's death, but now, of course, he'd been murdered by the hand of the infidel. Then he added, 'And this is only the beginning, the big one is yet to come.'

Henry paused the screen and looked at Donaldson, then back at the grainy image.

'That guy, that lad,' Donaldson said, 'was born in the UK, educated here, was at college in this town until a couple of months ago – when apparently he quit for no reason . . . but now we know why, don't we?'

'What about his parents?'

'I haven't met them,' Donaldson said, 'but they own a shop in Bispham and from all accounts they're devastated.'

'What about the parents of the lad in custody, the one you stopped?'

'Zahid Sadiq?' Donaldson wiped an eye with a finger. 'His parents are both doctors from Preston, one in a practice here in Blackpool. I have briefly met them. They are . . . it's beyond words, really . . . cannot believe their precious son had been radicalized. Seems both boys lived double lives. They didn't even know they'd been to Yemen. Which is where this was probably shot.'

An overwhelming sadness descended on the three of them.

'Intelligent lads, nice lads – outwardly,' Donaldson said. 'And although it sounds clichéd, in the hands of a manipulator like Jamil Akram, they didn't stand a chance. He's sent so many people, kids like these, to their pointless deaths.'

'And when he appears on the scene, it's usually a portent,' Henry said.

'Yep.'

'So how did they come to meet him in the first place?' Henry asked.

Donaldson shrugged. 'Probably via a local mosque. Dunno.' He sounded completely depressed.

Henry clicked the mouse and dragged the video back a few seconds as Rahman, now dead, finished his triumphant speech about his planned glorious death with the words, 'And this is only the beginning, the big one is yet to come.' The screen went blank.

Henry felt slightly guilty about having to abandon Donaldson that evening. It was clear his friend wanted to talk things through, mull it all over, but Henry had other plans. First of all the murder squad had to be debriefed. Everyone was due in for an update and a download at nine p.m. Then, from what was gleaned, Henry and Rik had to work out the strategy and tasking for the next day. There was no way he would be finished before eleven.

When he explained this to Donaldson, the American had instantly suggested a late night whiskey in Henry's conservatory, but Henry had bluffed his way out of that. At least that is what he thought he'd done until Donaldson tilted his head and gave him a squinted look of suspicion. 'Have you got a date?' he said. 'Or are you seeing a hooker? Which one?'

'Just a rendezvous with a friend,' Henry said tightly.

'A kissin' friend?'

'None of your business, pal.'

'So you're getting back on to the hey-ho?'

'Just a friend.'

'Anyone I know?'

'Why would you?'

Donaldson shrugged his broad shoulders. 'I need an early night, anyhow. I'm bushed.'

'Good idea.'

'Hey, pal,' Donaldson said. The two men locked eyes meaningfully. 'If I'm right, it's fine with me. No judgements from this
neck of the woods.'

'I know.'

'But I still want to talk to ya, brainstorm a bit, yeah?'

'Fine.'

The debrief went smoothly. Each pair of investigating detectives pooled their accumulated knowledge of the short and, as it
was turning out, rather sordid life of Natalie Philips. Not that
her lifestyle made any difference to Henry. He particularly hated
it when young people came to sticky ends, hated the thought of
a young life snuffed out and the death of possibility. In any
murder inquiry, he gave his all. In the case of a youngster, he
pushed even harder.

Some good stuff came up. Ex-boyfriend Lewis Kitchen had
been found and was due to be pulled in tomorrow. The name of
the teacher who supposedly had the hots for Natalie had been
unearthed and was also going to be spoken to next day. Some
of her friends had been interviewed and a clearer picture of her
life was emerging, in that for the past few weeks she had with-
drawn from her mates and was being secretive about who she
was seeing. There was a stumbling block with her computerized
social network contacts, the detectives being unable to access
her Facebook account, from which she had recently de-friended
most of her contacts. Henry took the opportunity to reveal what
had been found inside Natalie and that DNA tests were in the
database queue for the three unidentified sperm samples. He told
everyone that although Mark Carter remained a good suspect,
this investigation was by no means over.

Afterwards he and Rik did next day's tasking and Henry brought
the murder book up to date, which in turn brought him to eleven
fifteen p.m. Uneasily he picked up his mobile phone and sent a
text, receiving a reply only moments later that said, 'YES'.

She was waiting for him in the bar of the Hilton Hotel. It was
quiet, just a few lonesome looking businessmen staring glumly
into spirit glasses, and Alison Marsh sitting in a corner reading
a novel. She closed it as he walked across the bar and they smiled
warmly, but uncertainly, at each other. Internally he had a very
warm glow and a sudden sense of euphoria, even though his throat

seemed to close up. She laid the book on the table in front of her, her eyes playing over the weary Henry, now slightly dishevelled after another long day. There was a glass of red wine on the table and Henry asked her if she wanted another, finding his voice sticking in his closed throat and unable to form any coherent words.

Seeing his discomfort, she said, 'JD on the rocks?'

'Coming up,' he declared after a cough. He made to turn to the bar, but Alison rose to her feet and touched his arm.

'In my room,' she said huskily. 'It's all prepared.'

They looked at each other.

'The time for talking's over, Henry.'

And he realized it probably was. When they had met the other night for a drink in the same location, he had poured out, for the first time to anyone, his grief about losing Kate. Alison had listened, allowed him to download, and for him it had been an incredible release. For the first time he had told someone about Kate, their ups and downs, the bad way he'd treated her, the fact that although they had divorced she stuck with him through it all and eventually they had remarried. And been happy. Then she had been struck down by something evil and ferocious which was more than a match for her grim determination to stay alive. He spoke for almost an hour, non-stop, then had suddenly looked into Alison's eyes before melting into her arms and holding her tightly. After that they talked about her husband, Robert, the soldier killed in Afghanistan.

'So I kind of know what you're going through,' she'd said gently. 'I know everyone's different, everyone reacts differently to the unexpected, or expected, death of a loved one . . . but I do know what it's like.'

They parted with a hug that night.

Henry could not get her off his mind, even though he fought grimly with the guilt, the recentness of Kate's death, and about how others would react, his daughters in particular. In the end, he knew he had to be true to himself.

He took her hand as they walked out of the bar. His legs were dithery. His whole being was trembling. They rode the lift in silence, Henry just holding Alison's little finger as they stood side by side.

Moments later they were in her room.

Then they kissed and the JD on the rocks had to wait for a while.

She lay tucked into him, her arm across his chest, fingertips touching his left shoulder and the raised scars where he'd been blasted by the shotgun, now well over a year ago. Six inches to the right and his heart would have been shredded, and he would have been the first to die, not Kate. But he had survived and the wounds healed.

It had been through Alison's nursing skills that he'd come away from the incident so well.

She raised her eyes. 'That was lovely.'

'Short and sweet,' he admitted.

'Just right under the circumstances.'

His head moved down and he kissed her mouth, loving the taste and texture of her very soft lips. A surge of blood gushed through him and her hand left his shoulder and slid silkily down his body to grasp him, causing a moan to emerge from the back of his throat, then from hers.

'Gorgeous,' he whispered.

With amazing dexterity she was suddenly on top of him, moving gently, and he was entranced by her looks.

His mobile phone rang at half past midnight. Henry grunted, carefully extracted his right arm from under Alison's neck, and sat on the edge of the bed. He had been on the verge of a deep sleep. He glanced at Alison, who muttered something, but kept her eyes closed. Henry sifted through his clothing which was discarded across the floor. It had been ripped off with abandon, as had Alison's, and he grinned like a juvenile at the memory, especially when he picked up her bra. That had been one of the great moments.

The phone continued to ring – still *Miss You* by the Stones. Have to change that, he thought. Maybe *Mixed Emotions*.

Finally he found the infernal device, plucked it out of his inner jacket pocket, and it stopped ringing. He muttered a curse.

The display said, 'Unknown number'.

'Bugger,' he said, laid it on the bedside cabinet. He needed the toilet, but was reluctant to go, particularly when Alison reached out and scraped her fingernails gently down his back.

'Who was it?'

'No idea.'

'Kiss me,' she ordered him. He twisted around and she had a lovely crooked smile on her face. 'I need kissing.'

Henry thought about saying something witty, but decided against it. He needed kissing, too, so he lay down next to her, cupped her face and lowered his mouth to hers and they explored, teeth, tongues, lips and wetness. It wasn't just a lust-driven mashing, which it had been initially. It was slow and slithery and Henry, amazing himself, found that he was responding yet again.

And then the phone rang. *Miss You.*

He snatched it up, dropped back on to the pillow and answered it. Alison propped herself up on an elbow and bit into his nipple.

'Christie,' he hissed through clenched teeth, and Alison suppressed a wicked giggle.

'It's me, your prime suspect.'

Henry held the phone away from his ear and squinted angrily at it. He put it back. 'Mark – it's way past midnight. This better be good.'

'It's about Natalie.'

'What about her?'

'I was going to tell you stuff about her – until that twat annoyed me.'

'DI Dean?'

'Yeah, him.'

'OK – what were you going to say?'

Alison continued to suck and lick his nipple like it was a mini lollipop.

'Her likes, her preferences.'

'What do you mean by that?'

'She liked Asians, Pakistanis . . . well, she'd started liking them recently.'

'And?'

'I've seen the picture of the guy who was shot on the motorway, yeah?'

'OK.' Henry sat up. Alison backed off as he held up a hand to keep her at bay.

'And the picture of the lad locked up in London now, the suicide bomber guy.'

'Yeah?'

'They were the ones she liked.'

ELEVEN

After just two hours' deep sleep, Henry stirred at six o'clock, detached himself from Alison's grip – she rolled over with a disgusted grunt – and padded into the bathroom, picking up his discarded clothing on the way. He dressed, then left without disturbing her, his mind still zinging with confused thoughts about the relationship.

He needed to get home, shower, shave and change into fresh clothing, then get into the MIR before anyone else landed. This, he thought, as he climbed into the Mercedes, was going to be a long day.

He arrived home less than ten minutes later, the streets of Blackpool virtually traffic-free at that time of day. Karl Donaldson's huge Jeep was parked on the driveway alongside Leanne's Fiat 500. This car had belonged to Kate and Leanne had inherited it. Henry swallowed a fresh gulp of guilt at the sight of the Fiat, and just for a moment he wondered how the hell he was going to explain himself to Kate, arriving home at this time of day, bedraggled and with bloodshot eyes. Then he remembered. He shook his head, but the gulp stuck in his throat as he let himself quietly into the house.

He heard the running of a shower from the main bathroom. It was unlikely to be Leanne, so Henry knew it would be Donaldson up and ready to face the world again. The guy had boundless energy and no doubt had already been for a three mile run. Fit, good-looking bastard, Henry thought.

Lifting one heavy leg after the other up the stairs, Henry sidled into his bedroom like a naughty teenager sneaking home. Still feeling the guilt. He undressed, and when he heard the other shower stop, he got into the en suite shower, turned it on hot and stood for a very long time under the driving jets.

Twenty minutes later, fresh as a daisy, newly clothed and with everything trimmed, including nose and ear hair, Henry walked into the kitchen where Donaldson was pouring a mug of freshly filtered coffee. The toaster popped up as Henry entered. His friend gave him one of those knowing looks.

'Say nothing,' Henry warned him.

Donaldson's eyebrows arched as he considered this, then he said, 'You know I can't do that, don't you?'

Henry poured himself a coffee whilst Donaldson buttered the toast and dropped two more slices into the toaster. He hummed irritatingly, a cheeky grin on his face, then armed with food and drink made his way to the conservatory to eat.

Henry joined him a few minutes later, similarly equipped.

'Work colleague?' Donaldson probed. Henry remained mysteriously silent. 'Hooker?' Still nothing. 'Second cousin twice removed? We are, after all, in the backwoods here?' Nothing. He squinted at Henry. 'Can't be a cougar – you're the one who's too old.'

Henry bristled, but oddly enjoyed the tease.

'Supermodel?' No response. 'You know I'll find out, I'm a superb FBI agent for God's sake.'

'Stop.' Henry raised a piece of toast threateningly. 'Stop right there. I'm pretty screwed up about it as it stands.' This was an ironic thing for Henry to say. His history of extramarital relationships would have made most observers draw the conclusion that Henry hadn't cared very much about Kate's feelings when she had been alive, so now that she was gone, what did it matter? He just knew it did.

'Who is she?' This time Donaldson's probe was gentle.

'Alison Marsh.'

'The barmaid?' Donaldson said. He had met her at the same time as Henry in the blood-soaked village of Kendleton.

'The landlady, to be more precise. The owner of a very nice country pub stroke hotel.'

'And a woman with a dark secret.' Donaldson made a pistol shape with his fingers.

'Aye, maybe . . . whatever.'

'But she is very nice. How . . . er?'

'Call out of the blue.'

'Could it be serious?'

'Who the heck knows? I don't think I'm handling it very well.'

'It's early days.'

'That's part of the problem, I reckon.'

'What? Social niceties? Henry, this is me, your biggest pal.' He leaned forwards with his toast. 'Screw social niceties and let whatever is going to happen, happen. If it's a fling, then so be it. Screw each other senseless. If it's serious, well good for both of you. She deserves happiness and, what's more important to me, so do you.'

Henry regarded him open-mouthed. 'I thought you were an FBI agent, not a relationship counsellor.'

'I can turn my hand to most things . . . except DIY, much to Karen's annoyance.'

'OK, bud, thanks for the ass-kicking.' Henry bit into his toast, then with his mouth full said, 'I've something that might interest you.'

'This is a legitimate question,' Henry said to Mark Carter. 'Are you just pissing us about, or what?'

Mark looked affronted – and angry. 'I'm telling you the truth, man.'

'Start talking, then.'

The interview was monitored by Rik and Donaldson via an audio/video feed into the DI's office. The picture on the monitor wasn't brilliant but the speech was clear enough, and when Henry drew the interview to a close, the two men leaned back, looked at each other, but said nothing as they watched Henry and Mark vacate the interview room down in the custody office.

Rik poured Donaldson a coffee, one for himself and one for Henry, who was expected a few minutes later when he'd re-bailed Mark.

Although Henry hadn't arrested Mark this time, he wanted to re-bail him, so he led the lad back to the custody office, only to find a man arrested on a warrant was being booked in, so they had to wait.

He and Mark stood patiently at the back of the room, waiting for the custody desk to clear. Henry had a few papers rolled up in his hand, and was tapping his chin thoughtfully when Mark said, 'Are those the photos of the guys?' Henry nodded. 'Can I have a look again?'

Mark had already seen the photographs of Sadiq and Rahman and confirmed they were students attending the same college that he did and that he'd seen them talking to Natalie in a more than friendly way. That was the basis of what he'd told Henry – that he knew the two Asian lads by sight, not personally, and that Natalie knocked around with them in the dining rooms and common room. And that it had got him mad.

Henry handed the photos over absent-mindedly. He was busy rolling this new information through his mind, wondering if it was important or just juvenile tittle-tattle. Mark opened the sheets and looked at them and said, 'Yeah, these are the guys. Geeks, I'd've said.' Then he said, 'Who's this guy?'

'Who?' Henry looked and realized he had inadvertently handed Mark a photograph of Jamil Akram which was also in his file. Mark was studying the photograph intently. It wasn't a good one, a bit grainy and blurred, a surveillance photograph that could have been taken on the other side of the world.

'This one.'

'Why?' When Mark hesitated, Henry sensed he was back-tracking then. 'Why?' Henry said forcefully.

'I . . . er . . . saw Sadiq and Rahman and Natalie with this guy.'

Henry dragged him by the collar straight back into the inter-view room they'd just vacated.

'Speak.'

'Uh, remember I said me and Natalie did it on her mum's rug?'

'How could I forget – I'm constantly trying to purge my mind of the image.'

'Well, it was for old time's sake. But I was still mad and I wanted to know what she was up to . . .'

'So?'

'I hid and waited, and then followed her when she went out. She got a bus and I followed her into town, then she got another bus up to North Shore.'

'How did you follow her?'

'On my bike. Pretty easy. Buses don't go that fast. Anyway, she got off at North Shore, so I dumped my bike in a backyard and legged after her on foot, and next thing she's walking up to a flat, when the two geeks come out and there's a load of kissing and huggin' and stuff. Fuck, I thought *they* didn't do things like that in public. Y'know – Asians.'

Henry rolled his eyes. 'Where was this?' Henry mentioned the name of a road and Mark confirmed it. 'Then what happened?'

'Then that other guy, the older one, came out of the flat and the geeks introduced her to him.'

'And you saw all this?'

'Uh-huh. I was hid behind a wall. I'd got pretty good at stalking her.'

'Then what?'

'She went back into the flat with Rahman and the bloke, and Sadiq set off walking in my direction. I just slid off then. Bet they were all fucking her,' Mark snorted.

'And you're certain this was the man?' Henry held up Akram's photograph.

Mark nodded. 'Who is he?'

'A very bad man.'

Henry's coffee had gone cold. He looked at Donaldson and Rik Dean, who themselves were looking pretty stunned. They had watched the whole thing on the AV feed.

'Well?' Henry said.

'Pure gold,' Donaldson said.

'I've never been impressed with him,' Rik said. 'He's a little shit and could be lying to save his own backside. He only knows Sadiq and Rahman because they went to the same college as him.'

'You really are a cynic,' Henry said.

'You mean you're not?' Rik exclaimed. 'You must be going soft in your dotage.'

Henry grinned. 'Whatever . . . that said, we now need to interview Sadiq down in London. I promise I won't lose sight of the fact that Mark's sperm was inside Natalie . . . but I know he wasn't her killer.'

'I think he's clean,' Donaldson said.

'And I suspect everyone,' Rik said.

'You remind me so much of a younger me,' Henry said.

'Ugh!'

'Where do we go from here, then?' Donaldson said. 'I only ask, because if you can get to interview Sadiq, I'd like to sneak in on the back of it, particularly after this little revelation.'

Henry pouted. 'It's unlikely they would allow you into

Paddington Green even if they let me in, especially if they've already blocked you.'

'Maybe we could get him back up here?' Rik suggested. 'That's what we'd do normally.'

Henry pondered for a moment, then said brightly, 'I know – let's go and annoy the chief constable.'

For a brief second he took stock of himself and found he was unaccountably happy. He was having an interesting time at work, his personal life was also . . . interesting. Actually, both areas were quite fun and he thought he might just delete his 'Intention to Retire' report. And the prospect of winding up FB was also highly appealing.

Three quarters of an hour later Henry entered the office on the middle floor of the headquarters building at Hutton that housed the staff officers and admin team for the chief constable and the deputy chief constable. The room acted as a firewall and had to be negotiated like a level in a video game if one wanted to get in front of the chief or the dep. Their offices – inner sanctums – were accessed from here, a door at either side of the room; to the left, the chief, to the right, the dep.

The chief's staff officer had changed recently. The role had been taken by a female chief inspector that Henry knew quite well, but from whom he did not expect any quarter. She glanced up from her computer as he breezed in and plonked himself down next to her on the chair positioned at the end of her desk.

'Morning, Henry,' she smiled.

'Deb,' Henry said, returning with one of his best lopsided boyish smiles, designed to soften the heart of any woman. At least that was what he hoped. 'How are you? Settling into the job?' She had only been in post a couple of months.

'Fits like a glove.'

'Pity about the boss?' he said. She smiled.

'What can I do for you?'

'Need to see him.'

She shook her head. 'Zero chance.'

'It's very important.'

'The dep might be free – in about three days.'

'Has to be the chief.'

She leaned her chin on her hand and studied him. 'Which bit of "no" don't you understand? I can make an appointment, but it'll be next week now.'

'He is in, though?' Henry jerked his head at FB's thick office door.

'All the divisional commanders are in with him, the finance director and the head of HR. Apparently the government has decided to cut our budget by twenty percent and they're brainstorming how. Long, long session.'

'I can feel the brain heat emanating from the room.' Henry held out his hands, palms out, as if he was warming them on a coal fire. 'All those dendrites zapping across their grey matter.'

The chief inspector laughed. 'I can't interrupt, Henry. I'm sorry. They're hunkered down for the day, lunch and everything.'

Henry's mouth curled thoughtfully. 'Shove a piece of paper under his nose for me?'

Henry had abandoned Rik and Donaldson in the ground floor dining room. He walked back to them with a shrug and sat down.

'He's busy, but I've left a message.'

Henry had his back to the door, so he was facing out with a view of the headquarters social club, known colloquially as 'The Grovellers' Arms'. The eyes of the two men with him looked back past him as FB entered the room, waving a piece of paper in his hand with irritation.

'Brief me. You've got five minutes, then I'm going back to that meeting where, I'm sure, my brain's going to implode.'

FB took the spare seat at the table, big, rotund, mustachioed, like Buddha's fifth cousin twice removed but much more wrinkly. He and Henry had known each other many years and their relationship was complex. FB had used Henry on many an occasion, mainly for his own ends, and there was no love lost between them. However, when things went to the wire FB had actually backed up Henry, which is what Henry was hoping for this time. But he wasn't banking on it.

Henry explained everything succinctly, as instructed. FB hated superfluous detail. The chief looked suspiciously at Donaldson, then back to Henry.

'You need to speak to the lad in custody because you have information linking him to a murder victim. Fair enough, and it should be possible to achieve. But why the Yank?' He thumbed at Donaldson.

'He could do with speaking to the lad, too,' Henry said, making FB snort derisively.

'But not about the murder of a girl in Lancashire?' FB said. 'No.'

'I'd guess it would be about Jamil Akram,' FB said. He looked at Donaldson again. 'They're freezing you out, aren't they?'

Donaldson nodded. 'I don't think the security services have grasped the implications of Akram turning up on the scene. And now with Mark Carter's identification, we have him clearly linked to Sadiq and Rahman, if he wasn't before.'

FB snorted again. 'Think you're wrong there, pal. They know it all and that's why they want to be the ones trying to squeeze every last drop of information out of that poor misguided youth.'

Donaldson's face fell. It was something he had suspected, but having it confirmed by a third party was like being hit by a truck.

Then Henry said, 'They want Akram for themselves.'

Donaldson's body slumped.

'Yep,' FB sighed. 'You'll not get a look in.'

'I know more about Akram than any of them,' Donaldson whined weakly. 'I've been after him for over ten years. Sadiq might know something extra that I can slot into the other pieces of my jigsaw. Something that will lead to his front door.'

'They won't let you talk to him. *You* might not get to him either,' FB said to Henry.

Henry's voice was indignant. 'I have every right.' He knew instantly he sounded like a probationer constable who only saw the world in black and white, right and wrong, not a grizzled old-timer who knew the world was as murky and grey as 1950s' London smog. 'Sorry,' he said, as all eyes turned to him.

FB went into deep thought, eyes a squint. 'How quickly can you get the DNA profiles done on the outstanding sperm samples?' he asked Henry.

'I managed to get Mark Carter's fast-tracked through a personal contact. I doubt I can repeat that.'

'Try,' FB said. Then his attention turned to Donaldson. FB's mind was also grinding hard on the subject. FB had been a career detective, rising up through the ranks in plain clothes, so he thought like one still. 'It would be helpful if the DNA profile from the blood on the plane could be fast-tracked, too, don't you think? I know . . .' he said, before Donaldson had the chance to point out that this was completely out of his hands because the sample had actually been taken by a Merseyside CSI and had been submitted through that force's channels. He leaned forwards. 'Can I just give you my line of thinking? We need power to our elbows if we're to have any chance of getting to interview Sadiq. First off, all the DNA samples taken from her body have to be profiled and ready for comparison. Four profiles, four comparisons. Mark Carter's is done, that leaves three – so what if the three belong to Sadiq, Rahman and Akram? What if all three of those guys had sex with her?'

Henry, Rik and Donaldson exchanged excited glances.

'The first thing we need to do is get Sadiq's and Rahman's DNA analysed.'

'We still have Rahman's body in the mortuary,' Henry said. 'And his DNA would have been taken as a matter of course.'

'But he's dead – and you can't speak to him,' FB said. 'But, yes, his DNA needs cross-checking with the samples. Then, if we get Sadiq's DNA analysed . . . if that comes back positive, then there's no way we should have any problems in getting to see Sadiq. And—'

Donaldson intercut, 'If Akram's DNA matches one of the samples from Natalie's body, then we're whoopin'.'

'That's only if these things match up . . . but if they do, then perhaps you can shoehorn yourself into Henry's slipstream.'

'I also think we need to have another look at Sadiq's flat,' Henry said. 'If Natalie was seeing the two lads as Mark suggests, it might be possible to find something in the property that relates to her. That'll help our cause, too.'

'Mm,' FB said dubiously. 'You might be too late on that score. That place is being gutted, packed and then sent off for detailed examination by MI5 and CT as we speak. You'll need to move quickly, otherwise it'll all go, then you'll have no chance.'

'Shit,' Henry said.

'Anything else I can solve for you?' FB asked. 'I need to get back to my budget meeting. We're just discussing FMIT, actually. Need to cut that budget by thirty percent.'

'What budget would that be?' Henry said. The Force Major

Investigation Team operated on a minuscule budget, the money to run long inquiries coming from other sources as necessary, not from the FMIT pot.

'We're wondering whether four superintendents isn't a bit OTT,' FB said. 'Two could probably be enough, so we could easily lose two of you . . . and as two of you could retire if pushed . . . just a thought.'

Henry's guts churned. Maybe quitting the job wouldn't be down to him after all.

'Anyway,' he muttered, 'thanks for your input, sir. Very valuable.'

'Happy to help. Once a jack and all that. Actually, I'm happy to help anyone, even the security services, but I was, and still am, miffed by the fact that they seemed willing to put my officers into danger without briefing them properly.' His eyes turned to Donaldson. 'You know what I mean.'

'Yes sir,' Donaldson said.

FB nodded then revolved away towards the door.

There was silence at the table.

Then Henry said, 'As it appears I have nothing to lose, I'm going to hijack any evidence from that flat and get a tame scientist to look for any traces of Natalie.'

Flynn had fished all the time that Boone had been away. Mainly from the beaches south of Banjul, on safari from early each morning to evening, using Boone's beat up Land Cruiser for transport. It had been a wonderful time. Being alone throughout the days was quite therapeutic.

After the fishing he returned to *Faye2* and following a long shower, shave and cold beer, made his way to Boone's houseboat to be cooked for by Michelle. It was worth watching her glide about the place in her loose flowing African dresses; sometimes the breeze blowing the fine fabric taut against her breasts or between her legs made it obvious that she wore nothing of note underneath and had shaved everything. She seemed oblivious to Flynn's sneaky peeks, but as each evening progressed and she drank a little wine, inhaled good quality weed, she became more flirty with him.

But that was as far as it went. From their conversations – deep and meaningful – Michelle seemed to have an almost spiritual insight into Flynn's soul, but not so much as to make him feel uncomfortable. It was obvious she was completely sold on Boone, and Flynn had no wish to spoil that. He was slightly envious, though, because he, Flynn, had no one. An ex-wife, a son he hardly ever saw and a woman he had loved who was now dead. That was his emotional footprint. He was seeing someone in Gran Canaria, but it was a relationship based on animal lust and he knew it was going nowhere. In the years following his divorce and his exit from the cops, he thought he would never want anyone to need him ever again, and vice versa. But as he aged – he was only a few years short of fifty now – he knew he wanted to spend his life with someone else, but that person eluded him.

Michelle had been reassuring on that point.

'Seek and you will never find. Just rest, relax, and the world will come to you,' she predicted over beer and cannabis. 'You are a good man, Steve Flynn. I can feel it here.' She placed a hand on to her groin. Flynn gulped. Then she removed it and put her palm on to her chest. 'And here.'

Flynn calmed down, but his hand was dithering slightly as he drew his beer to his lips and sipped.

They had eaten one of Michelle's wonderful chicken dishes, hot, spicy, aromatic, when the short wave radio in the galley squawked and Flynn heard Boone's voice calling.

Michelle dashed down to answer it whilst Flynn sat back in the comfortable wicker chair and let his food settle. He did not take heed of the conversation going on below deck and soon Michelle came back up, beaming happily. 'Boone is less than an hour away.'

Flynn raised his beer. 'I'll drink to that.' At that moment the evening breeze moulded Michelle's dress against her body, leaving nothing to Flynn's imagination. In his mind he said, 'And I'll drink to that, too.'

'I'll go and greet him.' Flynn rose from the second game of chess he and Michelle had played in the intervening hour, knowing he was beaten soundly again.

'OK. I'll warm him up some food.'

Flynn stepped off the houseboat, and sauntered down the pathway that clung to the riverbank which led to the next creek where *Faye2* was moored, and where Boone was easing *Shell* into her mooring alongside Flynn's boat. Flynn would have hurried along and assisted Boone to tie up, but the sight of the big old black Mercedes already parked on the jetty, plus the two big black matching men leaning on the vehicle, arms folded as they watched Boone manoeuvre the boat expertly into position, made Flynn pull up sharp. He was sure he hadn't been seen in the darkness, so he stepped sideways out of sight behind a couple of empty oil barrels stacked on one another.

One of the men caught Boone's mooring rope as he tossed it across the gap. Moments later *Shell* was secure and Boone played out the gangplank across to the quayside.

A man got out of the back of the Mercedes and dashed across on to the boat and had a quick conversation with Boone, who then took him inside the cabin. Flynn ducked low, peering around the barrels at the scenario some fifty metres in front of him, which was illuminated by a couple of lamp posts that cast a white, eerie glow on the tableau.

Flynn saw that one of the men lounging against the car had a machine pistol held at an angle across his chest. The wry look on Flynn's face said it all. What the hell had Boone got himself involved in now? Before he could answer, Boone reappeared on deck. Behind him was the man from the Mercedes supporting another man with a blanket over his shoulders. This was obviously the cargo that Boone had been to collect from God knew where. The man was apparently injured in some way and had to be propped up as he was led across the gangplank into the hands of one of the waiting men, before being placed in the back of the car. Flynn concentrated his vision on the man in the blanket and, just before his head ducked into the car, he got a one second look at his face.

A further mouth-to-ear conversation took place between Boone and the man from the car, then the latter slid into the rear of the vehicle and the other bodyguards – because that's what Flynn pegged the men as being – climbed into the car, which then set off with a spurt of red dust. He kept out of view as the car spun around in a turning circle, then drove towards him along the narrow road that ran parallel to the quay.

It was a big, battered old Merc. Flynn knew there were plenty knocking around Banjul, either driven as taxis or by gangsters. He instinctively read and memorized the number plate, noted an unusual dent in the rear wing and that the back bumper was twisted out at one corner.

Flynn stood up slowly and strolled towards the boat, whistling tunelessly as though nothing had happened. And maybe it hadn't, but Flynn was an ex-cop and still had a nose that sniffed out badness. And what he'd just witnessed stank rancid and rank.

Boone was reticent about the job. Flynn didn't press him, it wasn't his business. The guy was clearly exhausted by the journey and although he was ecstatic to see Michelle, and ravenously ate the meal she'd prepared for him, he was dead beat and crap company. He hauled himself off to bed within an hour of landing, leaving Michelle and Flynn alone on the deck of the houseboat.

They chatted until the early hours. Usual subjects. Love, life, food, religion . . . sex. At one thirty Flynn dragged himself up, complimented her on the food and her company, bowed like a gentlemen – having had a little too much to drink – kissed the back of her hand and left.

Twenty minutes later he bedded down on *Faye2* in the air-conditioned chill of the stateroom and was deep asleep almost instantly, but not before looking forward to the next day's fishing out on the estuary, his last day in the Gambia.

TWELVE

Boone had promised Flynn a wonderful day of fishing, then a slap-up meal at one of the beach hotels on the coast followed by a drinking session, after which they would crash out in rooms at the hotel. Then, after breakfast the following morning, they would wave bye-bye. Flynn had to get back to Gran Canaria to prepare *Faye2* for the summer season and the marlin runs. He needed to get the boat and his crew, Jose, the sour tempered Spaniard, ready for action.

Flynn woke early, and after a cool shower sat in the fighting chair with a breakfast of scrambled eggs on toast, accompanied by a cafetière of coffee and a tall glass of chilled orange juice.

He was feeling pretty tranquil. After the ructions of the last couple of years he was sanguine about life ahead. The midnight talks with Michelle had been very beneficial for him; her view of the world, the way she saw into his soul, then reached in and gently massaged what she found.

He sat back with his coffee, raising his face to the tropical heat, smiling. But just for a moment, unaccountably, his thoughts revolved around to Henry Christie of all people. This was the guy Flynn had blamed for hounding him out of the police almost six years ago and who had crashed back into his life a couple of years back at the same time Flynn's sordid past had intruded.

Flynn shook his head to rid his mind's eye of Christie, his face now scowling, thinking that if he never met Christie again, it would be too freaking soon.

Flynn grunted, collected his breakfast things, rinsed them off, then hopped on to the quay and started the short walk to Boone's houseboat. He glanced at the deck of *Shell* and saw Boone hadn't mopped the deck properly last night. There were some droplets of blood on the white decking, dried and brown now. Definitely blood, Flynn thought, pausing, recalling what he'd witnessed last night. Flynn couldn't have known that the injury was a wound of some sort, but the blood confirmed it. His face screwed up, thinking about men with guns and the brief glimpse of the injured man's face as he got into the car. Flynn had seen him clearly, his eyes as sharp as they'd ever been. So who was he?

He walked on and five minutes later he was at the houseboat, once more amazed at how brilliantly it had been refurbished. Nice one, Boone, Flynn thought, and smiled brightly at the figure of Michelle who was on deck, sipping juice and reading a paperback.

She saw him, tipped back her sunhat and placed the book down. Her smile was radiant and Flynn caught his breath, not for the first time, at her beauty. Nice one, Boone, he thought again. Don't screw this one up.

Michelle hugged him and he could not stop himself from loving each second of the short embrace, feeling every contour of her body, even though today she was wearing a cut-off T-shirt that showed a few inches of her midriff, and three-quarter length jeans, not one of her wispy dresses.

As they parted, Flynn said, 'Where is the old rogue?'

'Gone into town. He said he wouldn't be long and for you to wait. The fishing will be great, he told me to say.' She rolled her eyes.

'Did he mention what he'd been up to?'

Michelle frowned, not quite understanding the question, so Flynn rephrased it slightly. She said, 'No, he tells me nothing.' But she did not seem put out by this. Boone was clearly a man with secrets that she was prepared to tolerate. 'I need to shower,' she told Flynn and picked at her T-shirt. 'You relax, make yourself comfortable – help yourself to a drink if you want.' She smiled and went below.

Flynn was slightly narked at Boone's absence, having been anticipating a day heaving in tarpon again, but there was nothing he could do other than chill. He heard a door close below decks – the bedroom, he guessed – and after giving Michelle a few moments to get in the shower, he went below with the intention of getting a drink from the fridge.

He helped himself to chilled mineral water and added some fruity cordial, stood there and took a long draught of it. He glanced around the living area and saw a laptop computer on a small desk tucked in one corner, the screen saver pulsing out exploding stars. Flynn wasn't particularly drawn to computers but he thought he might take this opportunity to check his e-mails. He was expecting one from his son, who he hoped would be visiting him next month in Puerto Rico. He sat in front of the laptop and tapped the enter key. The screen saver disappeared, but a log-in screen appeared asking for a password.

Flynn cursed, sat back and sighed – but spun quickly in the chair when the bedroom door opened and a very naked Michelle stepped out.

'Oh – jeez, sorry,' Flynn gasped, trying to avert his eyes.

Michelle stood at the door, completely unfazed by the encounter. 'You want access to the computer?'

'I . . . I . . . thought I might check my messages.' Flynn began to rise, but suddenly Michelle was right behind him, leaning over his shoulder, her breasts pressing into his shoulder blades, her amazing scent invading his sense of smell, almost overpowering him in a subtle way. She reached over and her fingers tapped on the keyboard. Flynn froze, certain that Boone would come back at this very moment and witness this little scenario.

'Just tap in BaBaGee1234,' Michelle said into Flynn's ear. She entered the password, her breasts still crushed into his back, then stood upright, gave a little laugh and walked back to the bedroom. Flynn, despite the danger of death, still had a serious rush of blood and could not help himself turning to ogle her bottom. She glanced back over her shoulder before Flynn could look away. She gave him a tinkle of a wave and disappeared.

Flynn exhaled, unaware he'd been holding his breath.

The computer was displaying the pages that Boone, presumably, must have been browsing earlier. There were a lot of Google news searches, all on separate pages. Flynn, though not all that curious, selected one and when he realized what he was looking at, his heartbeat stepped up a few notches. His lips popped open and his whole body stiffened with terror and foreboding. He tabbed from screen to screen, his eyes scanning the pages that Boone had been reading.

Flynn wasn't sure how long he'd been looking at the computer when he heard footsteps crashing on to the deck above and the voice of Ray Boone screaming, 'Shell, Shell, we need to move. Shell, we need to get the fuck out of here!'

Flynn spun, a curious mix of emotions in him. Guilt at looking at Boone's computer, the same at having seen Michelle naked, and puzzlement about what Boone was yelling about.

Boone slid down the almost perpendicular stairs and crashed into the living room, gasping, rasping for breath, red-faced and exhausted. He clutched his chest.

'Shit, you're here,' was his reaction on seeing Flynn.

Boone ran across the room and yanked a drawer out from a cabinet, turned it upside down so the contents fell out.

'You need to fuck off now,' Boone said. 'Just like I'm doing.'

'Darling, what's going on?' A be-robed Michelle appeared at the bedroom door. Boone glanced at her, his face contorted with desperation. 'Get dressed – just don't ask, do it. Pack a few things in a holdall – you might just have time. But do not, repeat, DO NOT, arse around. Well? What are you waiting for, you silly bint?'

Michelle blinked, stung by the insult, confused by the orders and urgency. She went back into the bedroom.

Flynn said, 'Boone – what the hell's . . .?' He did not finish the sentence. Flynn saw the reason for the drawer being yanked out and upturned. Fastened by masking tape to the underside of the drawer was a pistol and two spare clips of ammunition. Boone ripped the tape away, fitted a magazine into the gun, drew back the slider and eased the first bullet into the chamber.

'You get the hell out of here,' Boone said. 'I don't have time for chapter and verse – just go, now. Michelle? Where the fuck are you? Come on, *come on*.' Boone turned back to Flynn. 'Go, please. I'll catch up with you sometime. Just leg it, pal. Michelle!' he bellowed. 'Christ.'

'Boone?' Flynn said.

'I fucked up. OK? I need to get to the boat and away from this stinking shithole. Run – now, Flynn. I can't make it any plainer.'

Michelle emerged from the bedroom, hurriedly re-dressed, with a small holdall in hand, a concerned and puzzled expression on her face which morphed into something else – terror – when she saw the gun in Boone's hand.

Boone grabbed her arm. 'Do you want to be with me?' He shook her.

'Yes I do.'

'Then we need to go now.'

'OK,' she said, her big eyes wide with fear. 'Let's go.'

'To the boat, Flynn. Get going.'

Flynn wasn't about to hang around any longer. He already had the feeling that too much time was being wasted. He recognized a hunted man when he saw one. He shimmied up the steps on to the deck, the two others behind him. He hurried towards the gangplank but he stopped as a black Mercedes skidded in the dust on the quayside, maybe a hundred metres away from the house-boat, as close as a vehicle could get, just behind Boone's Land Cruiser that had been left at a skewed angle, abandoned by Boone, the driver's door open.

Four men climbed out of the Mercedes, all dressed in summer shirts, shorts and sunglasses. The summer attire didn't somehow seem to go with the weapons they were openly carrying. They were varied. An AK47, an H&K machine pistol and two similar weapons Flynn did not recognize. All did similar jobs. That of firing short deadly bursts of bullets designed to rip people to shreds. Each also had a pistol in a pancake holster at his hip.

Boone came on deck, Michelle in tow.

A shout went up from the men – a primeval roar, really, as when a human being locks on to his prey – and they fanned quickly out, bringing their guns across their hips into firing positions. The weapons burst into life.

Flynn dived, Boone dragged Michelle to her knees. She screamed. Bullets thudded into the deck, furniture and fittings, and the glass-topped cane table disintegrated spectacularly.

Boone fired off two shots from his pistol, wayward, unaimed panic shots.

Flynn raised his head cautiously to see the men now line abreast, walking towards them. They would be here within seconds. They halted as one unit and again raked the boat with gunfire. Flynn slammed himself to the deck, bullets whizzing dangerously above him, inches at most, smacking into the superstructure and furniture, spinning one of the chairs around.

Boone dragged Michelle behind Flynn. Just a glance over his shoulder and he saw her petrified eyes, but had no time for sympathy or words of reassurance. Now was the time to keep moving, to try to stay alive, although both aspirations were becoming less likely as ammunition continued to crash around them.

Boone rose, fired six shots double-handed at the oncoming men. He caught them by surprise this time, and with a bit more accuracy. One reeled away, dropping his weapon and clutching his arm. A hit. Boone loosed off the remainder of the seventeen shot magazine, forcing the men to keep their heads right down, until the hammer clicked on empty and the slide locked open. He flicked the magazine release and let the empty container clatter on to the deck.

'Run to the front of the boat and jump,' he said between his gritted teeth, fitting the spare magazine into the handle and yanking the slide back to reload the chamber.

Flynn grabbed Michelle and they scuttled along the deck like crabs. Boone rose again and emptied half the new magazine at the men. They were not so brave under fire, their line and cockiness had gone to pot and they were hiding behind any cover available. At the same time, the painful screams of the one who'd been winged could be heard as part of the general cacophony.

One of them ducked behind a barrel.

Boone swung his gun purposely at him and fired at the barrel.

It had previously contained fuel for the boats and was now virtually empty – with the exception of fumes, ideal to be ignited by a spark to become a deadly bomb.

Within a microsecond of Boone's bullet entering the barrel, it exploded with a huge, spectacular burst of red-hot flame and torn, jagged metal, and the man cowering behind it was thrown, alight, across the quayside, spinning like a grotesque Catherine wheel, his shape black against the blast, ten feet off the quayside into the creek, where he splashed down with a fizzle.

The heat whooshed across Flynn's shoulders as he leapt across the gap from the prow of the houseboat on to the quay, landing with the agility of a big cat, stooping and turning to Michelle to encourage her to follow him.

She jumped the gap easily, dropping on to the quay. No need for Flynn to steady her. Boone was just behind.

The only problem they had in running away was that they were now completely exposed to the two remaining, active gunmen and there was at least another hundred metres to sprint before there was any kind of cover for them.

Flynn checked over his shoulder.

Michelle was a foot behind him, Boone twenty, both with terror on their faces. Boone's arms were pumping, his face glowing from the exertion that must have been affecting his heart. He looked like he might explode with the same ferocity as the barrel and Flynn had a parallel thought about the weak heart beating within his friend's chest.

'Go,' Boone screamed at him.

Flynn's head jerked forwards. He vaulted what seemed to be an old railway sleeper left diagonally across the deck. Michelle followed easily.

There were more shots, Flynn ducking instinctively as he.felt them zing by just above his head.

Then a sudden bad feeling hit Flynn, making him stop and turn – only to see that Boone had been shot and was half-lying, half-kneeling across the railway sleeper. His left shoulder had been blown apart. Boone dragged himself up and looked at Flynn. Then there was more shooting as, sixty metres further back, the uninjured men came on relentlessly.

Boone's head angled up, and a bullet struck the back of his skull. His face exploded from the inside out, as the bullet, having bounced around his cranium at a thousand feet per second, tumbled crazily and exited, removing Boone's nose and mouth.

Michelle screamed. She too had stopped to look. She ran back to Boone, his body now prostrate across the sleeper, blood pooling under him, body twitching.

Michelle ran quicker than Flynn could reach out to stop her.

'We can't do anything,' Flynn shouted, but to no effect.

She sank to her knees by Boone's shattered head and a dreadful wailing sound erupted from her.

The gunmen had stopped running now, were approaching at an easy, confident stride, their shoulders rolling. Then they stopped twenty metres short of Boone and one of them raised his weapon. Flynn saw it was the H&K.

'No!' Flynn bawled, believing the gun was going to be fired at Michelle, who at that range would be torn apart. He moved towards her, then realized his mistake. The machine pistol was aimed at him, not her, and as this dawned on him, he reacted. Using his forward momentum, he curled away and launched himself off the quayside into the brown, brackish water of the creek which he knew was deep enough to dive into.

As his feet left the ground, a bullet impacted his left side and turned what would have been a graceful dive into an uncoordinated messy spin of arms and legs, like a gull being shot out of the sky. He hit the water hard, went under, inhaling and swallowing huge mouthfuls of the muddy concoction.

He writhed painfully as he sank. Unable to see a thing, he kicked out frenetically with arms and legs, feeling like he'd been hit by a baseball bat connected to an electricity supply.

He fought panic, realizing that it would land him in a dirty watery grave. The first thing he had to do was remain calm, surface and purge his lungs of what he'd swallowed, even though that action could result in death, too.

But he had no alternative. He had to go up and hope the guys weren't serious about finishing him off.

With a huge effort that sent an explosion of pain through his side, he kicked upwards and broke the surface, choking and spluttering. He opened his eyes and was momentarily confused at finding himself surrounded by darkness. Air sucked automatically into his lungs and he realized he'd surfaced right underneath the slatted wooden boards that formed the unsteady quayside.

He trod water, looking up, knowing that his upsurge to the surface must have made a noise, his coughing and spluttering not having been exactly surreptitious.

His side hurt. He inhaled and spat out – quietly – and saw no blood in his saliva, giving him hope he hadn't been shot in the chest. However, it was fucking creasing him and as he rocked gently in the water, holding position, his ribs felt like they were scraping together like tinder. Maybe the bullet had just gouged him. His self-absorbed musing stopped.

Footsteps on the planking six feet above his head. Shadows moving. Talking, muttering.

Flynn kicked across to one of the stanchions, pile-driven into the mud, holding up the quay, and hugged it, trying to keep his breathing even, trying not to emit any pathetic squeaks of pain.

The gaps between the planks were uneven – it was a shoddily built structure and Flynn had a theory that it was the *Ba-Ba-Gee* keeping it upright. Sunlight shone through some of the wider gaps between the planks, whilst other planks tightly abutted each other.

He could see the soles of shoes right above him, hear urgent whispering and Michelle moaning further down the quay. The men had stopped, now no longer talking. They were listening, trying to locate Flynn.

He heard a slide being pulled back, then slotted back into place, one of the scariest noises in the world. A gun being loaded, ready to fire. Flynn could not say which weapon it was until it opened fire.

It was the AK47, the Kalashnikov, the widow-maker, Russia's present to the world. The man holding it opened fire and Flynn recognized its very individual signature noise. Whoever was firing it was doing so randomly down through the quay, spraying bullets through the planks into the water below. A guessing game. They had easily worked out they hadn't fatally shot him, and that he must now be underneath them, cowering in the water.

They got that bit right.

The bullets tore through the wood, splintering it. Flynn gripped the stanchion and hoped for the best.

Then the gun did exactly what he would have prayed for. Flynn heard the firing mechanism clunk and jam and the bullets stopped as suddenly as they'd started. The AK47 was a very robust weapon, but it had to be lovingly maintained and decent quality ammunition was always best. Flynn guessed that neither was the case here.

The shooter cursed. Flynn could hear the man trying to loosen the slider and drag it backwards to clear the problem.

After taking a deep breath against the agony in his side, he pushed himself away from the upright, silently he hoped, and started to breaststroke quietly under the quay, pushing his way through the debris that had accumulated on the surface. This included a lot of floating rubbish, polystyrene cups and, grue-somely, the carcass of a dead boar. Horrified, Flynn reared away from this, trying to contain a gagging reflex in his throat. He kicked away, remaining underneath the quay, moving further and further away from the houseboat which he could still see behind him. The water was still muddy brown, but was warm, and he noticed he was leaving a trail of blood, already attracting little fish that fed in a frenzy of tiny splashes. He knew he had to get out, dry off and see what damage had been done. He was feeling weak and woozy now.

He grabbed another stanchion, paused, looked back, listened, watched. He groaned noisily when a shot of pain tore at his ribs, like a lion had scraped a claw along them, then inserted the same claw for an extra jolt. Working his way around the stanchion, he found a thin rope ladder tacked to it. Flynn grabbed hold of the bottom rung and slowly eased himself up until he could raise his head just above the quay and peer back to the scene of the incident.

He watched with horror.

One man was kick-rolling Boone's body to the edge of the quay, his lifeless limbs flailing with each revolution of his body.

Another man was holding Michelle down on her knees, his hand wound tightly in her hair, causing her face to warp in agony as she was forced to watch the other man flatfoot Boone's body off the quayside into the water below.

A third man, the one shot by Boone, stood as witness to this, his right arm dangling uselessly by his side, blood dripping from the wound.

When Boone's body splashed into the water, they turned their attention to Michelle, who struggled to break free from the man holding her hair. He held tight.

Using the last of his waning strength, Flynn hauled himself on to the quay and rolled quickly out of sight behind a low wooden fence that surrounded two large waste disposal bins. He squatted low and pulled up his shirt to inspect his own wound.

He almost fainted when he saw a huge chunk of his side had been gouged out. Steeling himself, he touched it warily, gasping and nauseous, using his wet fingers to probe. There was some relief when he was sure the bullet had not entered him, but if this was what it was like to be winged, he didn't recommend it. There was a lot of damage and blood was pouring out. He pulled off his T-shirt, rolled it into a ball and held it against the wound.

Keeping low, he started to work his way back to the next creek where his beloved *Faye2* was moored next to Boone's boat. He knew he was leaving a trail of wet footprints and spats of blood, and he hoped it wasn't a trail the men would even look for. But he moved quickly, with a loping sideways gait to compensate for the agony he felt in his side.

By the time he reached his boat he was gagging for breath, light-headed, legs dithery and weak. But he knew he didn't have the time even to think about treating himself.

If the bad guys were thinking about coming for him, the trail he'd left could have been followed by a child and he didn't want to take the chance of them turning up. He jumped on board with the mooring rope, turned the hidden cut-out toggle and started the engines. They came to life first time. Then, with a wistful glance at *Shell*, Flynn crept out of the creek and into the main river channel, setting out west towards the estuary and open sea. Once there, he steered north and fixed the autopilot that would take him right to the harbour mouth at Puerto Rico, and would automatically steer a safe route through any other shipping they might encounter.

Guilt burned away at him like a laser for leaving Michelle to her fate, which, he thought bleakly and in a clichéd way, would be worse than death . . . followed by death. But he knew he could not have saved her without being killed himself.

He stripped off in the cabin, and seeing his blood dripping on the floor reminded him of how Boone had failed to clean the blood on *Shell*, the boat he'd named after the love of his life. Flynn thought of the irony of the name of his boat, *Faye2*. Faye was his ex-wife's name. Not the love of his life.

Then he stepped into the narrow shower to clean himself off and treat the wound, hopefully discover it wasn't life threatening.

It had been a terrible thing to leave Michelle behind. The expression on her face as the men approached her was already etched in Flynn's mind. As was the image of Boone's face as it exploded after being shot in the back of his head. Flynn cleaned himself mechanically, thoroughly . . . knowing that he would return to the Gambia sooner rather than later, and that his friends would be revenged.

THIRTEEN

They had been too late.

After the HQ dining room meeting with the chief constable, Henry, Rik Dean and Donaldson had driven quickly back to Blackpool and to the flat that Sadiq and Rahman had been using in North Shore. It had been stripped clean, like vultures had been on a wildebeest carcass. Everything had gone, every scrap of furniture, every strip of carpet ripped up and taken away, along with all the food, crockery, cutlery and toilet rolls. All that remained were the bare bones.

Henry had not been surprised. The forensic scientists who worked for the security service would take all the stuff and recreate the rooms based on their notes, photographs and videos, at some secret location outside London, and they would be able to take their time in assessing what they had. Everything would be combed, read, tested, analysed and the results fed back to MI5.

He had wandered through the tiny lounge, the one bedroom, the kitchenette, the toilet, hoping that something had been missed. He tried pulling up floorboards, easing skirting boards away from the wall with his fingertips, looking into what fitted cupboards remained, those things that were part of the fabric of the flat that could not be removed.

Donaldson, exasperated, simply stood at the door with his hands on his hips, shaking his head and continually telling Henry that it was no use. He had experienced the scientific thoroughness of the security services before and knew, to their credit, they were beyond excellent. They wouldn't have missed anything. Where their professionalism fell down was on the operational side of things, the intelligence gathering, dissemination and use. That was where it all turned to shit.

'I know, I get the picture,' Henry said when, for the zillionth time, Donaldson had said, 'It's no good.'

Donaldson had eventually mooned around the flat, as though someone had stolen his puppy. In the tiny toilet he had leaned on the wash basin and looked at the square above it on the wall where a mirror had been fixed, but had also been taken away, leaving an unpainted rectangle of paint. He blinked as something crossed his mind, but was then gone. He tried to chase it, but the thought was elusive and probably meant nothing.

They left the flat muted, returning the key to the landlord, who said he hadn't even been in it himself since and wasn't looking to re-let it any time soon. Apart from anything else, he wanted the furniture back from the spooks.

'Well,' Henry breathed, 'what next?'

The 'What next?' turned out to be frustration upon frustration. Despite FB's representations, Beckham, the MI5 man, refused to let anyone near Sadiq, who he described as a prized and vulnerable asset. There was also the suspicion that he wasn't even being held at Paddington Green police station any more.

FB, to his credit, did keep up the pressure until Beckham relented slightly a week down the line.

Henry had been sitting in his own office in the FMIT block at headquarters, looking forlornly at the dry-wipe board on the wall. The problem for him was that, although Lancashire wasn't the murder capital of the world, people still had a nasty habit of killing other people, as well as committing other serious crimes that came under the remit of FMIT.

Since Natalie Philips's body had been discovered, Henry was now dealing with two other murders and what looked to be a series of brutal rapes that seemed to be connected. Each of these offences required time and effort, and a very straight dose of panic-free thinking. It was just as important to find the villains in these new cases as it was to discover who murdered Natalie.

And Henry was wobbling a bit.

It did not help that he was being distracted, in a good way, by Alison Marsh. He had met up with her a couple more times and they had ended up fucking each other like the world was about to end. He was still very confused about his feelings for her, and although both of them were simply happy shaggers at the moment, he suspected that in the not too distant future there might be the requirement to ratchet the relationship up a notch, from *lust* to *lurv*. He wasn't sure he was ready for that and as such their trysts had remained clandestine.

He was also having constant run-ins with Leanne and her on–off boyfriend. His daughter wanted the 'lowlife shit' – Henry's description – back in her life, but Henry was dead against it. He refused the guy access to his house and it was getting to the point where he was going to have to ask her to up sticks and move out. It was another thing he didn't really want to have to deal with because Leanne had been totally there for him after Kate's death.

And now there were new cases to deal with. The murders were fairly straightforward domestic ones, but still needed steering and overseeing. The rapes he had inherited from a DI in Blackpool who, the rumour was, on discovering he had a serial rapist operating on his patch, had gone on stress leave never to return to work. Henry thought there would be a need to jack up a full-time team to crack them . . . which seemed like a good job for Rik Dean.

He looked back down at his computer screen, logged on to his e-mail. It showed eighty-five unread messages, many tagged with 'urgent' flags. He ignored them, minimized that screen and opened a file on the desktop marked 'Retirement'.

He opened it and read the few lines.

He could re-date it, print it out, sign it and submit it, and would probably be pulling a police pension in six weeks. Get out of this mind-blowing situation. Draw the pension – half his salary, more than most other people earned – draw the lump sum and simply fuck off. Maybe go live with a woman who owned a very nice pub in a nice village that got snowed in every winter.

He sighed, glanced at the board again and thought about what Donaldson had said to him. And knew he would have to be pushed to leave the job.

He closed the file just as his office door clattered open – no knock – and FB bundled in without warning. Henry, who had a view from his office window across to the front of headquarters, was a little miffed. He'd been so engrossed in his internal monologue that he'd failed to spot the chief trundling across. If he had done, he would have made certain he wasn't in the office.

'Henry.'

'OK, boss? Come to fire me?'

FB chortled, his double chin wobbling. He took a seat opposite Henry. 'No such luck, but I'm working on it.'

'Cheers,' Henry said flatly. 'To what do I owe the pleasure?' Having known FB for such a long time, some of the formal barriers were blurred and, up to a point, Henry knew he could get away with being relaxed and a bit cheeky, certainly during a one-to-one.

'Bit of a result from our friend Beckham down at the Box.' Box being an informal term for MI5. Henry perked up. 'As you know MI5 has basically taken control of everything related to the flat and Sadiq and Rahman, and that includes the results of the DNA tests.'

Henry's mouth twisted. 'I know.' That MI5 had commandeered the blood sample taken from the seat of the plane from Las Palmas and the one taken from the dead Rahman made him seethe. Donaldson was also fuming, but even despite formal protestations from the FBI, the British security services had not budged. They were like a kid in a classroom, covering their work so no one else could copy it. They were also keeping the result of the DNA test on Sadiq to themselves, and consequently Henry was banging his head against a brick wall in his efforts to trace Natalie Philips's killer. At some point he assumed that MI5 would have to relent to the pressure and allow access to the results and to Sadiq, wherever he might now be. Even if the lad's DNA did not match what had been found inside Natalie, Henry wanted to speak to him.

Henry waited for FB to reveal all.

'It's better than nothing,' FB said, preparing him.

'Go on . . .'

'Sadiq's DNA matches one of the sperm samples from Natalie.' Henry's ring piece constricted, as did his throat.

'And the DNA sample taken from the blood on the plane matches another of the sperm samples.'

*   *   *

'So Sadiq and Akram had sex with Natalie sometime before she was murdered,' Karl Donaldson said. 'Jeez.'

'That's if the blood from the plane actually belongs to your friend Akram – yes,' Henry confirmed.

'You know it does,' Donaldson said. 'So three out of the four samples have now been identified – Mark Carter, Sadiq and Akram?'

'Leaving one unidentified,' Henry said. 'As yet.'

'When are you going to interview Sadiq?'

Henry paused. He was on the phone to Donaldson, bringing him up to speed with developments. The American was back in London – had been for over a week now – and was still making representations to MI5 without success. He had been warned by his superiors to back off and not make waves. Henry's unexpected news caused a resurgence of hope within him, as he'd almost swallowed his anger and was about to get back to his day job, hoping that Akram would step into his cross hairs some other time. This chance, he'd thought, had passed him by.

Henry's voice was blunt. 'I'm not.'

'What? What the hell?' Donaldson stopped, unable to believe his ears. At that exact moment he was walking along in the sunshine on the River Thames embankment, threading his way through the tourists in the vicinity of the London Eye. He leaned on the wall by the river and stared across at the Houses of Parliament.

'Whilst they confirm the DNA matches, they say I still can't interview Sadiq face to face. I can e-mail down a list of questions and one of the MI5 interview teams will put them to him. That's the best I can do, and while it's bollocks, it's the only way I've got at this time.'

'I'm staggered.'

'Karl,' Henry said pointedly, 'he's obviously more to them than simply a murderer. You've lectured me about the bigger picture before now and that must be what all this is about. National security . . . maybe he knows a lot of . . . stuff . . . and having him dragged through the courts to face a murder charge isn't what they want. If in fact he did kill Natalie. He might have had sex with her, but didn't necessarily kill her.'

'But it needs the detective on the case to get into his ribs, not some detached dick brain reading from a cue card.'

'Tell me about it . . .'

Donaldson went silent for a moment, then said, 'They're up to something.'

'Yep.'

'Bastards,' Donaldson whined. 'They don't have the right to . . .'

But his words were cut short as his phone signal died.

Henry looked quizzically at his phone but nevertheless completed the sentence, speaking into a disconnected phone. 'The right to what? Treat us like mushrooms and feed us on shit. Sorry pal, but they think they do.' He hung up.

Standing under the shadow cast by the London Eye, Donaldson jiggled his phone, feeling that his line to Akram was receding with each passing moment. He wasn't enjoying the sensation.

He had pretty much done what he could, even flying out to Las Palmas to grill the detective at the airport and make his own enquiries as to how Akram might have got off Gran Canaria and what the onward destination might have been. He had found nothing. The terrorist could easily have left the island by any number of air or sea routes. Donaldson's nosing around the few private airstrips yielded nothing, nor did any information come from the sea ports he visited. Problem was the island was dotted with numerous tiny ports and it was impossible to keep tabs on everyone who came and went. Donaldson's educated guess was that Akram had left by sea, which meant there was the likelihood he'd gone to the African mainland and then back to the Middle East. Impossible to track down.

Donaldson leaned on the embankment wall and stared at the water of the Thames. His mind tossed everything around and he knew he was missing something in his equation, the something that had come to him when he and Henry had visited Sadiq's flat in Blackpool. But he couldn't for the life of him pinpoint what it was.

He stopped shaking his phone, checked a signal was back – yes – and tapped out a text message, paused thoughtfully before sending it – *should he, shouldn't he*? – but then pressed send and it flew away into the ether: 'MESSAGE SENT'.

'Shit,' he winced, suddenly wishing he could recall it. Too late. 'Oh God,' he whispered, 'I hope I haven't screwed this up.'

He made his way to a riverside cafe, ordered a filter coffee, sat out in the sun, and waited. If it was going to happen, it would be in the next half hour. He could afford to wait that long, but no longer. Then a text landed on his phone. One word: 'COMING'.

She arrived fifteen minutes later. Donaldson had an iced coffee waiting for her.

'Karl, darling,' she said, and leaned across to kiss his cheeks, before sitting down opposite him. Edina, his discreet contact at Whitehall, smiled at him, always with a hint of lust in her eyes. Donaldson thought she must be a lonely woman and that it would be nice to see more of her as a friend, but he did not want to compromise her any more than their relationship did already. He guessed she got some excitement from seeing him occasionally, in a James Bond sort of way, and passing on the odd snippet of information was perhaps a bit thrilling. Then she said, 'It's just a feeling, nothing I can prove, but I think they're on to me.'

'Ahh,' he said. 'Look, I'm sorry. I don't want to make life difficult for you. You didn't need to come.'

'No, darling, it's OK. It's not like I'm a double agent for the Russians. You are the only one I ever say anything to, and that's because I like you, and because it's only ever about one man that everyone wants to bring down – Jamil Akram. I know why you want to catch him and if I can do anything to help you, then I will.'

Donaldson stared at her for a few moments. She was more than good-looking, one of those women whose appearance took a bit of time to permeate, but when it did, the effect was lasting. 'You don't need to do anything more,' he said. 'Let's just have coffee and say bye.'

'No, no, I do.' She screwed up her nose. 'I'm going to resign anyway. We, Hugo and I, have a pile in Monaco that needs some TLC. I'm going to go and supervise the renovation.'

'When you say a place . . .?'

'Well, slightly more than a place . . . more a villa . . . a big villa. A palace, really. So those are my plans. So what can I do for you? One last thing?' She held his gaze meaningfully.

'Why is MI5 not sharing anything about Blackpool?'

Mark Carter was due in to answer his police bail that evening, as a result of which Henry Christie decided to meet, greet and re-interview the lad together with Rik Dean. His plan was to get a long, detailed interview completed this time, put some pressure on Mark and if nothing came of it – such as a confession to killing Natalie – Henry would release him with the warning that if any other evidence came to light that fingered Mark, he would be rearrested. Keep the sword hanging over him. Always a good police tactic.

During the afternoon, Henry brought himself up to speed with his other ongoing investigations and spent some time with Rik, who Henry had decreed would take on the serial rapist case.

It was one of those jobs that was beginning to bubble and rouse some media speculation. Henry, having had it thrust on him, wanted to do something about it before it blew up in his face, as such things often did. If not dealt with immediately and seen for what it was, the police could end up looking like idiots in about ten years' time, still trying to chase their tails and solve a hundred offences instead of just three.

He and Rik tossed around a few strategies, mostly coming back to resources and the lack of them. If they *could* throw resources at it, then they'd have a good chance of getting a result. That was the problem with everything, though. No resources.

'At least we know they were all committed by the same individual,' Henry said, looking at the report on the DNA samples. One man had indeed carried out the three reported attacks. Henry raised his face to Rik, who was sitting across from him. They were in Henry's office at HQ reviewing exactly where the investigation stood – up to the point where the original DI investigating had gone sick – and, as ever, coffee was being consumed. 'I'm surprised this offender isn't on the database, being such an obviously violent person. Surely he must have some previous.'

'Wouldn't be sitting here if he was on the database,' Rik pointed out.

'OK, it was a pretty obvious point to make,' Henry conceded. 'Any pattern to the attacks?'

Rik scanned the analysis of the crime reports. 'Night-time, between eleven and one. Lone women, young ones, teens, early twenties, attacked in areas where there are no CCTV cameras.'

'Deliberately chosen, or just lucky?'

Rik shrugged. 'An area he knows, I suspect. All in the vicinity of Garstang Road on the way out to Poulton. Two of the women were dragged into Boundary Park, one on to some playing fields. No independent witnesses to speak of.'

'Dates?' Henry frowned.

'One a month for the last three months . . . well,' Rik scrutinized the reports more closely, 'that's one every four weeks . . . each progressively more violent, but each woman threatened with a return visit and a horrific murder if they reported the assaults. This is a guy we need to catch.'

'Bastard,' Henry whispered. They looked at each other. 'So if this pattern continues, when would he be due to strike again?'

'This week,' Rik calculated. 'Although he hasn't done so far, unless it hasn't been reported.'

'No set days?' Henry asked. Rik shook his head. Henry pouted. 'Could it be a shift worker of some sort, out on a break?'

'That's something I'll check, see what businesses are operating around that area twenty-four hours.'

'I wonder how many he's actually carried out?' Henry mused.

'What do you mean?'

'The reported ones are always the tip of the iceberg . . . the terror factor makes a lot of victims clam up. Any chance of pulling an operation together for a couple of nights this week?' Henry asked in vain hope.

Rik screwed up his face. 'I could possibly muster a few bodies tonight, but it's a late request. Maybe more tomorrow, but then we hit the weekend and everybody's stretched.' He checked his watch. 'I'll see what I can do, but don't hold out much hope.'

'We need to plan something for next month.'

Rik nodded and gathered all the paperwork together. 'I'll get home for some tea, then I'll see you at Blackpool for Mark Carter, seven thirty?'

Rik left. Henry picked up the phone to call a detective sergeant at Preston who was dealing with one of the domestic murders Henry was overseeing. He needed an update . . . and that was how the rest of Henry's afternoon unfolded, checking up on progress. Then it was six and he had a sudden, gut-wrenching thought that he hadn't called Kate to let her know he would be late home.

It was only as he unthinkingly tapped the first digit of his home phone number that he remembered. Suddenly he was overwhelmed by a feeling of despair and emptiness, heartbroken by the realization that it was a call he would never have to make again.

In the same time zone, about three thousand miles to the south on the west coast of Africa, Steve Flynn steered *Faye2* out of the deep Atlantic Ocean and into the wide mouth of the Gambia River. The journey from Gran Canaria had been uneventful, even his overnighter in Nouadhibou. Here Flynn had refuelled, taken on fresh supplies and had a long, uninterrupted sleep.

The Gambian capital, Banjul, was on his starboard side and he sailed past with disinterest, his eyes cold as granite under the brim of his baseball cap. He angled *Faye2* upriver and cruised slowly past many creeks, surveying them with binoculars, until he found one he wanted. It was deep enough and contained a badly constructed wooden quayside against which he manoeuvred and tied up his boat. He had noticed it on his previous visit to the country, but had never imagined he would be returning to use it.

The heat was heavy and cruel in the early evening, although the sun had virtually disappeared over the western horizon.

Flynn poured himself a long, iced cola and rolled his hips as he drank it, still feeling the pain of the gouge-line ploughed by the bullet along his ribcage, nicking bone as it went. The wound was healing well but had a way to go yet. But he was mobile enough to return to the country from which he had fled like a rat being chased by dogs.

He had abandoned a dead friend and left that friend's lady in a horrifying situation, and did not even yet know if she had survived it. She could well be as dead as Boone, and that was what Flynn expected.

His guilt was gut-wrenchingly physical. Tearing him up.

Boone had been dead for certain, his body kicked like a dog into the creek. But Michelle *had* been alive and maybe she had survived. He knew he could not have helped her at the time, but that didn't make him feel any better.

Which is why, after a horrendous return to Gran Canaria and some convalescence there, he was right back in the Gambia as soon as he was fit, with one thing on his mind.

He downed the last of the cola, the ice chinking against his teeth, then vaulted off the boat, tucking the 9mm Glock 17 into the waistband of his three-quarter length trousers, pulling his shirt over it and pushing the silencer into his pocket.

Henry did not bother going home, unable to face the house, empty or otherwise. He'd spent about half an hour staring into space at his desk, his mind empty and dull. Eventually he clicked into action, roused himself with a sorry shake of his head and pushed himself up from his chair, which was like trying to lift a lead weight. He gathered his stuff and made his way to his car, sat in it for a while and experienced more guilt at having acquired such a fancy machine for what, it seemed, was the cost of Kate's life. He knew he would not have owned such a beast if she was still here. It would never have entered his head. The Mondeo had been more than adequate.

The Mercedes engine barely made a noise as he drove up the avenue away from the FMIT block, towards the HQ building. At the junction he was faced with a slight dilemma: turn right and exit, or go straight on to the sports and social club, aka The Grovellers' Arms. The beer was cheap but at that time of day, between five and seven, it was full of office staff and bosses, none of whom he cared to mix with. He rarely socialized with other cops, other than a few close friends, and was a bit worried now that he'd reached the rank at which others might want to brown-nose up to him. The thought worried him. He had always disliked rank and authority, yet was now part of the establishment. Sort of like Mick Jagger accepting a knighthood.

With that in mind, he selected a very old Rolling Stones album from the in-car iPod, from the days when they were the bad boys, and swung the car right, spurting under the rising security barrier quickly, because he never quite trusted it. Then, to the strains of *Gimme Shelter*, he hit the road.

He joined the traffic heading into Preston, bearing left after crossing the River Ribble, out towards Blackpool, past Preston docks. He enjoyed the drive in the new car, although his left shoulder was giving him some gyp, the one which had been peppered with shotgun pellets during the blood-soaked stand-off in Kendleton, where he first met Alison. A slight sweat came at the memory of his lucky escape.

As he drove he did his retirement sums again. The house was now paid off. The pension would be good. He could buy a dog

. . . Or maybe just keep going until they forced his hand? Then he could come back as a cold case consultant on half the salary, no responsibility and all the fun.

In Blackpool he turned into the KFC on Preston New Road and parked in one of the wide grill bays. Once inside he stood at the back of a long queue and kept an eye out for Mark Carter, who was nowhere to be seen. He ate in the restaurant, glumly avoiding standing on the chips on the floor, having had to wipe the table before sitting at it. But the food was OK and gave him that short energy burst he needed.

At seven thirty he was at Blackpool nick in the CID office with Rik, awaiting a call from the public enquiry desk to say that Mark Carter had answered his bail.

He chatted with Rik about the serial rape inquiry, and whether he had sorted anything out for later. The DI looked sheepish.

'Singularly unsuccessful. Tomorrow night, maybe, plenty of bodies about, but tonight, too short notice.'

'Which means?'

'Uh, well, after we've finished with Carter, I'll get changed into my scruffs, grab the crappiest CID car I can find and troll about myself until midnight.'

'Yourself?'

Rik nodded.

'Keeping obs for a rapist?'

'Yep.'

'Not exactly the well-resourced operation I had in mind,' Henry sighed. 'Tell you what, I'll come with you. Wouldn't expect you to do it alone.'

'Seriously?' Rik sounded doubtful. 'Only thing is, every time I go out on a job with you, I seem to end up getting injured.' He was referring to the times when he'd been stabbed once and shot once, each time out with Henry.

'You're still alive, aren't you?'

'Just.'

Henry winked, checked his watch and picked up a desk phone, dialled the front desk and asked if Mark had shown his face. Negative. Cradling the phone, Henry checked his watch again and decreed, 'I'll give him until half eight, then I'll go looking.'

'Probably done a runner,' Rik said. 'Guilty and all that.'

*   *   *

It was a ten minute walk to the creek in which Boone's house-boat was moored. As Flynn turned on to the unstable quayside, his insides seemed to drop from a great height. The tropical evening had drawn in and his way was illuminated by lamp posts along the quay which varied in strength. Some flickered, some glowed dully, others cast intense white light. Even so, Flynn could clearly see the big shape that had once been the *Ba-Ba-Gee*, Boone's houseboat and home.

The old concrete barge was tilted at a forty-five degree angle away from the quay, like an immense, dead, beached whale. It had been completely gutted by fire and everything that had been so lovingly and expensively refurbished by Boone – upper and lower decks, the outside seating area, the galley, the bedrooms – was all destroyed. All that remained was the seemingly inde-structible concrete hull, half sunk in the water.

Flynn approached the wreck slowly.

Inside he was cold and raging. Outside his skin had tightened on his skeleton, and now his breathing was laboured and he started to dither.

He walked alongside the barge and up to the point on the quay where the fleeing Boone had been shot in the back of the head. His body draped across the old railway sleeper that was still there.

Flynn stooped to one knee and touched a bullet hole in the planking, slipping his little finger into it. Then he looked up sharply, his face distorted by venomous anger. He came upright slowly, carried on walking along the banking to the next inlet where Boone's fishing boat *Shell* had been moored. Flynn had originally moored *Faye2* alongside, such a long, long time ago. A light year away. Since then he had been shot, and managed to make it back to Gran Canaria, where a discreet Spanish doctor had treated the wound and taken an excessive amount of money to keep quiet. During his recovery, Flynn had done his research, remembering the Internet pages that he had briefly looked at on Boone's laptop in the seconds before the man himself had rushed back, pursued by desperate killers.

Splattered all over the news pages that Flynn had accessed back in Gran Canaria was the face of the man he'd watched getting off Boone's boat. The man who had been injured, the same man suspected of involvement in the planning of terrorist activities in the UK. The man who was now wanted by the authorities and whose name was Jamil Akram.

Flynn had only seen his face briefly from his hiding place behind some oil barrels, but he was convinced it was Akram. His eyes were as good as they'd ever been, honed by five years of searching sun-glistening waves for the sight of blue marlin on the move.

It wasn't a difficult equation for Flynn to work out.

Boone was clearly still in the cargo trade. He had brought Akram back to the Gambia from wherever – the news reports, Flynn noticed, were sparse on the details of where Akram might have gone to. But Boone was involved. Old habits and all that shit, Flynn had thought. Boone was just keeping his hand in, making money as and when. It was in his blood. That's what he did. And it had led to his death because the men who came after him were the ones who had been guarding Akram.

So what had Boone done to incur their ire?

He'd delivered the package. But then what? The fact was that Boone had been browsing pages on his computer about a man who, it was alleged, had been helping some young Islamic fundamentalists to cause carnage in Blackpool, a place Flynn knew well. He'd been a cop there once. Had lived with his wife there – until it had all gone wrong.

Flynn concluded that Boone hadn't known who he was transporting at first. Then he'd found out. And had that knowledge killed him?

Flynn asked himself again – what had Boone done to bring about his death?

The answer was a guess. Boone was a hothead, a guy with an eye for the main chance and not above blackmail.

Could that be it? Had he discovered the true value of his cargo and gone to demand more money, or had he threatened to go to the authorities? Or both? Flynn could imagine Boone combining the two with the subtlety of a bull elephant's charge.

What Flynn had also found interesting in the news reports he had read was a name that cropped up a few times – that of Detective Superintendent Henry Christie who had been at the scene of the police shooting of one of the suspected terrorists. Henry Christie – a name Flynn could conjure with all day. But, interesting as the name was, Christie was peripheral to Flynn's own investigations and intentions.

Flynn had healed quickly, one of the benefits of being fit and healthy. The gouge the bullet had taken out of him had been closed, meshed and bandaged by the tame, money-driven doctor. Then, with the assistance of liberal doses of good painkillers, sunshine and alcohol, and a festering desire for retribution, Flynn had reached a stage where he thought he could act.

And now he was back in the Gambia. He didn't care what the reason was for Boone's death, he just knew that he didn't deserve to die in that terrible way. And what of Michelle? Not knowing her fate had been gnawing away at Flynn intensely.

He turned into the creek and stopped abruptly.

Boone's boat was still tethered there, apparently unscathed. Flynn's heart whammed in his chest. He truly had not expected this, especially having just seen the wreck of the houseboat. At the very least he thought he would find a burned-out husk or no boat at all.

But here she was, *Shell*, rocking gently in the creek water alongside the other boats moored here.

Had she been commandeered by Boone's killers? Did she now belong to someone else?

He moved quietly in his soft-soled deck shoes, his right hand snaking to the small of his back, fingers clasping the handle of the Glock which he extracted slowly and held down by his hip.

There was no sign of life on board, but the boat looked OK.

Instinctively he dropped into a defensive crouch as he approached the stern, where he stopped and listened. Heard nothing.

It was a short leap on to the aft deck, sidestepping the fighting chair. He landed with hardly a noise and stood completely still, listening again. He approached the sliding door that led into the cockpit and tried the handle. The door slid open an inch. He opened it further, wide enough for him to step through into the cockpit. To his right were the wheel and controls, to his left the bench seat and bait area. Ahead was the door, beyond which were the steps leading to the galley and living accommodation.

He crossed to this door and tried the handle. This was locked.

Flynn swore under his breath, took a step back to weigh up the door which was made of thick UPVC in a frame, rather like the back door of a house. In his time as a cop Flynn had booted down many doors, although it had become progressively harder. As a drugs branch detective, entering premises through locked doors was a regular occurrence. In the old days, most doors could easily be removed by size elevens and determination. But as UPVC and multi-lock doors became more common, the cops had become more sophisticated, in a rough sort of way, in their attempts to batter them down. The door Flynn faced that evening was of the newer variety, and even though it was on a boat it was still substantial. He doubted his ability to kick it open using the flat-footed method – but was going to give it a try anyway.

He angled himself side-on to the door, gritted his teeth, and got into the mental attitude required to boot down the door.

But at that moment he felt a gun barrel pressing into the back of his neck, just below his trimmed hairline, at the point where his skull connected with his spine. Flynn did not move an inch, other than to open his fingers when a voice said, 'Drop your gun.'

FOURTEEN

Mark Carter had not answered his bail and Henry was fuming, convinced he could be doing better, more interesting things than hanging around in a grotty police station. Although when he analysed that thought, he wasn't exactly sure what. As Alison was back at her pub in Kendleton, he wouldn't be with her, so the probability was that the only place he would be right now would be alone, splayed out on the settee at home gripping a beer and trying to get his head around why Kate had loved soap operas so much. Or maybe propping up the bar down at the Tram & Tower, his local, bending the ear of Ken, the landlord, who'd become a bit of an unwilling listening post for him.

Maybe being annoyed at the police station, waiting for someone to answer bail, wasn't such a bad option.

He checked his watch for the umpteenth time and looked across at Rik Dean, who was busying himself with paperwork.

Then his mobile rang and the display read, 'Unknown Caller'. Henry said, 'Bet this is him . . . Henry Christie.'

'Detective Superintendent Christie?' came the crisp, upper-class tones that Henry recognized instantly: the spookmeister, Martin Beckham. Henry snatched the pen from Rik's fingers.

'Mr Beckham, hello – at last.'

'Mm, this is only a courtesy call.' Beckham sounded unwilling even to speak and Henry guessed he was doing so under pressure from some other quarters. 'You sent a list of questions and some requests concerning Zahid Sadiq.'

'Oh yes . . . when was that? I'd almost forgotten.'

'Sarcasm will get you nothing,' Beckham's voice hardened. 'Just to say that our interviewers questioned him on your behalf and he made no comment, so I'm afraid that's where it ends.'

'He made no comment?' Henry asked incredulously. 'His ejaculate was found inside a female murder victim and you allowed him to make no comment?'

'That is the situation.'

'In that case, I need to come and interview him properly, like I should have been allowed to do in the first place.'

'Are you suggesting that my interviewers are less than competent?'

'What I'm suggesting is that an investigator with a feel for the brutal murder of a teenage girl needs to speak to this guy, who must be seen as a prime suspect until I'm satisfied otherwise.'

Beckham gave a harsh laugh. 'I may point out to you that the ejaculate, as you so delicately put it, is only one of four specimens found inside a girl who, it would appear, was of loose morals and may well have been the author of her own downfall.'

Henry tugged his collar, feeling the redness of anger shoot up his neck. 'Can I quote you on that?' he asked, trying to keep his voice level. 'She is a murder victim and I have a job to do, and, as far as I can see, you are obstructing justice.'

'The bigger picture, Superintendent. I assume you've heard that term before?' Beckham said patronizingly. 'Sadiq is an asset in the war against terrorism and you will not have access to him.'

'I know all about the bigger picture, but in this case there is no bigger picture than finding out who killed an innocent teenager,' Henry responded.

The line went silent.

Beckham said, 'Maybe when we've finished with him, you can have him.'

'And what will be left of the poor misguided bastard?'

'Not much, but that's the best I can do. And if you want my opinion, he didn't kill her.'

'What about Akram? Don't forget his sperm was also found inside her.'

'How would I know?'

'When can I have him, then?'

'To be determined, dear boy,' Beckham replied, keeping up the patronizing tone.

Henry was almost crushing his mobile phone, but he controlled himself and asked, 'There is something else. I also asked you to check the items that you seized from Sadiq's flat to see if there were any DNA traces of the dead girl on any of the stuff.'

'There was no trace of anything relating to the girl,' Beckham said. 'It looks like she was never there. In fact there wasn't really much of anything there.'

'OK,' Henry said, and he ended the call.

'Nada?' Rik said, as Henry placed his phone down on the table.

'Zilch,' Henry confirmed, wishing he knew a way around the situation. He paced the small office. It was an extreme idea, but the media was a possibility. Go to the papers, slag off MI5? He dismissed that. Apart from the fact it was likely the story would be suppressed from the highest level, he would find himself deep in the mire – shit that would probably follow him into retirement. His anger subsided – a little – and he checked his watch again. 'I think I'll go and see if I can collar Mark Carter. I need somebody to shout at. Coming?'

Rik shook his head. Henry handed him his pen back, not having used it, grabbed a set of keys for a CID car and headed down to the police garage. There was no way he was going to drive his Mercedes around the hellhole that was Shoreside estate. He wasn't bothered if the wheels disappeared from a police car.

They decided on a new location for their next meeting later that evening.

Donaldson made certain he wasn't followed and insisted Edina did the same. Trouble was, Donaldson knew that the 'Watchers', as the surveillance branch of MI5 was called, were the best in the world. They could tail even the most surveillance conscious target without ever revealing themselves. However, basic precautions could be taken, such as stopping abruptly, false window-shopping to look at reflections rather than the display, doubling back and looking at faces, as well as ducking into shops through one door and leaving via another. Edina was unfazed and said she knew what to do.

When she appeared at the Spanish restaurant in a medium-sized shopping arcade just off Victoria Street, Westminster, at eight that evening, she looked beautiful and relaxed. She had strolled the mile or so from her apartment close to the Home Office, overlooking the Thames.

They shared paella, food that Donaldson loved. It was a good one, a mix of seafood and chicken, freshly prepared. The accompanying Spanish beer complemented it perfectly. As Edina scraped a spoon across the paella pan for the tasty burned layer on the bottom, Donaldson asked, 'Can we talk now?'

She had drunk the best part of the bottle of Rioja. Her eyes glistened as she placed the spoon into her mouth and chewed the burned rice that coated the pan.

'I can't actually answer the question you asked about Blackpool, but I can tell you one thing. There were three of them.'

'What do you mean?'

'Not two, but three.'

Donaldson sat back.

'Three boys, not two.' Her words were slightly slurred but clear. 'The two you caught – Sadiq and Rahman – and another one who had been brainwashed or radicalized or whatever it's called. As far as I can gather, his whereabouts are unknown, as are the whereabouts of Jamil Akram. But they believe this little escapade isn't yet over. That's why they're keeping a tight reign on Sadiq, but so far he's told them nothing useful.' Edina chuckled. 'A teenage boy is holding out against some of the world's most experienced interrogators.'

'I saw you run,' she said accusingly. 'You left me to die.'

'Could you possibly point that thing in another direction?'

Steve Flynn was sitting on the bench seat in *Shell*'s cockpit and the woman after whom the boat had been named was perched on the fighting chair, a double-barrelled sawn-off shotgun resting across her lap, but loosely aimed at Flynn's groin. If it had been discharged, even if he had survived the blast, he would be minus his genitals.

'You left me behind, ran off,' she said. 'I saw you climb back on to the quayside. Then you ran away.' The aim stayed the same.

Flynn said, 'I couldn't have helped, Michelle. I'd been shot . . . may I?' He wasn't sure why he felt the need to do this, but he eased up his T-shirt and peeled back the dressing to show the ugly red, raised scar across his ribcage. 'I was unarmed. I thought I might be dying anyway. I could hardly move. I would've been no use. As soon as I made a move, I would have been killed. I was too slow. I knew Boone was dead. I just had to hope that they wouldn't kill you as well, because I knew even then, that if I lived, I'd be coming back.' He replaced the dressing and pulled his shirt down.

Michelle raised the shotgun and trained it on Flynn's chest. The double hammers were cocked and her finger was curled across both triggers.

Flynn stopped breathing. 'Michelle, I'm back. I came back,' he whispered.

'You left me,' she accused him. 'You left Boone.'

'He was dead. Don't forget, I saw him die, too.'

Flynn recalled the first time, not so very long ago, that he'd seen Michelle. It had been on the day he and Boone had returned from a day's tarpon fishing. He had been stunned by her radiant, free beauty. He also remembered those moments before Boone had hurtled back with the devil on his tail, how Michelle had unashamedly leaned over him at the laptop, naked, her breasts nuzzling his shoulder blades. A vibrant, beautiful woman. Now completely changed by recent events. Her chocolate brown skin had lost its lustre, her face gaunt, bearing the faded marks of a brutal beating. Her eyes seeped terror. Her whole body seemed shrivelled and wasted. Everything had somehow been battered out of her.

'Do you know what they did to me?'

Flynn shook his head, nostrils flaring, eyes flickering between the double-O barrel ends and Michelle's face. A tear formed at the edge of her left eye. A perfect, glinting droplet that rolled down her cheek, leaving a track.

'They beat me and they raped me,' she whispered.

'I'm sorry.' Flynn swallowed. His voice croaked.

'They beat me and they raped me . . . again and again.'

Flynn swallowed drily now, his mouth and throat like acid. Michelle's forefinger jittered on the triggers.

'But that didn't matter.' She removed her finger from the trigger and wiped away the tear with the back of her hand. 'Rape doesn't matter to me. I've been raped a thousand times. I was a prostitute, you see. A good one. Men have always had their way with me, and as far as I was concerned it was always rape. But I learned to live through it. I've been abused since I was seven. By men. Eventually it meant nothing. I have been beaten, too. Many, many times, by angry men.' Another tear formed, trickled down. She wiped it away. 'Beating means nothing, either, because no one could ever beat the spirit out of me.' She lifted her chin challengingly.

'Shell,' Flynn started to say, and moved slightly.

She jerked the gun at him. He became rigid again.

'Those men raped me. They did it on the jetty and in the houseboat. They held my face over the side of the jetty and fucked me from behind so I had to look at Boone's body floating in the bloody water. His face was looking up at me, what was left of it. The fish had already started to eat him.'

'Shell,' Flynn said again.

'What those men took from me was my hope. Boone was my future. He was my way out. He saved me and I loved him for it. They took him from me . . . and you – YOU – left me . . .'

'Shell,' Flynn said again for the third time. 'I'm back. I couldn't save Boone and I couldn't have saved you.'

Her head began to shake from side to side, then her chin fell and her whole body sagged as though, this time, the spirit had left her. The gun fell out of her hands on to the deck.

Flynn swooped down and knelt in front of her, encircling his strong arms around her now frail body, which shook and juddered uncontrollably. He held on and her thin arms went around his neck, crushing him ferociously. She started to howl and Flynn kept a tight hold as she broke down completely, her head buried into his chest. He stroked her hair, now coarse and straggled and stale, cooing, 'It's OK, it's OK,' softly, and other useless words into her ear. Such as, 'I'm here now.'

As if that was any sort of reassurance to her.

'I prayed you'd come back,' she said, her voice muffled and broken. 'Prayed hard, prayed to God you hadn't truly deserted me.'

'Tell me who these people are,' Flynn whispered. 'Tell me their names. Tell me where I can find them.'

'Will you destroy them?'

'Oh yes.'

The evenings were getting longer and on Shoreside the gangs had started to gather again. Henry drove on to the estate in the CID Focus and was instantly spotted and ID'd by the four youths on the first corner he drove past. They had been pushing and shoving each other, generally larking around. When they saw him, they ended their boisterous shenanigans and eyed him fiercely. Two of them fished out their mobile phones. One started to text, one took his photograph. Henry knew these guys were the sentinels for this entrance to the estate, a bit like lookouts for the Hole in the Wall gang – and this estate was pretty much as lawless as the Wild West. In fact a lot of cops referred to it as Dodge City.

Henry gave the hoodies a broad smile and drove on.

He was looking for Mark Carter, who lived on the far perimeter of the estate in a house once occupied by his mother, which, Henry had learned to his surprise, had been bought by her from the council and the outstanding debt on it had been paid by a mortgage insurance policy when she'd been murdered. Mark now lived there alone.

He drove past the fenced off remnants of a parade of shops that had been systematically razed to the ground by local vandals. Then past the house owned and occupied by the Costain family who presided over the estate like warlords, controlling most of the criminal activity therein. Henry was sure that his photo had been beamed to one of the Costains.

Then he was on the avenue on which Mark lived.

He drew up outside the house, which was in darkness. Didn't seem like anyone was at home. Still, Henry never took anything for granted. He walked up to the front door, eyeing the windows all the time for signs of movement, then tapped on the front door and rattled the letterbox. The door opened slightly at Henry's touch. He pushed it fully open and called out, 'Mark? It's me, Henry Christie,' from the threshold.

Behind the door was a stack of unopened mail. Henry switched on the hall light and bent down to pick it up. Scanning through it he saw quite a few official looking envelopes that smacked of final demands, which made Henry wonder how Mark survived. The house might have been paid for, but bills still came in and a two-bit job at a fast food restaurant wouldn't go far in paying for its upkeep. Could well be on benefits, too, Henry thought.

'Mark,' he called again.

He checked the downstairs rooms, found no sign of the lad.

He was upstairs on top of his bed. The bedroom floor was littered with beer cans and a couple of supermarket own-brand whiskey bottles. Henry stood on the crunchy crust of a half-eaten meat pie – hard, like stepping on a cockroach – and wafted away the aroma of exhaled booze, sweat, urine, farts and vomit, smells Henry readily associated with cell blocks.

Mark was fully clothed, lying in the recovery position, on his side, one knee drawn up, clasping a can of cheap lager. He was snoring and dribbling at the same time.

Henry walked across to him, raised his right foot and prodded him with his toe. No response. He prodded a little more firmly and said, 'Mark.' The lad groaned, rolled on to his back and quarter-opened his eyes, which seemed to be stuck together by some kind of mucus. He looked dreadful. 'Jeez,' Henry muttered and managed to step smartly back out of range.

It was the stomach heave that gave him the warning. Mark spun back on to his side and his projectile vomit splattered on the bedroom floor like a pan of thick vegetable soup being hurled across a kitchen.

Henry half-dragged Mark out of his room, sidestepping the reeking pile of vomit, and into the bathroom. He heaved him into the shower, fully clothed, then turned it on full blast. The icy rods of the water jets shook Mark, semi-conscious up to that point, into some sort of life, demonstrated by a scream and a scramble to get out of the cubicle with a lot of cursing and swearing. Despite getting his sleeve wet, Henry held him back easily as the water gradually lost its chill and warmed up, then became hot, and the struggling teen gave up the fight with a resigned but vicious glare at Henry, who he called a bastard repeatedly. Then he said, 'OK, OK, let me get my stuff off.' Henry released him and backed away.

'Get your sorry arse showered and get into some new clobber.'

Henry reversed out, closing the shower door as he went.

Mark rubbed two round holes in the steamed-up glass door and looked balefully out through them.

Edina hadn't actually said much, Donaldson mused as he walked back down Victoria Street after they'd finished dinner, but what she had revealed set the American's mind chugging. He rewound back to the morning he had managed to prevent a suicide bomber causing death and destruction in the middle of Blackpool, and almost caught one of the world's most wanted terrorists, whilst another suspected bomber had been shot dead on the motorway.

So there had been three of them.

Three would-be suicide bombers? Is that what Edina meant? Was that what she had heard in passing?

He flagged down a cab and instructed the driver to get him to the American Embassy.

'Look what the cat kicked out,' Henry said at Mark's eventual appearance in the kitchen doorway.

Mark scowled and sloped across to the sink where he ran the cold tap for a few seconds before bending over and angling his mouth underneath the flow, swallowing and then spitting out a mouthful of water. He wiped his face with his hands and said, 'What are you doing in my house?'

'You're under arrest for not answering your bail.'

'Oh, fuck.' He held himself up against the sink. 'Completely forgot.'

'Forgot you were on bail for murder?'

Henry had filled the kettle, which he switched on, and found two clean mugs on the drainer. Mark sank on to a chair by the unstable breakfast bar.

'Yeah, forgot.' His head was in his hands.

'Got pissed instead?' Henry heaped some instant coffee into the mugs. 'How long have you been asleep?'

'Dunno. Started drinking at three this aft, after I finished work. Probably zonked out about six.'

Henry watched the kettle boil.

'I didn't do it, you know.'

'Well, that would be the point of answering bail, wouldn't it? So we can have a chat about things in more detail.'

Mark, head still in his hands, eyes closed, had changed into fresh clothes. 'I need to clean up that spew.'

'Oh yes,' Henry said. He poured the boiling water into the mugs, then handed one to Mark who sniffed it; his head reared away from the aroma.

'Ugh – hate coffee.'

'Take a sip.'

Mark did so, tentatively. 'Yuk, needs sugar, lots of it.' He stood up, unsteady, and crossed to a work surface on which there was a sugar bowl. He heaped a lot of sugar into the coffee, Henry watching him as he did so. Mark managed to drink some of the resultant mixture.

'I've got to come with you, have I?' he asked Henry. 'I didn't do it, honest. Ask one of the brown musketeers,' he mumbled.

'What?'

Mark shook his head. 'Nowt.'

'Right, tell you what. I'll do a deal with you.'

Mark eyed Henry suspiciously. 'Like with the devil?'

Henry sighed. 'Get your room cleaned up, get yourself some food down you, watch a bit of telly, go to bed and then turn up at the nick at nine tomorrow morning, bright, sober, ready to roll.'

'That's your deal?'

'Second option – I drag you down to the nick right now and trap you up for the night. You've had a skinful and I'd say you're not fit to interview, so maybe a night in the cells would do you some good. And, as horrible as it might seem now, your vomit will be easier to clean up while it's still wet. Once its dried, it'll be a complete nightmare.' Henry cocked his head at Mark.

Mark sighed. 'I'll take option one.'

'Good.' Henry pointed at him. 'If you're a minute late, I'll drag the whole thing out for the day, understand? Be on time and we'll sort it, OK?' Mark's mouth curved downwards. 'I'm doing you a favour here.'

'I haven't left the boat since . . .' Michelle started to say. She was in the front passenger seat of Boone's old Land Cruiser, a vehicle that had seen much better days, but kept going. Flynn was driving and they were entering the environs of Banjul, the Gambia's capital city. The streets teemed with people and traffic, fairly typical of an African town. Progress was slow, the heat tremendous and the air-con unit knackered. Flynn sweated heavily.

'I understand,' Flynn said for the umpteenth time, coaxing her gently along. He'd explained he had fleetingly seen the man that Boone had returned with from wherever, and that he thought that person would probably be well gone by now. But he expected that the small man who had helped the man off the boat, and the heavies – the ones who had returned to wreak havoc and death – would still be local.

Flynn had described the small, besuited man. Immediately Michelle exclaimed, 'That's Aleef.'

'Aleef?'

'Mamoud Aleef . . . he's a fixer, a middleman, makes deals, takes a cut.'

This conversation had taken place a little earlier on the deck of *Shell*. Michelle had sobbed heavily for what seemed like a very long time before it had all subsided and Flynn had pushed her gently away from him, wiped her tears with his thumbs, reassured her and listened to her story. The fear, watching them destroy the houseboat, the rapes, the beatings. And also how, when the police came later, they simply sneered at her, dragged Boone's body out of the water and that was the last she saw or heard.

'I need you to help me find these men,' Flynn insisted. 'I wouldn't know where to start. You need to point me in the right direction.'

She nodded. 'I will.'

Flynn had described to her what he'd seen when he'd gone to meet Boone arriving back from his hurried, mysterious journey. How he'd hidden behind barrels and watched the tough guys lounging by the big old Mercedes, the little man – Aleef – helping to transfer the injured man from the boat into the car. He had seen all their faces, they hadn't seen him, and he had since managed to identify the injured passenger.

'Who was he?' Michelle asked.

Flynn then told her about the computer pages Boone had been browsing and when he'd got back to Gran Canaria, he'd found the same pages – and more.

'A man on the run from the British cops on terrorism charges. I'm certain it's a guy called Jamil Akram.' He watched Michelle's face as he said the name, but saw it meant nothing to her.

'Boone brought a terrorist back from somewhere?' she mused thinly.

'Seems so.'

'The utter fool. But why did they come after him? Surely he had done what they wanted?'

Flynn sighed, knowing Boone's character of old. 'I don't know for sure, but my guess is he didn't know who his cargo was until he read the news and saw pictures of Akram. Then suddenly he puts it all together . . . and . . .' Flynn's voice trailed off.

'He went for more money. Blackmail,' Michelle said, showing that she too knew Boone pretty well. 'I'm sure the small man you describe is Aleef. He's been around a long time, but in the shadows . . . he's a businessman, got lots of henchmen. But I'm shocked he's linked to a terrorist.'

'Money,' Flynn said. 'How do you know him?'

'Just do. He flits around the clubs, where he does a lot of his business . . . where I used to do my business. Until Boone gave me a future,' she concluded resentfully.

'Take me into town and find this Aleef. I'll take it from there.'

The prospect of stepping foot off *Shell* and going into town clearly scared her. 'I haven't left the boat since,' she said then, and when Flynn finally got her into the Land Cruiser, which he'd found to still be in working order, she continued to repeat the mantra all the way into town. She was plainly terrified of being out and about again.

'They threatened to kill me,' she said, turning her face to Flynn, half-hidden in the shadows, but her eyes were wide open. He swerved the Land Cruiser to the side of the road and said gently, 'I'll take you back. I'll try and find them myself.' He was being honest, not manipulative.

'No, no,' she insisted. 'I'm doing this for Boone. They destroyed him and though I am saddened to say it, I want this, I want them dead, Flynn.' She then looked forward, jaw set hard, a totally different woman to the one he'd met less than two weeks before, now transformed and changed for ever by the trauma she'd experienced. 'Do it,' she said.

*　*　*

Donaldson was back at the American Embassy. Alone in his office, he was watching the DVD of the video that had been released by al-Qaeda of Rashid Rahman, the young man who had been shot dead on the motorway, who was ranting on about how he would take the fight to the infidel.

His wish – *'To take as many unbelievers as possible so they may go to hell and I to heaven . . . and this is only the beginning, the big one is yet to come.'*

The words, as ever, sent a shiver through Donaldson's bones.

'What a waste,' he sighed and skipped the disc backwards and watched it again, leaning forwards, closely studying the image, this time with the sound turned down, his head shaking sadly at the terrible loss of a life. Then he noticed something that made him sit upright and think back to the moment he had spotted the other would-be terrorist, Zahid Sadiq, walking along Blackpool promenade, showing all the outward signs of being a suicide bomber. Inappropriate clothing. Robotic walk. The mouth chanting, mumbling his last prayers. Eyes fixed, staring ahead. And something else . . .

Donaldson shot forwards again, froze the image and pressed print screen.

'You didn't find him, then?' a smug Rik Dean asked.

Henry had driven back to Blackpool police station to drop off the CID car, which had made it unscathed off Shoreside. He'd bumped accidentally into Rik, who had changed into some rough clothing and was making his way to the police garage with the keys for, as he described it, 'the shittiest police car in there'. A turn of the millennium Nissan, tucked away in a dark corner, which no one used unless absolutely necessary. It should have been changed long ago, but cost cutting meant that if it had gone, there would have been no replacement, so the CID clung on to it as a last resort. It came in useful for jobs like tonight – keeping obs – but it wasn't something you turned up in if you were out to impress.

'I did, actually, but he needed to sleep it off.'

'Pissed?'

'His life's going down the pan – literally,' Henry said. 'I've arranged for him to come in first thing in the morning.'

'And you think he'll turn up?' Rik's voice said *he* didn't.

'Yep.'

'Henry, you're too soft with that lad. It's not your fault his sister OD'd, his brother's a dealer and his mum got whacked.'

'I know, but I think we have some sort of obligation to him.' Henry sighed. It was an old conversation.

They were face to face in a narrow, poorly lit corridor just outside the custody office. A section van reversed in and two uniformed cops dragged a belligerent drunk out of the back doors. Another body for Blackpool police station's prisoner sausage machine that processed over 12,000 each year.

'Anyway, I'm going to give it a couple of hours.' Rik dangled the car keys at Henry. 'Until midnight, then I'll find somewhere for a nightcap. You still coming?'

'If you want some company,' Henry said.

'So long as you don't go all social worker on me about Mark Carter.'

'Promise.'

'And I drive you home to get changed. Not certain a suit is the best attire for observations.'

'OK . . . and I thought we could talk about shagging, y'know, like blokes do.'

Rik said, 'I'll go for that.'

Flynn and Michelle drifted from bar to bar, drinking soft drinks and sitting in dark alcoves from which they could keep watch for Aleef. It was hit and miss, no guarantees, but at least they were doing something. Flynn felt better about that. He was a man of action and some violence and moping about did not suit him. He needed this. Inside him, the desire for revenge was like a caged beast wanting to be set free. Even if Boone hadn't been killed, had somehow escaped, Flynn would still have gone after the men who had shot him.

He and Michelle sat close to each other, knee to knee. She kept her face lowered in the shadows as much as possible. The hot, dusty streets of Banjul were thronging with bodies, quite a few white faces in amongst the Africans, so Flynn was not too obvious. No one paid him any heed. Banjul drew in holiday-makers and he was simply a man in a crowd who might have picked up a whore. Nothing unusual about that.

Except Flynn could not even start to visualize Michelle as a prostitute, even though she had once been one. It was very hard for him to make that mental leap.

However, there was only a handful of clubs that tourists frequented and these were not the ones Michelle guided him into. These were dark, dingy, basement hovels, hotter than the streets, crammed with people, the smell of sweat and dope overpowering. The music was loud and African, with driving beats and an air of menace.

Michelle clung to him as she steered him into a club that had no name over the door and had two evil looking bouncers guarding the place. Inside it was a crush, impossible to move other than by sliding intimately past other customers. A haven for groping accidentally on purpose, and pickpockets. There was a minuscule dance floor, which was heaving, and a long bar at which Michelle and Flynn chiselled out a space. Flynn shouted his order, then rotated to rest his back on the edge of the bar whilst Michelle tucked herself tightly alongside him. Flynn's eyes roved, spotting the pimps and hookers on the prowl, drug dealers too, and lots of clients.

Michelle tiptoed up so her mouth was at Flynn's ear. 'Boone liked this place. It's where I met him.'

Flynn nodded, somewhat surprised at the admission.

'He took me away from it,' she added, and dropped back on to the flats of her feet.

Flynn's eyes adjusted to the darkness and the flashing disco and strobe lighting, and he saw a line of alcoves along the wall opposite, deep recesses in which couples groped, and glimpsed occasional flashes of male ecstasy, female hands tucked down men's trousers, the jerk of gratification.

He turned away from the sight and faced the bar as the drinks came. Michelle's arms encircled his waist and she clung to him. He draped an arm around her shoulders and gave her a reassuring hug, then glanced diagonally across to the far corner of the bar where a man sat on a stool, a beer in his hand, a woman in a shiny dress dancing slinkily on the spot in front of him as he watched with lustful eyes.

Flynn tilted his head and spoke out of the corner of his mouth so Michelle could hear his words.

'That's one of the men,' he said, his lips hardly moving. He turned her slightly. She saw him and Flynn felt her convulse and

spin back into him with a moan of anguish. It was one of the
men from the Mercedes. One of the ones who had killed Boone,
shot at him, then raped her. He could have been the one who
had winged Flynn.

'What do we do?' Michelle asked.

'We leave, I watch, I wait . . . I follow. Get the drift?'

'And me?'

'You go back to the car, lock yourself in and wait for me. If
I'm not back within an hour, go back to Boone's boat and wait
there. I'll be back. Sometime.'

FIFTEEN

'It comes to something when officers with our length of service
and rank are sitting in a crappy police car at bloody near
midnight, keeping obs. Surely we've got something wrong
somewhere? This is a job for the younger, keener, more energetic
end of the policing family. Not old lags.'

'Speak for yourself,' Rik Dean said. 'You've got a lot of years
on me, pal.'

'But you know what I mean,' Henry whined. 'The principle
of two relatively high ranking detectives doing what we're doing
. . . I dunno . . . unseemly, not right.'

'I'll have it sorted for tomorrow night.'

Henry slouched down in the passenger seat of the Nissan,
which had springs that had collapsed completely and others
that stuck in his spine like corkscrews. It wasn't far off midnight
and now it was all wearing a bit thin. Conversation had
started sprightly enough. Not, as it happened, about sexual
intercourse, but the other usual things that cops talked about
on boring obs. The physics of the universe, how insignificant
human beings were in the grand scheme of things, the power
of the moon, the credit crunch and other such mind-blowing
topics. Heavy stuff, about which they knew very little but
spouted a lot. However, that had petered out as they drove
fairly aimlessly around the north shore area in which the rapes
had taken place.

It was pretty hit and miss and Rik had already decided that the officers who were due to be out tomorrow night would be more specific in their tasks.

Not much was moving. Not many cars. Not many people.

As they drove out in the general direction of Poulton-le-Fylde, they spotted a car coming in the opposite direction that Henry recognized as they passed side by side. He got a look at the driver, who he also recognized.

'Corrie run,' he said.

'Eh?'

'That car,' Henry jerked his thumb over his shoulder. 'It's the plain car from Poulton.'

'And how would you know that?' Rik asked. He hadn't clocked the car.

'Because even though I had a mini collapse at the scene of Natalie Philips's murder, I did notice the car that the PC who had found her had been driving.'

'Oh.'

'Don't remember the PC's name, though I sort of recall talking to him. He was pretty upset.'

'Paul Driver. He found her by the crematorium gates.'

'That's the one.'

They continued their slow patrol, parking up here and there. A few kids were out on the streets. A couple of lads, a couple of girls, maybe walking home from a pub. Then they saw one lone female walking swiftly and with purpose. Not really many targets for an opportunistic rapist, if that is what the offender was. But maybe a quiet night was the best. Fewer targets, even fewer witnesses.

Henry checked his phone – again – slightly disappointed he didn't have anything from Alison. Maybe she's just used me, he tried to rationalize. But he knew that wasn't true. She was honest, genuine, quite bloody gorgeous and wonderful.

Points which suddenly hit the nail on the head for him. His guts lurched as he suddenly realized how lucky he had been to meet Alison and get into a relationship with her. He knew he couldn't afford to lose her.

'Once more round the block,' Rik said, 'then let's call it quits.'

Henry nodded. He was concentrating on sending a text. It began, 'SORRY ITS LATE. CAN WE TALK? B HOME IN BOUT AN HR'.

As an afterthought, he added, 'xx' so it could not be interpreted as one of those, 'We need to talk, it's time to end it' texts.' If he got one back without a kiss, he would be worried.

He found Alison's number in his phone's contacts list and after a moment of hesitation, pressed send, then raised his head from the task to see where Rik was taking him.

And then he saw the car parked up.

'What's he doing here?' he said. He craned around to look as Rik drove on past the car that was parked on the roadside, in amongst a line of other cars. Henry did not see anyone in the car and Rik obviously did not know what Henry was talking about.

'Who?' Rik said. He'd reached the next junction. They were on a nice, well-established housing estate just off Garstang Old Road. If Rik drove straight across the junction, he would reach a T-junction at which a left turn would take him out towards Poulton, and right back into Blackpool.

Henry, ignoring his questions, said, 'Go across here, pull in and switch everything off.'

'Eh?'

'Just do it.'

Rik complied, drove across, pulled in to the side of the road and parked about twenty metres along the next avenue, doused the lights and turned off the engine. Henry wound down his window – electric ones not being standard on the old Nissan – and adjusted his door mirror manually to give him a view back up the road.

'What is it?'

'That plain car from Poulton is parked back there in that line of cars.'

Rik jerked his head and squinted at Henry. 'Your point being?'

'What's he doing there?'

'Don't know. Maybe he lives there. Maybe he's popped home for a brew. Maybe he's shagging, maybe—'

Henry held up his right hand. 'Stop. Too many maybes. Whatever he's doing, he's off his patch.'

'But he has to come off his patch to do the corrie run.'

'I know that, but he's taking the piss here, isn't he?'

'Henry – why are you bothered? You're not his sergeant. Did you never sneak off for a brew now and again – or something else?'

'All the time. But I'm a superintendent now. I have double standards and I'm therefore above that sort of thing.' Henry wasn't actually too bothered what the PC was up to, simply curious.

Rik's mouth snapped shut, then he sighed. 'Do you want me to talk to the inspector at Poulton tomorrow? I'd kind of like to get that nightcap now, you know? I don't get paid overtime.'

'Nor do I.'

'But you earn almost twice as much as me.'

'Stop bickering, will you?'

Rik murmured something incomprehensible, but was annoyed.

Henry finely adjusted the mirror, slumping in the seat for a clear view back up across the junction, enough to see if anyone approached the car along the pavement, but not necessarily if they came at it from any other direction. Rik also slid down his seat and adjusted his door mirror, so between them, they pretty much had it covered.

'This just seems absurd,' Rik said.

'Have you got the number of Lancaster comms in your mobile?' Rik muttered that he had. 'Then call them and ask them to radio PC Driver and ask him for his current location.' Although geographically adjacent to Blackpool division, Poulton-le-Fylde was actually in Northern division, the HQ of which was Lancaster, where the divisional control room was situated. Logically it would have made more sense for Poulton to belong to Blackpool as it had much in common with the resort, but such were the vagaries of political boundaries on which policing areas were more or less based.

Rik found the number and dialled.

As he was speaking, Henry's own mobile bleeped with a text landing. It was Alison. Nervously he tabbed it open.

It said, 'TIME DONT MATTER. THINKING OF YOU. LOVE YOU. WANT TO TALK. XX'.

Oh my God, Henry thought, and a shudder ran through him.

Rik was speaking to Lancaster comms room. 'Yeah, uh, can you tell him that DI Dean wants to see him at Poulton police station?' Rik gave Henry a desperate what-the-hell-am-I-supposed-to-say expression. 'OK, I'll hold.' Rik then snatched up his PR from the door pocket next to him and tuned it over to the radio channel used by Lancaster just in time to hear an operator call PC Driver's collar number and ask for his location.

There was a long pause, then the operator repeated the call.

Then Driver responded. 'Yeah, just leaving Blackpool nick, en route back to Poulton, correspondence run.' Henry and Rik exchanged a surprised look. 'Can I ask why?' Driver said.

'DI Dean on the line, would like to see you at Poulton.'

'Any reason?'

'Stand by.'

The comms operator came on to the line and asked Rik the question. He said, 'It's a slightly delicate matter, not suitable for the airwaves. Just tell him I want a quick word on a personal matter.'

This was then relayed to Driver, who came back, 'I'll be about half an hour. I have a job I need to attend to on the way back.' His voice was cool and not harassed.

'I'll pass that on,' the operator said, and did so.

Henry pouted and said, 'Fibber. Vinegar strokes.'

There was no guarantee that the man would even leave the club. He seemed pretty comfortable, lording it at the bar. Nor was there any guarantee that if he did leave, Flynn would be able to follow him anywhere of interest or without being sussed. As much as he wanted to confront the guy, he also wanted the other men involved in Boone's death. That was the problem with life: no guarantees. As Boone had found out. As Flynn had once discovered when he lost the woman he loved. Life was the dealer of a pretty shitty hand sometimes.

The club door opened. Flynn leaned back in the doorway opposite, deep into the shadows. Several customers tumbled out, laughing. But not the man who interested him.

Flynn exhaled. The Glock, silencer fitted, was uncomfortable in his waistband.

A police Land Rover rolled slowly down the street, past the club, past where Flynn stood. Two uniforms on board. He tensed but the officers were more concerned with eyeballing women on the street.

A further stream of customers stumbled into the club exuberantly.

Flynn had been waiting forty-five minutes now.

He did not really have a plan. Yes, he wanted retribution against the men who had killed Boone and destroyed Michelle's life, and almost killed him in the process. But beyond that he wasn't certain. Really he wanted to find all the men together, the two who'd survived unscathed, and the one who'd been shot in the arm by Boone. The fourth one, Flynn assumed, had perished in the explosion caused by the bullet being fired into the fuel barrel. Flynn also wanted Aleef, who he was sure, was behind the whole incident, middleman or not.

Three killers, one businessman.

Flynn relived the killing on the quayside, the faces of the gunmen seared into the front of his brain for ever.

And he waited patiently.

He was good at that. Having been a soldier, then a detective, he was accustomed to watching and waiting without getting bored, then leaping into action. It was a learned skill, but one that had been absolutely necessary in the way he'd chosen to live his life.

The club door opened.

Several people surged in front of Flynn along the pavement at that exact moment, obscuring his view. He did not want to break cover, but he caught a glimpse of the one man who came out of the door, then turned quickly left, then left again into the narrow alleyway that ran along the gable end of the club building.

A single figure. A big guy. That was all he saw. It was enough. It was the man.

Both detectives slouched well down in their seats, so their shapes could not be seen, other than by close scrutiny.

Rik muttered, 'So what, he's been for a quickie.'

'Yeah, well, let's put the shit up him.'

Looking back by using the door mirror, Henry spotted a figure walking towards them in the distance. The figure – it was a man – stopped on the footpath. Henry could not make out any of his features using the mirror, so he looked over his right shoulder between the seats. The man had stopped next to the unmarked police car, a Vauxhall Astra, then took a step sideways so he was standing behind the vehicle.

Rik, too, had turned to look over his shoulder. His head and Henry's were side by side, ear to ear.

It was impossible to ID the person, but the assumption they both made was that it was PC Driver returning to his car, having been rudely interrupted by comms and the fake summons to go and see the DI who was waiting for him at Poulton nick.

The hatchback of the Vauxhall opened and the man bent down out of sight behind it, obscuring him and what he was actually doing.

'What's he up to?' Henry whispered.

'Can't tell.'

The hatchback closed with a thud. The figure got into the car. They heard the engine start up. The headlights came on and the car pulled out from between the other parked cars.

'Get down,' Henry said.

He and Rik quickly slid low into their seats, their heads under the level of the windows. The Astra zoomed quickly past them, up to the next junction, and turned left without stopping, heading away from Blackpool.

Rik fired up the Nissan, waited for the Astra to go out of sight, then set off without lights up to the junction and turned left, when he flicked on his sidelights and saw the Astra was now well ahead of them on the otherwise quiet road.

Henry sat up, flicking his fingers at Rik in a 'Gimme' gesture and said, 'PR, please.' Rik handed the radio across, which was still tuned into Northern division's channel.

'Superintendent Christie to PC Driver at Poulton, receiving?'

There was a pause. The brake lights flashed on the Astra for a split second. Then, 'Receiving.'

'I'm at Poulton awaiting your arrival with the DI. Do you have a current location and ETA?'

Again a pause. 'Amounderness Way, Fleetwood. ETA, five minutes.'

'Roger that.'

'Can you tell me what it's about boss?' Driver asked.

'Nothing to worry about,' Henry assured him. Then he said, 'Superintendent Christie to the Poulton section mobile currently driving the plain Astra on Garstang Road towards Poulton, give me a call.'

This time the pause stretched to complete silence, but the Astra sped up noticeably. Henry repeated the message and added, 'Please pull in, I want to talk to you.'

Rik had responded to the Astra's turn of speed with a mirrored surge from the Nissan which, worryingly, left a dirty black cloud of exhaust fumes behind. The Astra did not stop.

Henry said into the PR, 'Please pull in now. We are behind you.'

Still no response, so Henry called up Lancaster comms who had obviously been listening. 'Detective Superintendent Christie to Lancaster, please ask the patrol in the Poulton Astra to pull in now. I need a word.'

Comms relayed the message again and got no response. The operator asked Henry, 'Are you certain it's a Poulton section vehicle, sir?' It was a question posed with great delicacy. Just for a moment, Henry had a wave of self-doubt. Was he making an arse of himself here? Was this the same car he'd seen at the scene of Natalie's murder, the one used by the PC who had found her? Or had he got it completely wrong?

'Yes, I'm certain. It's an Astra, registered number . . .' Henry reeled off the number of the car.

'Roger that,' the operator said.

'Tell him to pull in again, please. We are behind him and I'm getting cross now.'

Rik flashed the headlights and the Astra then indicated and slowed down. Rik came right up behind it as it stopped. Henry jumped out and told Rik, 'You stay in here until he gets out.'

'Henry,' Rik whined, 'don't you think you're overdoing this?'

'At the very least he deserves a bollocking,' Henry shot back, and walked quickly to the passenger door of the Astra, which he yanked open. A spurt of relief shot through him when he saw it was PC Driver behind the wheel.

'Boss,' he said.

'Get out, let's have a chat. Switch off the engine.'

Driver blew out his cheeks, killed the motor, climbed out and trudged slowly around to Henry on the footpath, ready for a super's bollocking.

'You lied,' Henry said.

'Uh, yes, sorry boss.'

Henry saw he was dressed in uniform trousers, boots and shirt. His epaulettes were missing, as was his tie. He was breathing heavily and his armpits were wet with sweat.

'What were you up to?'

Driver looked around for inspiration, then admitted, 'Just popped in to see a girlfriend.' He sighed with defeat. 'Sorry.'

Henry nodded.

Rik climbed out of the Nissan and came around to them. 'Henry, a word.' He beckoned him to one side.

Henry said to Driver, 'Stay there.' To Rik he said, 'What is it?'

'Blackpool comms have just been on. A patrol's attending the report of a young woman who hasn't returned home from an evening out. I think we should leave this, and go and have a look-see. Could be connected with why we're out here tonight. Just rollock him and have done, eh?'

'OK, OK,' Henry said and walked back to Driver.

The PC blurted, 'Look boss, I'm sorry. I know I sneaked off my patch, but it's not the crime of the century, is it?'

Henry gave him one of his hard, boss-like stares. 'Take this as a warning.' He jabbed his finger at Driver. 'But I'll be having a word with your sergeant.' He spun regally away on his heels and took a step towards the Nissan, when he heard a dull knocking noise that didn't make any sense to him. He stopped and also heard a sort of murmuring sound, and then another dull knock.

Rik was leaning on the open driver's door of the Nissan.

'You hear that?' Henry said.

Rik shrugged. 'What?'

Another knock.

'There – again.' Henry turned slowly back to Driver, who was watching him, a look of horror on his face. A tapping noise. Henry listened, his head tilted, and then he said to Driver, 'Open the hatchback, please.'

'Why?'

'Open the fucking hatchback.'

Driver came slowly to the back of the car; Henry stood next to him.

'Like I said, why?' Driver demanded.

'Open it.'

'There's nothing to see.'

'Open it,' Henry growled.

Driver hooked his fingers underneath the lip of the hatchback and released the catch. The hydraulic mechanism slowly lifted it with a hiss, taking up the parcel shelf and exposing the storage area, illuminated by a small light on either side.

Driver did not move then.

Henry looked in, horror-struck. His head flicked up and he locked eyes with Driver, who instantly lurched sideways to run. Henry grabbed out for him, missed and took a handful of fresh air as Driver ducked.

Henry shouted, 'Get him.'

Driver was fast. Two strides and he was across the footpath, leaping over a low wire fence on to the playing field beyond.

Henry charged after him, clearing the fence cleanly, but with the agility of a dray horse. He landed heavily, slightly skew-whiff, but powered on, keeping his balance.

Rik was right behind, ready to support Henry with his actions, even if he didn't quite know what was happening.

Driver ran, zigzagging across the close-cropped field, towards the utter darkness at the far side. Henry knew if Driver made it ahead of him, there was a good chance he would disappear into the night.

He couldn't have that. He upped his speed, focused and gained on Driver, who was only a few feet ahead when Henry – digging out something from his old rugby days – hurled himself at the fleeing man. For a brief moment – in mid air – he thought he'd misjudged distance and speed, but his outstretched right hand latched on to Driver's belt, his fingers tightened into a fist and Henry hauled the man down to his knees. Keeping up the momentum, Henry scrambled on to him, flattening him face down and kneeling hard between his shoulder blades.

Rik arrived, still unsure of what was happening. Gasping, Henry held out his hand and wriggled his fingers. 'Cuffs,' he said.

Henry and Rik dragged Driver back across the field. He struggled ineffectively between the two detectives, who then pulled him over the fence and forced him into the back of the CID car. They then returned to Driver's vehicle, the hatchback of which was still raised.

The girl inside was gagged and bound, feet and ankles taped together, duct tape across her eyes and mouth. Even so, Henry recognized her as the girl they had seen earlier, walking quickly, and alone, through the streets.

*   *   *

'I want you to be honest with me,' Karl Donaldson said.

'All right – I do not appreciate you calling me at this time of day.'

'Don't worry, I won't keep you long.'

'How the hell did you get my number anyway?'

'You gave it to me once – when we were friends, remember?'

'Only vaguely,' Martin Beckham said with annoyance. Donaldson had woken the man up with the late night call, but at that moment he didn't give a damn.

Donaldson was still at his desk in his office. He had the phone on speaker and was leaning back in his big comfortable leather chair, hands clasped behind his head, ankles crossed on the edge of the desk.

'What is it you want?'

'One question. An important one.'

Beckham sounded resigned. 'What?'

'The flat the two lads were in. You and your team stripped it bare for forensic reasons.'

'Yes.'

'What did you find down the drains?'

'What do you mean?'

'I mean, when your expert team went through the place, what did you find down the drains?'

Beckham paused, his weary brain clicking over. 'Tell me what you're getting at?'

'What did you find down the drains?' Donaldson repeated slowly. 'That's what I'm getting at.'

'Nothing.'

'Is that nothing as in we looked, but didn't find anything? Or, nothing as in we actually didn't look at all?'

'We didn't look,' Beckham admitted.

Donaldson dropped his feet on to the floor and tipped forwards to tap the disconnect button.

Flynn trailed the man down stinking, poorly lit alleyways, virtually devoid of people, other than the dark mounds that were the sleeping forms of beggars under cardboard and sacking. He managed to keep close tabs on him using distance, shadows and the very obvious fact that the man wasn't expecting to be followed, a factor that counted for a lot. He was on home turf and it was pretty much a fact of life that when people were comfortable in their surroundings, being followed was one of the last things they ever considered. This principle applied as much to Mafia bosses as it did to hired killers.

The man kept going, taking Flynn further into the city. The problem for Flynn was that while the strip he had started out on was comfortable, with white faces in the crowds, these streets were not. Even darkness and a good tan could not disguise Flynn's skin colour and ethnic background. White European through and through, he looked out of place in the backstreets of Banjul, especially late at night.

Then the man turned into a building and was gone from sight.

Flynn came to a halt, sank into shadow, considered his position, then stood in a dark recess on the opposite side of the street.

It was a fairly typical style of building for Banjul. White, square, shutters on the windows, just one level to it, a flat-roofed bungalow. Flynn could not work out if it was a home or a place of work. Its whole appearance was alien to him.

The door the man had entered looked flimsy, easily kick-downable. Light showed from the angled gaps in the Venetian-style shutters at the windows.

Then Flynn noticed the car parked a little further down the street. The big, old, black Mercedes. Its sight jolted him. The car that the injured man had been helped into from Boone's boat, the one that Boone's killers had later turned up in.

Flynn crossed the street quickly and flattened himself against the wall next to the door. The Glock was now in his right hand, held at his thigh, and he wished he'd had the foresight to bring along the shotgun that Michelle had almost killed him with. It would have been effective in a tight space. He reached for the handle and turned it slowly. Locked. He emitted an exasperated gasp of frustration, then stood directly in front of the door, turned the handle with his left hand and leaned his weight on it with his left shoulder.

As he guessed, it was flimsy. He felt very confident he could open it easily, but it would make a horrible noise as he forced it down.

He hated the lack of planning and wondered if it would be better to back off now. Recce the place in daylight, work out the logistics and practicalities. See who came and went. How many people would be inside, what the inner geography was like . . . all the sensible things.

Unfortunately he did not get the chance to withdraw. That decision was taken out of his hands because as he stood there dithering, his mind whirring and tumbling as to the best approach, the door opened and he was instantly face to face with the man he had followed from the club, who was putting something into the inside pocket of his jacket, looking as though he was on the way out again.

In those circumstances the outcome of such a surprise encounter was usually determined by the one who reacted first. The one who was ready.

The man's face dropped and a frown knitted his thick eyebrows together – and he hesitated, not immediately computing anything, not recognizing Flynn, not even beginning to understand why a white man was outside his door. By that time it was far too late for him.

Flynn, by contrast, reacted instantly.

He was bigger, stronger and much fitter than the guy, who himself wasn't small and unfit by any means.

Flynn's left hand shot out, grabbed the man's shirt at his chest and in the same movement brought up the Glock and rammed the muzzle of the bulbous silencer into the soft under part of the man's wide chin.

He did not waste time with words.

He went for action, brutal force, speed.

He forced the man back into the premises, knocking him off balance, running him backwards on his heels.

Behind the door was a hallway of sorts. Three doors off. Using what little intelligence he had gathered from his short external inspection of the front of the building, Flynn thought the door to the left could be a living room of some sort. The one directly ahead was a kitchen – Flynn had glimpsed a sink beyond the open door – and the one on the right could be a bedroom. The one that concerned him in these opening seconds was the one to his left, because that was the one which was lit up.

Flynn powered the man backwards, then jerked him to the left and ran him into this room, which had no door to it.

With a massive heave, Flynn pistoned out his left arm and let go of the man's shirt. He staggered, tripped and landed on his backside.

Flynn took in the rest of the scenario. To his left a man lounged on a huge, dirty beanbag. This man had a bandage around his left bicep, his arm in a sling. This was the one Boone had managed to shoot on the quayside.

Next to him, on the remnants of a battered armchair, was another man, a cup of something in his hand, which he spilled as Flynn came in through the door. This was the second, uninjured gun man.

On the right, sitting primly on a dining chair, was the smartly besuited Aleef.

The man in the armchair threw his cup aside and started to rise – his right hand picking up the revolver that was lying on the chair arm.

The Glock came around. Flynn fired twice at the man's body mass. Two shots, quick succession, double-taps. They struck him perfectly, less than an inch apart, entering his heart, left and right ventricle, shredding the organ, the power of the impact smacking him back in the chair.

The beanbag man scrambled across the floor towards the AK47 propped up against the wall by an electric radiator. Flynn swivelled less than forty-five degrees, fired again. The man was side-on to him, his body mass a smaller target, so Flynn shot him in the side of the head, a temple shot, again a double-tap that entered the left side and exited at a downward angle, making a hole about as big as a drinks coaster. He jerked sideways, dead.

Flynn came around. The man he had forced into the room was lying on his side, his legs drawn up to his chest in a tight foetal position, cowering and whimpering.

Aleef, on the dining chair, had not moved. Flynn jerked the Glock at him, causing him to wince, dread on his face as he braced himself for the inevitable death that was coming. But Flynn swung the gun back around to the man on the floor and aimed.

'No, no,' he pleaded, his hands palm out.

Flynn shot him twice.

Then he turned to Aleef. 'Are you armed?' Aleef shook his head. 'Get up.'

He stood, legs wobbling, and looked at Flynn, but then his eye line flickered slightly over Flynn's shoulder. He tried to disguise this, but Flynn saw it, recognized it for what it was, dropped a shoulder, spun round and was faced with the horrific sight of another man coming for him with a double-handed hold on a panga, the broad-bladed, deadly African machete. It was a weapon originally designed for use in sugar fields or for clearing jungles. More recently it had become a lethal weapon, responsible for thousands of horrific deaths and punishment amputations on the continent.

What made it even worse was the appearance of the man who was brandishing the weapon. His face was horribly disfigured, burned and melted, and Flynn knew this was the man who had been caught up in the explosion caused by Boone's bullet exploding a fuel barrel that the man had been seeking cover behind. He had been blown into the creek where Flynn assumed he had perished. Clearly he had survived, obviously to be deformed for the rest of his life.

The panga was held high and was slicing down at Flynn. Had it caught him before he'd turned, his head would have been sliced cleanly open.

But Flynn had caught Aleef's look, turned, leapt backwards as the panga came down and just missed him, leaving the burned man wide open for a millisecond, an opportunity that Flynn did not miss.

He shot him in the chest. The shot was hurried, and Flynn shot slightly high, the bullet breaking the man's collar bone and spinning him away like a top. The second shot was even higher and removed most of the left side of his face.

Flynn stood there for a moment, controlling his breathing, then he looked at Aleef, who emitted a little squeak.

Flynn stepped over the dead men at his feet and gestured for Aleef to go ahead of him out of the door. Flynn came up behind him, slammed him up against the wall and frisked him quickly, expertly, getting close to the man, inhaling the cheap aftershave of which he stank.

'You're a very bad man,' Flynn breathed into Aleef's ear.

'I'm just a businessman. Who are you, what is this?'

'Who else is here?' Flynn demanded, ignoring Aleef.

'No one.'

Flynn jammed the barrel of the Glock hard into Aleef's spine at the small of his back. 'Truth?'

'Honestly.'

Flynn gripped Aleef's jacket collar and steered him out of the room into the hallway. He checked the room to the left, found a basic kitchen and a bathroom/toilet beyond. Then he manhandled Aleef into the next room, directly opposite the living room.

It was empty.

Flynn switched on the light with the butt of the Glock, a low wattage bulb dangling from a frayed length of wire in the middle of the ceiling.

A thin single size mattress was on the floor in one corner of the room with a grimy, bloodstained sheet covering it. Flynn glanced around quickly and saw a small pile of bloody bandages and dressings discarded in another corner, flies buzzing around them. In another corner was clothing, a rolled up shirt and trousers and a pair of sandals. Next to the mattress was a plastic tray containing some crockery and cutlery, and next to that was a metal frame on wheels that held up an empty saline drip bag. Two other empty drip bags were in a bin, together with syringes and their packages. There was also a hessian prayer mat on the floor.

Flynn computed all this, putting together everything he knew and had witnessed, everything he'd read.

'Where is he?' Flynn asked Aleef.

'Who?' Aleef responded innocently.

Flynn buried the muzzle of the Glock into Aleef's spine.

'You know who.'

'I . . . don't know . . . I don't know what you're talking about . . . look, please allow me to go . . . I don't know what this is about. I haven't done anything.'

Flynn backed off a step then brutally side-footed the back of Aleef's right knee, causing the leg to fold and the man to drop on to his knees with a cry. Flynn pressed the gun into the back of Aleef's head.

'I said where is he?'

'Gone . . . he's gone.'

'Gone where?'

'I don't know, sir, I don't know,' Aleef wailed.

Flynn forced him down to the floor, so the side of his head was crushed against the rough surface of the prayer mat.

'Where is he?' Flynn asked again, his instinct telling him that this mission of revenge for the death of a friend might have become something much more serious on a much larger scale.

'Gone, gone,' Aleef said, tears welling up in his eyes.

'Who is gone? What is his name?'

'Akram . . . Jamil Akram,' Aleef confirmed.

'And where has he gone?'

'To finish what he started.'

SIXTEEN

'Suited and booted and now he's in the traps with a gaoler watching over him. He's asked for the duty solicitor, so we'll just wait for him to land.'

Henry nodded as Rik explained this and they walked down the dingy corridor towards the exit that would take them to the underground police garage.

'Did he say anything?'

'No, just blubbered a lot.'

Henry pushed the door and the detectives walked out into the chilly garage. They made their way across to the plain Astra that had been used by PC Driver. Henry now had the key and clicked the remote to unlock it. As they approached the car they were pulling on latex gloves. Henry lifted the hatchback under which they had found the trussed up girl and looked at the items remaining. The girl was now in hospital being looked after by a policewoman, her parents on the way to the station. She was a mess.

In the hatchback was a Nike sports bag that had not been looked at yet. Other items in the boot, untouched as yet by the detectives, included a full face ski mask with eye holes, a pair of overalls, a pair of trainers and a roll of duct tape.

Henry's mouth turned down distastefully. 'What do we know about Driver?'

'Not that much yet,' Rik answered. 'Just recently transferred up from Wiltshire, apparently, posted straight to Poulton . . . apart from that, I don't know him. I suppose it'll be a morning job for accessing his HR file.'

'Not unless we knock up the HR manager.'

'True,' Rik concurred, liking the thought. 'How did the chief take the news?'

Whilst Rik had been booking the prisoner into custody, Henry had done his duty by informing the people who needed to know about things like a police constable being arrested on suspicion of rape and abduction. He'd phoned the divisional commanders of Blackpool and Northern divisions, the on-call ACC and the chief himself, all of whom had been tucked up in nice warm beds.

'Grumpy old man at being woken up. Like prodding a hibernating grizzly. But more irate at being told one of his finest had been arrested for such serious offences – but also pleased it might take us somewhere with the rape investigation. A real conflict of emotion.'

The two men looked from item to item in the hatchback, then Henry carefully unzipped the sports bag.

'He must have been getting out of these overalls when he was at the back of the car, when we couldn't see what he was doing,' Rik said.

'Which is why he only had half his uniform on. Caught in the act.' Henry hooked his forefinger on to the zip and gently pulled the sports bag open, peered in and shone his mini Maglite torch into it. 'Shit,' he said. He reached in and slowly extracted a long, fine silk scarf, held it up and then looked at Rik, who even in the crap garage lighting went noticeably pale.

'Trophy bag,' Rik gulped.

Henry nodded slowly. 'This looks incredibly like the scarf that Natalie Philips had around her neck on the photo her mum provided for us.'

'I know,' Rik whispered. Both men could have been sick there and then.

Henry's mobile rang. He slowly replaced the scarf back into the bag and answered it.

'Henry – you awake?' It was Karl Donaldson.

'I am now.'

'Good, can you speak, or are you . . . y'know?'

'I am just a bit busy, actually. Police work busy.'

'Henry – do you know what time it is?'

'Yeah, well as they say on TV, crime won't crack itself.'

'But you're a superintendent! Aren't you supposed to be tucked up, beddy-byes? You're not setting a good example.'

'Never have done . . . anyway, why're you still up? You've been living in this country long enough, surely you're not still suffering from jet-lag?'

'Funny guy, huh? Even us Yanks work late occasionally.'

'OK, banter over and out. What do you want?'

'That apartment those suicide bombers were using?'

'Apartment?' Henry said. 'That's a bit strong. Even calling it a flat is pushing it.'

'You know what I mean.'

'Just teasing.'

'You got any CSIs on call could do something for me?'

'At the flat? Hasn't it all been done?'

'Yep, at the flat.'

'When, now?'

'Yes, and you might need a plumber, too.'

'Karl – what the fuck are you talking about? It's late and I'm dealing with something unpleasant.'

'I wanna stick my fingers in a U-bend.'

'Why, exactly?'

Donaldson told him but he sounded like he was talking with his head in a bucket, and though Henry listened hard he only got half a tale. Irritably, Henry said, 'Where are you now?'

'M6 northbound, just passing Rugby.'

'Two hours away,' Henry calculated, even on empty roads and especially in Donaldson's hulking four-wheel drive monstrosity. Henry pondered a second, mulling logistics. 'Tell you what, head for my house and I'll meet you there. Get a couple of hours sleep, nothing's going to spoil in the meantime, and I'll arrange to meet a CSI at seven this morning. How does that sound?'

'Too lazy, but I'll go for it.'

At the same moment as Henry ended that call, Steve Flynn was making a call on his mobile phone to a number in the UK.

The phone in the bedroom rang out shrilly, but only the man in the bed stirred and reached out for it, almost knocking everything off the bedside cabinet in his grogginess. The woman next to him, his wife, turned over and dragged the duvet off him and continued to snore softly.

'Un-huh,' the man said.

'It's me, Steve Flynn – and don't you dare fucking hang up Jerry.'

The man in the bed, Detective Constable Jerry Tope, squinted at the bedside clock and muttered something which, though indecipherable, was clear in its meaning.

'I take it you're in bed,' Flynn said.

Tope gave an affirmative grunt and said, 'Whajjawan?'

Flynn managed a slight grin. 'Get yourself out of there, away from the warm clutches of your lovely missus, and get your brain working – I need to pick it.'

'And if I don't?'

'Just hand the phone over to Marina, and I'll have a little discussion with her.'

By that time, Tope had sat up and swung his legs out of bed, the phone to his right ear, his left hand scrunching his face into life.

'I can't talk to you, Flynn, you get me in shit,' Tope whined.

'If you don't talk to me, you'll be in real shit – personally and professionally, guaranteed.'

Tope glanced at the sleeping mound in the bed, exhaled wearily and said, 'Give us a second.'

He stood up and padded out of the bedroom in his PJs, his top tucked neatly into the bottoms, cursing the fact he had ever become involved in a cover-up with Flynn.

Way back they had been police buddies, colleagues verging on friends, in the halcyon days before Flynn fell out with the police hierarchy and became a pariah. After a particularly riotous night out in Preston, a Tuesday, on one of those nights known colloquially as 'Grab-a-granny', when it was alleged that slightly older and more experienced women were out on the razz and were easy prey, Tope, amazing himself, had done something very silly with a lady who *was* actually a grandmother – at the ripe old age of thirty-four. It was a sordid tryst that ended up with Tope pleading with Flynn to provide a cover story for him in order to put his highly suspicious wife off the scent. Flynn had done him the favour, saved the marriage and Tope had learned a very salutary lesson.

What neither man expected was that Flynn would eventually use this piece of knowledge to prise information out of Tope after leaving the police. Flynn had only done this on a couple of desperate occasions and, in truth, got no joy from doing it. But it was certainly handy to have a lever on someone like Tope who worked as a DC on the Intelligence Unit, which gave him a position of great knowledge. It also helped that Tope was also a highly skilled interrogator of computers. A hacker, in other words.

'What is it?' Tope asked bluntly, sitting down heavily on the settee in the lounge.

'Serious stuff. I need some information.'

'I will lose my fucking job,' Tope hissed. He looked around to check he wasn't being watched by the surveillance branch.

'Not on this one, you won't. This time it's commendations all round.'

'Not with you, Steve.' Tope's voice rose towards hysterical.

'OK – how does this grab you as an opener? Where is Jamil Akram?'

The phone went silent as Tope digested this. 'Who?'

'Don't fuck with me, Jerry, or I'll catch the next flight to Blackpool and come knocking on your door.'

'I don't know where he is.'

'Does anybody?'

'I wouldn't know, would I?'

'He managed to get out of the UK and disappear, didn't he?'

'Common knowledge.'

'After he'd set up two stupid lads as suicide bombers.'

'If you say so.'

'I do. Look, I'm not screwing around here,' Flynn growled. 'What would you say if I told you I knew where he'd run to, where he was less than forty-eight hours ago and where he probably is now?'

'I'd say talk to Henry Christie.'

'That twat?'

'First name that came to mind . . . er . . . er . . . yes, him. If you purport to know so much, you'll know he had some serious involvement with one of the suicide bombers. He's a good port of call.'

Flynn closed his eyes in despair. Being told to speak to Henry Christie was like being told to stuff razor blades into his mouth – painful. Ever since he had left the cops under a cloud of suspicion, Flynn had harboured a festering dislike and distrust of Henry, who he saw as the person who'd pushed him out of the job. Not that Flynn really had evidence to back that up, but Henry was a good target for his ire.

'Give me his number.'

Tope did so and Flynn ended the call.

Flynn was still in the bedroom of the house in Banjul. Four dead men lay in spreading pools of blood in the living area and Aleef, the middleman, sat shaking in one corner of the room, his face a bruised, swollen and bloody mess. He nursed his left hand, the little finger of which had been bent backwards and snapped like a dry twig by Flynn. He had been prepared to go for every single finger, one at a time, but Aleef had screamed, pleaded for mercy and promised to tell him everything he knew. Just let him live.

Flynn turned slowly back to him like the devil and Aleef whimpered under his gaze.

Over three thousand miles to the north of Flynn's position, a communications operative/intelligence analyst based at the government listening station, GCHQ, in Gloucestershire sat back in his comfortable chair and removed his earphones. He held up a finger and signalled to his supervisor, who rushed down from her raised dais and leaned over his shoulder.

'What've you got?' she asked.

Interview room one. Henry and Rik sat on one side of the bolted down table. On the opposite side sat Driver and the duty solicitor. The audio and video tapes were running, the camera recording the interview was fitted high in one corner of the room, protected by a fine mesh grill. Rik had done the introductions and made it clear that the interview was being carried out at this time of day with the consent of the accused and his solicitor.

Henry watched this introductory phase. His mobile phone was in his jeans pocket. It vibrated. He removed it and surreptitiously checked it, but the caller ID said, 'Unknown number'.

He frowned, slid it back, then focused on what was being said, before remembering he'd told Alison he'd be home by now.

Rik folded his arms. 'You know why you've been arrested, you've agreed to talk to us; what would you like to say?'

Driver was in the spacious zoot suit, the billowing paper forensic suit and slippers, provided for him after his clothing had been seized. He sat with his hands clasped between his thighs, rocking slightly, a hunted expression in his eyes.

'No doubt you've found it,' he said.

'Found what?'

'The scarf.'

'Which scarf?'

'The one in the holdall.'

'You need to explain its significance,' Rik said, revealing nothing. It was always better to let the prisoner do the talking. Let them fill in their own gaps.

'It's the one I took from Natalie Philips.'

There was a beat. Henry's arse twitched. Rik said, 'Go on.'

Driver shrugged pathetically, beaten and knowing it. 'I was on a corrie run –' he uttered a little snort – 'I saw her sitting on the kerb, carrying her shoes, barefoot.' He sounded wistful. 'She looked upset. I stopped to see if I could help her, y'know, me being a cop and all that.'

Henry's chest cavity seemed to tighten up as if a corkscrew was winding his insides around. His phone vibrated again.

'Anyway, she got in the car. I said I'd take her home.' Driver's voice was now monotone and emotionless. 'I knew I was going to rape her.'

Silence in the room.

'And after I raped her, I knew I had to kill her. You see,' he raised his face as though he was explaining something simple and straightforward, 'she was the only one who knew I was a cop. That's why she had to die. The rest didn't know – like her tonight. She wouldn't have known I was a police officer. Change of clothing. Plain car. Radio off. Mask on.' He tapped his nose conspiratorially and Henry had to stop himself from flying across the table and beating the little shit to a messy pulp.

'How many more are we talking about?' Rik asked.

'Seventeen.'

Flynn looked at his phone angrily, then at the still cowering Aleef, nursing his finger, now swollen to tennis ball size around the joint.

'So what happened?' Flynn said.

'I need medical attention,' Aleef bleated.

'What happened?' Flynn ignored the plea. 'Why did your men come after Boone?'

'They are not my men.'

'Who gives a fuck whose men they are?' He stepped across the room, towering over Aleef, who pressed himself back against the wall. 'Tell me what happened.'

'Boone . . . I hired him on behalf of someone else, to take someone up to the Canary Islands.'

Flynn held up a hand. 'Just . . . just stop there. Tell me straight or I'll get very upset with you. Straight is the only way you have any chance of surviving.'

'I'm just a middleman,' he wailed.

'So you keep telling me.' Flynn shoved the muzzle of the Glock into Aleef's inner right thigh, angled it at forty-five degrees against the muscle. 'Femoral artery,' he said, looking directly into Aleef's tearful eyes. 'I shoot, you'll bleed to death within minutes. You'll feel your life being sucked out of you. Do you want that? Are you a religious man?' Flynn could smell the sweat of fear pulsating from Aleef. 'No, I didn't think so, except when it suits, I'll bet. Going to heaven's not on your agenda, is it?'

'You'll kill me anyway, just like you killed them.'

'I saw those men kill my friend, that's the difference here. Then again, if I find out you sent them . . .'

'I didn't,' he blabbered. 'I swear I did not . . .'

'Then what happened?'

'Boone came back for more money, to my office. He'd found out who the passenger was and wanted danger money, plus ten thousand dollars extra, or he would be going to the police.'

'And . . .?'

'I could not afford that, but that wasn't the problem. His problem was that one of those men –' he pointed to the heap of bodies in the living room – 'was in the back office, listening. Boone only just got out of my office alive and they all went after him.'

'So who are those men? Who do they work for?'

Aleef shrugged helplessly. 'I'm just a middleman. I was asked to get a man from A to B and I found Boone to do it for me. I knew he took people and drugs, and his reputation was as good as any other. He just got greedy.'

'Where is your office?'

'Why?'

Flynn screwed the muzzle of the gun harder into Aleef's thigh.

'Just . . . just down the street.'

'How much money do you have stashed away there?'

'Why?'

'If you ask why again, I'll just shoot you.'

'Forty thousand, mixed currencies, sterling, dollars, local,' Aleef gabbled quickly.

'That'll do nicely.'

'What? You're going to steal from me?' he asked in disbelief.

'Every last sou, you bastard.' Flynn stood upright and gestured with the Glock. 'Up . . . lead the way . . . do anything stupid and I'll blow your spine apart.'

'Y–you're going to steal from me?'

'Your money or your life . . . so tell me, who did those guys work for?'

Aleef struggled to his feet. 'Al-Qaeda, I suppose.'

Flynn flicked open his mobile phone and redialled Henry Christie's number.

Karl Donaldson reached Knutsford services on the M6 with tiredness overwhelming him. He pulled off the motorway and bought himself a large black coffee laced with sugar, and a doughnut, hoping the sugar rush would push him onwards.

It hit his system quickly, probably giving a greater high than a bag of street-bought cocaine could have done. He jumped into the Jeep and was on the motorway a minute later, not really knowing what he was setting out to achieve.

Henry Christie was a dyed in the wool Rolling Stones fan. His first memory of the group was grainy black and white TV pictures of them on 60s' programmes such as *Ready Steady Go* and *Top of the Pops*. He'd been hooked by their music and shenanigans since about the age of six and been with them ever since, his constant companions through all his own ups and downs, loves and losses. The cover of their mid-seventies album, *It's Only Rock and Roll*, featured a painting of the Stones looking like they'd just staggered out of a night club at four in the morning, the worse for wear from every excess imaginable.

Which is how Henry felt when, two hours later, he and Rik emerged from the interview room after a marathon with a newly identified sex offender, Paul Driver, a police constable who used the position and freedom of movement that came with being a patrol officer to stalk, hunt, overpower and rape numerous women. His victims, all chosen at random, lone females walking home, had been subjected to brutal, sustained, degrading, terrifying attacks that would scar them for life.

Up until Henry inheriting the inquiry, only three victims were known about. Driver divulged fourteen more, all of them probably too scared to come forward. Nine of them in the Swindon area of Wiltshire.

Henry knew there would be even more.

Driver had been a cunning predator and had prepared himself for each attack in terms of clothing, a hood, gloves and even condoms. The detectives learned that he timed his attacks to take place every four weeks, to coincide with his shift system, the week when he would be on nights.

He used the correspondence run from Poulton to Blackpool in the early part of the week to search for victims. These were at times when the police, generally, were less busy and he could use his down time to attack – but not in his own division, always in Blackpool.

The reason why Natalie's attack had been out of sequence was that Driver had volunteered to cover for a colleague that night.

Driver had still done the correspondence run, but it hadn't been on his agenda to commit a crime that night.

He still took the opportunity to have a cruise around Blackpool and in so doing had encountered Natalie sitting on a kerb, obviously upset, bawling her eyes out, wiping away the tears with her silk scarf.

Driver stopped like a cop should have done.

His usual MO was to spot potential victims, park up in the plain car, get out of his uniform – under which he wore his anti-forensic clothing – pull on his gloves and mask, stalk, then drag the girl away to rape her.

But Natalie was out of sequence, unplanned, but impossible to turn down.

'I wasn't going to do anything, just be a good cop,' he told Henry and Rik. 'Help her, take her home . . . let comms know what I was doing . . . as you would, but once she was in the car, it all changed and I knew I had to have her.'

Henry said, 'What did she say to you?'

He blew out his cheeks. 'That she'd fallen out with her boyfriend, even after she'd had sex with him, and an older man, too . . . and let him watch . . . Jeez, that news went straight to my cock!' He laughed perversely. 'Even cut his hair for him,' he added.

Henry saw Rik grip the edge of the table. Henry touched his arm.

'Then it was a haze. Always is – and next thing I knew, I was holding her down and I'd done it and she was squirming. Problem was she knew I was a cop. I was still in uniform. I was in a cop car. I mean, how brilliant was that? She was in the car, she was wearing a skirt right up to her fanny, and she expected me not to do anything?' Driver's voice was incredulous.

'You are a police officer,' Henry said stonily.

'And . . .?'

'I think you know the "and".'

'Anyhow,' Driver stretched and screwed up his face, 'I had to kill her, just self-protection, really. Couldn't afford for her to go blabbing. The others, you see, never knew I was a cop, but she did. She shouldn't have been there. It was all her fault,' he rationalized, and if Henry hadn't realized it before, he realized it at that point: he was in the presence of a psychopath who would never legally set foot outside some sort of secure unit for the rest of his life. If Henry did his job right – and that's what he fully intended to do.

Henry said, 'Did she scratch you?'

'Oh yeah, fought like a cat.' Driver tilted his head and Henry saw four fingernail trails, now faded somewhat, in the skin of Driver's neck, just under his left ear. He recalled how, at the scene, Driver, playing the part of the deeply affected cop who'd stumbled on a murder, had been rubbing his neck with his hand in a gesture that was obviously part act and which in reality was just to cover up his injury.

'What about DNA?' Rik had asked. Driver shrugged. 'You're on the database, every cop is. Sooner or later . . .'

Driver shook his head. 'Lancashire haven't got my DNA yet, since I transferred in from Wiltshire.'

'They would have eventually.'

'A bridge I'd cross when I got to it,' Driver said. 'Like I did when I was in Wiltshire.' He grinned smugly. 'It was easy enough to substitute someone else's and I would have found a way of doing it. I just would.'

Psychopath equals deceiver, equals manipulator, equals planner, equals problem solver, equals dangerous, Henry thought.

It was at Henry's insistence that the interview was terminated, much to the relief of the ashen-faced duty solicitor, clearly out of his depth, who must have been rueing being on that night's call-out rota. He could not have imagined he would end up representing a monster.

When Driver was back in his cell and under supervision, Henry and Rik leaned on the custody desk, both exhausted.

'Result?' Rik said. 'And I hold my hand up about Carter.'

Henry shrugged wearily. 'Result – but a million miles away from what we – I – thought had happened to her. I was sure she'd been murdered by an Islamic fundamentalist. I just thought that was it. But I'm still not completely clear on what went on there.'

'We might never know.'

'But we have to find out,' Henry said, knowing that side of the investigation still needed sorting – Natalie's relationship with Zahid Sadiq and Jamil Akram. He yawned, his brain now officially mushed out. He checked his watch and grunted. Almost six. 'Talk about goosed.'

'Mm. Where do we go from here?'

'Let's make sure he gets his rest quota. That'll give us some time to get our heads together and sort everything out, including speaking to Wiltshire about any undetected rapes down there. By teatime we'll have enough to charge him and get him to court for a three day lie down. If we plan it carefully, we'll nail the bastard to the wall.' He scratched his head, feeling gritty.

Rik was nodding and yawning.

Once again, Henry's phone rang. This time he answered it.

'Henry? It's Karl. You're not at home?'

'No, still at work. Blackpool nick.'

'Good. I can't sleep. Did you manage a CSI – and a plumber?'

'No, sorry, pal. I'll turn out a CSI now. Got a bit distracted. As for a plumber, what do you need?' Henry's eyes locked on to the man in blue overalls just entering the custody suite, whistling tunelessly. He wasn't sure of the man's official job title, but he was basically the odd-job man for the station, who carried out minor bits of decorating, cleaning, electrical and plumbing repair work. He was a janitor, in other words, and of course went under the nickname of Hong Kong, derived from Hong Kong Phooey, the police janitor in the cartoon Henry used to watch years ago. The janitor in that was actually a dog.

'Not much really . . . a handyman might suffice,' Donaldson said. 'Equipped with things for loosening bolts, I guess.'

'Spanners, wrenches, that sort of thing?'

'Those are the ones.'

'I'll see what I can rustle up,' Henry said, trying to hide the miserable tone of his voice. Bed was what he needed, not rooting about in some pipework underneath a sink. DIY had never been his strong point, much to Kate's chagrin. She was far better at it than him.

Rik had been listening. 'Want some help on that?' he asked. 'I don't think I could sleep right now, a bit adrenaline fuelled.'

Henry folded his phone. 'Any good with a monkey wrench?'

SEVENTEEN

Flynn hadn't meant to kill Aleef, but his hand had been forced.

Aleef led him to the first floor office he used as a base. It was basic, but very secure, with a thick steel, multi-locked door that took ages for the dithering Aleef to unlock, especially with his broken finger.

Flynn stood behind him, watchful and wary, not trusting him at all, and wanted to get moving. They had left the four bodies in the house, locked behind them, all the window blinds fastened as tightly as possible. It would not be long before decomposition began in the African heat, but at least the locked windows and doors would prevent the smell getting out for a while longer. Flynn didn't envy the person who would have to kick down the door and fight through a swarm of bluebottles.

Eventually they entered the office. Again, basic. Large wooden desk, a big comfy chair for Aleef and a plastic one for the client. Behind the desk, bracketed to the wall, stood the safe.

'Open it,' Flynn said, propelling Aleef forwards. He stumbled down in front of it, and dabbed a finger from his uninjured hand on the digital keypad, then turned the handle as it beeped. Flynn heard the heavy locking mechanism scrape back. Aleef turned to Flynn, despair on his face and in his body language at the prospect of losing his money.

'Who are you? Who are you who will leave me a pauper?' He sounded like a character from Dickens.

'That would be telling. Best you don't know.' He jerked the Glock. 'Carry on.' Aleef bent to the task of pulling open the safe. 'When did he leave?' Flynn asked.

'Who, sir?'

'You know who I'm talking about.'

'Ahh, that man. Maybe two days ago.'

'Did you arrange his travel?'

'Yes, sir.'

'How did he travel?'

'Air.'

'From where to where?'

'Banjul to Gatwick, England.'

'He just flew? Just like that?'

'Yes – on a false passport.'

'Also arranged by you?'

'I am a fixer,' Aleef said humbly.

'Actually, you are as much of a terrorist as him.'

'I'm a businessman,' he protested. Aleef pulled down the handle with a metallic clang and eased open the safe door. He came slightly upright and showed Flynn the contents: stack upon stack of cash, many currencies, all denominations, all carefully bound.

'That is what Mr Boone wanted.'

'Stand away,' Flynn said.

Aleef edged back a few inches, his eyes jittery. Next to the desk was a waste paper basket lined with a supermarket carrier bag. Flynn pulled the bag out with his left hand, placed it on the desk, took hold of its base and tipped the contents on to the floor. He handed the bag to Aleef.

'Fill it – dollars and sterling only.'

Colour seeped from Aleef's face. 'That is virtually all of my money.'

'Eggs in one basket,' Flynn winked. 'Now fucking fill the bag.' He pointed the gun at Aleef's groin.

Aleef swallowed and got to the task, half-filling the bag with many blocks of carefully counted money.

'How much?' Flynn asked.

'Thirty-two thousand US dollars, four thousand sterling.'

'Not even close to the value of a man's life,' Flynn muttered.

'His choice, not mine.'

Aleef suddenly swung the bag at Flynn, let go of the handle and it flew towards him, the money inside helping to propel it. Flynn ducked instinctively. Aleef's right hand came up holding a small calibre gun. Flynn realized that the weapon must have been concealed in the safe, obviously for moments like this, and Aleef had managed to palm it without Flynn seeing it. Sneaky bastard, Flynn thought.

But as sneaky and underhand as he was, he was slow and Flynn had not relaxed enough for someone like Aleef to get the better of him. As soon as he saw the gun moving, the Glock jerked up and two bullets from it slammed into Aleef's chest, knocking him back against the wall. He slithered down it, dead.

Flynn picked up the carrier bag, slammed the safe shut with a kick, and left the office after locking it up.

Within minutes he was back at the place where Boone's Land Cruiser had been parked, expecting to find it gone, but Michelle was still there, having ignored his instructions. Just as he knew she would. He climbed into the passenger seat and they exchanged a look.

'Just get back to the boat,' Flynn said, 'no questions.'

She nodded, started the engine.

'It might be better for you to lie low for a while. Can you do that?'

She nodded again. 'I have family in Sierra Leone. I can go there by bus.'

'What about by boat? Boone said you were a natural sailor. Can you pilot the boat?'

'He taught me.'

'On the ocean?'

'On the ocean,' she confirmed.

'Good – take the boat. It would be a crime not to.'

'But I don't have money. I couldn't afford to.'

'You do now.' Flynn held up the carrier bag.

Henry, Rik, Donaldson and a CSI entered the flat in Blackpool that had been used by Zahid Sadiq and Rashid Rahman, and visited by Jamil Akram, the bomb-maker. The landlord, awakened at such an early hour, had been surprisingly cooperative, and let the detectives in again, not saying a word. He still had not managed to re-let it, nor had he received any word about getting the contents back from MI5. He let them in and said he was going back to bed and not to bother him unless absolutely necessary. He also reconfirmed that no one had been in or used the flat since their last visit.

Once inside, Henry looked expectantly at Donaldson.

'Follow me,' he said. He led them towards the bathroom, a fairly disgusting room consisting of toilet, wash basin and shower cubicle, all tiled, but the grout stained with black mildew. It was just about big enough for Donaldson to step into and turn around. He slid his hand into his back pocket and extracted a folded sheet of paper which he opened out. 'I got the lovely Mr Beckham to fax this to me, obviously thinking he had nothing to lose by doing so.' He handed the sheet to Henry. 'An itemized list of property seized by his forensic team from this bathroom.'

Henry scanned the very short list. Two hand towels, a bar of soap, a roll-on deodorant, a shower mat. Henry shook his head, puzzled.'What's missing?' Donaldson said.

Henry looked blankly at his friend. He was too tired. 'Just tell me.'

'Other than soap, no toiletries.'

Henry's expression was still blank.

Donaldson sighed. 'What do you have next to your sink at home?'

Henry could have fallen asleep standing up. 'Like I said, just—'

'OK, I'll tell you. Shaving foam or gel and a razor, yeah?'

'Maybe they used an electric one.'

'Not in the complete inventory for the rest of the flat.' He tapped his back pocket. 'Got it here.'

'What are you getting at?' Henry's shoulders had sagged.

'Did you bring a wrench?'

'I've got it,' Rik said. He was behind Henry, who said, 'Even got the monkey.'

Rik held up a large adjustable wrench that Henry had acquired from the police station janitor.

'Gimme.' Donaldson took it from him, turned to the sink and went on to his knees in front of it. The pipe down from the plughole dropped into a plastic U-bend with large plastic nuts that were capable of being loosened by hand. They unscrewed easily after the first use of force and a moment later Donaldson stood up with the complete U-bend in his hands. He fitted the plug into the sink and then emptied the contents of the U-bend into it.

The water in it had obviously been standing for about a fort-night and was scummy and stinky.

'There,' he declared proudly, 'what do you think?'

Henry, Rik and the CSI crammed into the bathroom to have a look.

'Water. From a U-bend. What am I missing here?' Henry said.

Donaldson reached into his other back jeans pocket and pulled out four crumpled photographs.

Zahid Sadiq and Rashid Rahman. Two students prepared to give their lives for a highly suspect cause. There were two shots of Rahman: one that Donaldson had downloaded from the video, the other a close-up of his face on the mortuary slab after having been shot on the motorway. And two of Sadiq: a college photo-graph and a mug shot taken on his arrest.

'What's not in here?' Donaldson indicated the room.

'Shaving gear,' Henry said, as it started to dawn on him.

'What was not on their faces or heads when we got to them? Me in town, you on the motorway.' Donaldson held up the photographs for them to see.

Henry felt a lurch inside him. 'They were clean-shaven.'

'Exactly,' Donaldson proclaimed. 'Ready to be received into heaven. In fact, their whole bodies were clean-shaven.'

Henry thought back to Rahman's corpse in the mortuary. No pubic hair, no head hair, no armpit hair, legs shaved, face smooth.

Donaldson's eyes were wild.

But Henry said, 'That's not to say they didn't shave here. They could have done it in the shower.'

'I'll wager a million dollars of FBI money we won't find a trace of anything down that shower drain either. Which is where you come in.' He shot a look at the CSI, who nodded, knowing what his job was.

'Get on with it,' Henry said to the man, and he and Donaldson reversed out of the shower room into the living area. 'What are you saying?' Henry asked his friend.

'That one way of spotting a potential male suicide bomber is the lack of facial hair. And something else has been bugging me about that morning, even though I didn't really get a grip of it until now. This place was under police surveillance from quite early on. When I saw Sadiq walking down the promenade it was simply assumed that somehow he had either been out before the cops arrived to watch him, or he'd managed to get out undetected.' Donaldson shook his head. 'Even as ineffective as Lancashire Constabulary are, I say, to use one of your words – bollocks! It was never even thought through. The car they were supposed to be using was outside, tick! So they musta been here, tick! Assumptions, ass bites.'

'You're saying they weren't even here that morning?'

'This might well be their flat, but you're right. They prepared themselves and set off from somewhere else, which means they had a hidey-hole of their own elsewhere and that someone else was involved in this.'

There was a crash and cracking noise from the bathroom, then the CSI came out bearing the drainage pipe from underneath the shower tray. 'Nothing down here but scum. No trace of hairs.'

'And there would be a lot of hair,' Rik said.

Henry turned on Donaldson and said, 'How many musketeers are there?'

Puzzled, the American said, 'Three, I guess.'

'Exactly.' Henry, now rejuvenated, got out his mobile phone and opened it, at which moment it rang.

Flynn was in the wheelhouse of *Faye2*, heading out to sea from the estuary of the Gambia River. Fast.

'What?' Henry said, screwing up his face. 'Who?'

'Flynn, Steve Flynn.'

'What the hell are you calling me for? And at this time of

day?' Henry had little time for the man. Their history was rocky to say the least.

'That's not very nice,' Flynn said. He took a swig of the mug of tea he'd prepared, which tasted amazing in the present circumstances.

'I'm busy.'

'Got something for you.'

'If you're phoning to tell me you never stole that million quid – wrong time, wrong bloke.' Henry, now standing on the landing outside the flat, gave Donaldson a weary look, then said, 'Did you try to phone me earlier?'

'Yup.'

'Why? I'm not interested in anything you might have to say.'

'In that case I'll hang up, find someone who does want to listen, and make you look stupid into the bargain.'

'Look, Flynn, what the hell d'you want? I am seriously busy here.'

'Jamil Akram,' Flynn stated. Besides the mug of tea, he had made himself a couple of slices of thick toast coated in butter and marmalade. He folded half a slice into his mouth.

'What? Say that again.'

'You heard,' Flynn said through a mouthful of toast.

'Speak, now,' Henry said, and mouthed '*Jamil Akram*' to Donaldson.

'I know where he's been hiding out – and I know he isn't there any more.'

Flynn set the autopilot, slid off the seat and walked on to the rear deck of *Faye2,* sat on the fighting chair, mug in one hand, toast in the other, mobile phone clamped between his shoulder and ear.

'What? How do you know?' Henry asked.

'I think you should call me back,' Flynn said. 'Costing me money, this.'

'No – I don't want to lose the connection. I'll reimburse you.'

'That's what I like to hear.'

'Where are you? Can we speak face to face?'

'Only if you can get to the Atlantic Ocean, eight miles west of the Gambia.'

'Steve – Karl Donaldson's here. You know him, the FBI guy?'

'The Yank, yeah.' Flynn had met Donaldson the previous year

when all three of their paths crossed in the village of Kendleton when they found themselves in the middle of a gangster war zone.

'I'm going to put my phone on speaker, so he can hear too. He has a vested interest.'

'Anybody else there?' Flynn said. 'Not sure I want anyone else listening in.'

'Just me and him,' Henry lied. 'Trust me.'

Flynn guffawed and tossed his toast crust into the wake being churned up by the boat.

Henry pressed the speaker button and held the phone between himself and Donaldson.

'Steve – it's me, Karl Donaldson. How ya doing?'

'How do, buddy?'

'Whatcha got?'

'Just the basics, OK? And no nooky questions from you lot, OK? When you guys came across Akram, he had started his journey from the Gambia. After you screwed up his plans he returned here via Gran Canaria and Mauritania, where he recuperated from the gunshot.'

'How did he get off Gran Canaria?' Donaldson asked.

'Private airstrip north of Las Palmas, to Mauritania, then by sea to the Gambia where he holed up.'

The line suddenly went dead.

'Steve!' Henry said. 'Steve, fuck!'

'Still here,' Flynn's voice came back.

'How do you know all this?' Donaldson asked.

'Nooky question . . . no time for that, but there is something you need to know. He's—'

The line went dead again

'Oh great,' Henry uttered.

'Back again,' Flynn said.

'He's what?' Donaldson cut in.

'He's gone back to finish what he started. Check recent flights into Gatwick from the Gambia and a passport by the name of Masud Aziz. Say in the last two days. And that's as much as I know, take it or leave it. So watch your arses because he's one dangerous fucker. Do with that what you will. You've got a dangerous terrorist back on your patch.'

Flynn ended the call. He finished his tea and toast, then picked up the Glock and threw it out of the boat, together with the keys for Aleef's office. Then he went back to the wheel, checked the autopilot settings, and tried to relax.

The GCHQ operative who had picked up the mention of Jamil Akram in the conversation between Flynn and Jerry Tope had been waiting for more from Flynn's mobile number. And, when it came, he picked up the secure landline phone next to him which was programmed to automatically dial a number so that he could pass on anything further.

Martin Beckham thanked him for the information, ended the call and redialled another number that was answered immediately.

'Do we have any resources in the north of England, Lancashire in particular?'

The question was directed to MI5's operations manager who chuckled and said, 'Ironically, yes.'

'Why ironically?'

'We have an SAS unit training. The irony being they're on land owned by our good friend, Sir Hugo Marchmaine.'

'Ahh.' Beckham smiled. 'Are they ready to roll?'

'At a moment's notice, sir.'

When Beckham had finished briefing the ops manager, he hung up the phone and settled back into his bed. The figure next to him said sleepily, 'What's going on?'

'Nothing you need to know about. Now try to get back to sleep, Tom, my love.'

On the landing outside the tiny flat, Henry and Donaldson stared blankly at each other. Rik hovered close by.

Donaldson broke the silence. 'Where do we take it from here?'

'Talk to a murderer for a start,' Henry replied.

Ten minutes later Henry was entering the custody suite at Blackpool police station, Donaldson close behind. Henry walked straight past the custody officer into the cell complex.

Driver's cell door was open. A uniformed gaoler sat on a chair outside, keeping a suicide watch on the prisoner, who, still in the billowy forensic suit, was sitting up on the bench bed. The gaoler stood up, but Henry waved him back down, and stepped into the cell.

Driver looked up, his eyes raw. 'Come to interview me in a cell?' he dared. 'Out of order, isn't it?'

'I want to clear something up. Where exactly did you pick up Natalie Philips?'

'I don't know. I picked her up and killed her, isn't that enough?'

'Where, exactly, did you find her in the first place?' Henry insisted.

Driver held a thumb and forefinger to the bridge of his nose. 'I don't know. Somewhere just off the town centre. Not sure of the street name. I don't really know Blackpool that well.'

'If I showed you a street map, could you pinpoint it?'

'Maybe, why?'

'I think the time for you asking why is long gone, don't you?'

Driver glared insolently at Henry, then his expression altered slightly and he dropped his arrogance. 'Springfield Road,' he said.

Just on the northern edge of the town centre.

'And what exactly did she have to say about shaving her boyfriend?'

Driver shrugged. 'Dunno. Sounded sexy, though. Shaved him and his two mates, apparently.'

There was a street map underneath the custody officer's desk. Henry and Donaldson inspected it, Henry putting his finger on Springfield Road, which was about a quarter of a mile from where Donaldson had first spotted Sadiq on the prom, clean-shaven and ready to explode. It was at least a mile away from the flat further north that had been under police observation, the one Sadiq and Rahman were believed to have been in.

'She went with Sadiq to an address somewhere around here,' Henry said, his finger circling the street map. 'Had sex with him and Akram, then they ditched her after she shaved them from head to toe – is what I think. Which is when Driver found her.'

'OK,' Donaldson said. 'So they had access to the apartment under surveillance, but they sure as hell did not prepare for their last journey there.'

'Bingo,' Henry said. 'You said your insider found out there were three of them, not two – which fits. They used someone else's flat to prepare, and to have sex with Natalie.' He mulled it over, his mind suddenly alive again. 'We caught two of them, and you almost nailed Akram, which put a spanner in their works and obviously bomber number three was aborted.'

'And if what Flynn says is true, that Akram has come back to finish what he started, then there will be another one of them waiting for him. Akram himself won't be the third one, because he's the one who sends others to their deaths. So we were right – it's not over. He could be back in town right now, strapping explosives on to another poor schmuck. He needs to be there to push the buttons, metaphorically and literally.'

'Then again,' Henry said, 'we could be completely wrong.'

'I'd rather have egg off my face, H.'

'Me too,' Henry agreed. Henry led Donaldson back through the station corridors to Rik Dean's office, both wondering how best to come at the problem. Rik was in his office, and so was an exhausted looking Chief Constable Robert Fanshaw-Bayley. He had felt it his duty to turn out because of PC Driver's arrest.

'Morning, boss,' Henry said, his enthusiasm waning.

'And Mr Donaldson, too,' FB said. 'Sometimes I think you guys are joined at the hip. Anyhow, come in and grab a seat. DI Dean is just bringing me up to speed with PC Driver. Good arrest, Henry. Shame it's a cop. And you thought she might've been murdered by our terrorist friends.'

'Not a bad guess, based on the fluids inside her.'

'I know all that, but it wasn't them.'

'No, but I'm sure she was with them in the hours before her unfortunate meeting with PC Driver.'

FB nodded, then looked at Donaldson. 'And why are you back up in this neck of the woods?'

'Our terrorist friends.'

'Meaning?'

'Akram is back on UK soil,' he stated, then turned to Henry. 'I know this guy, Henry. I've been on his tail since 1988. He's here in town, I feel it. He finishes jobs, and whether it's today or next week or next month, a lot of people in Blackpool are going to die en masse, but my guess is sooner not later. He's a quick operator. It would have all been set up until we spoiled it. He won't hang around. He's a busy guy, lots of people to kill the world over, and, according to my sources, there is someone else involved.' He paused – a little too dramatically for FB, but it was to good effect – and turned to the chief, 'You need to launch a manhunt – sir.'

* * *

'Bastard laughed at me,' FB said. The chief had made a call to Beckham at MI5, while Henry and Donaldson went up to the canteen to order breakfast. He'd then climbed the stairs to the dining room, arriving red-faced and breathless and not a little annoyed.

A coffee and bacon sandwich were waiting for him and he dived on to them with gusto, tore a few mouthfuls from the sandwich, wiped his mouth and then declared Beckham's reaction to him.

Henry said, 'What did he actually say?'

'I told him we suspected another person was involved and he said, "What, three?" I said, "Yes, is that correct?" He said no, but wanted to know where my information had come from, and I told him I wasn't at liberty to reveal my source.' FB looked pointedly at Donaldson, who experienced an unsettling quiver through his intestines, and not from the look or the food. 'He laughed and said, "From a Yank, I'll bet" – then he clammed up.'

'Did you press him on that?' Donaldson asked. FB shook his head. Donaldson fell silent and Henry watched him working through this new piece of information.

'Two things,' Donaldson said at length. 'I think I've been fed a hook, line and sinker here. They ensure that Edina –' Donaldson held up his hand to stop FB's question ' – hang on a minute . . . they ensure Edina comes across some information that might be of value to me. In other words, they feed her what they think is false information to see if it surfaces somewhere, then they can backtrack it. And now it has surfaced –' he looked at FB – 'and now she'll need to really watch her ass. She thought they were on to her, now it's for sure.' He shook his head at the enormity of the situation.

'You said two things,' Henry reminded him.

'Oh yeah. Thing is, therefore, MI5 don't actually know there's a third party involved. They don't know. They made it up, like spies do, to feed the "enemy" – me – a line. *They don't know.* They knew about the two lads and about Akram, but they haven't yet worked out that they set off from another location, just assumed, like us all, they managed to get out of the flat without the cops seeing them. Shit like that happens. They didn't even check the drains. I'll bet their scientists haven't found any traces of explosives or anything in that flat – because the lads simply lived in it, but didn't operate from it.'

'Half-baked Intel,' FB spat. 'And if it hadn't been for you guys, Blackpool would have been blown to smithereens.'

Henry blinked. FB handing out accolades. Almost unheard of.

'It still might be,' Donaldson warned. 'Akram is back in town. Don't forget Rahman's video . . . "the big one is yet to come".' He exhaled. 'That said, I need to make a phone call and warn somebody.'

As Donaldson stuffed the remainder of his bacon sandwich into his mouth, swilled it down with his coffee and got to his feet, Henry remembered something. It was eight fifty and Mark Carter was due to answer his bail at nine.

'I need to move, too.' Then Henry realized something else that he'd nearly forgotten. He put a hand on Donaldson's sleeve. 'Come down to the front desk with me. Might be something, might not . . . make your call on the way.'

Hung over, Mark Carter sat disconsolately in the public waiting area of the police station. He rocked slightly whilst waiting for the chance to get to the front counter and present himself, but there was a queue and he wasn't in a hurry. His face fell when Henry appeared and beckoned him across. Henry opened the door for him and led him through to the custody office, booking him back into the system.

'Do I need a brief?' Mark asked when the question of his rights came up.

Henry said, 'No.'

'Can I trust you?'

'No. This way.' Henry steered him into an interview room and sat him down. 'We need to wait a minute for someone to arrive, then we need a serious talk.'

'Oh, it's just been fun up to now, has it?' Mark sneered.

'C'mon babe,' Donaldson whispered into his phone as he listened to it ring out.

Then a man's voice came on. 'Hello, Edina Marchmaine's phone . . . could I ask who's calling, please?' He had a southern accent and Donaldson was thrown slightly off kilter. Was this her husband, Hugo?

'Can I ask who that is, please? I'm calling to speak to Mrs Marchmaine.'

'My name is PC Archer from the Metropolitan Police.'

'What are you doing with Mrs Marchmaine's phone?'

'I'm sorry, sir, but you need to tell me who you are.'

Feeling this ping-pong could go on for a while, Donaldson said – with dread – 'An old friend . . . John Hancock from America,' a poor ad-lib, but all he could come up with there and then. 'We're due to have lunch today, Mrs Marchmaine and I.'

'I'm sorry,' the voice said, 'but Mrs Marchmaine has had an accident . . .'

'A bad one?'

'I'm sorry to say, sir, but she died in a fall from her balcony last night . . . you wouldn't happen to know—'

Donaldson hung up. He stepped aside as two office workers crushed past him on the stairwell. He had to grab the banister to steady himself and to swallow hard so as not to vomit.

EIGHTEEN

Henry could not understand what the look on Donaldson's face meant when he came into the interview room. He could see there was an expression of deep shock, but beyond that he didn't have a clue. Henry looked at his friend with his own brow deeply furrowed and asked, 'Are you OK?' Donaldson gave a quick shake of the head. Henry gave him a further – brief – puzzled look, then turned back to Mark Carter sitting at the interview room table.

'You guys know each other,' Henry said. Mark and Donaldson had met as a result of Mark having witnessed a hit and run that had involved an Italian mobster who was hiding out, and ultimately the FBI. 'I won't waste time on introductions.'

Henry expected Donaldson to offer at least a handshake, but nothing came.

Mark squinted at Henry, alcohol-induced pain behind his eyes, and said, 'Big guns, eh? Brought in the Yanks.'

'Mark, serious this,' Henry said. The lad shrugged insolently.

Donaldson, seemingly in his own world, leaned back on the wall. To Henry, he seemed to have lost his focus all of a sudden. Ten minutes before he'd been excitedly jigsawing the pieces together, now he looked as though he didn't give a damn. *Phone call*, Henry thought. He said, 'I'll get straight to it—'.

'Hang on,' Mark interrupted. 'First off, *do* I need a brief, or what? Second, I haven't heard you caution me. Third, why's the tape not turned on?'

There was a rapid blur of movement as Donaldson erupted without warning. He shot across the gap between him and the teenager, and before Henry could react, Mark was hoisted by his throat off the chair, which went over with a clatter, and found himself pinned hard against the back wall. Donaldson's face was less than an inch from Mark's, his features contorted with fury.

'Listen, fucker,' he growled, 'don't make the mistake of thinking this is anything like a police interview. It isn't. This is about terrorists who kill fuckers like you. So sit and answer these questions or I'll make a point of seeing you outside these walls, then you can answer my questions.'

Donaldson swung Mark back around, righted his chair for him and plonked him back down into it.

Mark rubbed his neck, gasping for air, having realized that Donaldson was something different and dangerous. Nervously Mark said, 'Look man, I didn't kill her. Honestly.'

Donaldson had returned to the wall, arms folded, as though he had expended no effort.

Henry, stunned for the moment, had not moved. He swallowed and wondered if he might sneak out of the room and submit his 'Intention to Retire' report before he lost his job. He cleared his throat. 'We know you didn't. This is about her, but in a different way. You need to answer everything I ask truthfully, even if you're repeating gossip, OK?'

Mark's eyes darted to Donaldson as though he expected another attack. 'Just ask, OK?' he said, keeping his eyes on the American, though addressing Henry.

'Remember you talked about Sadiq and Rahman being like the musketeers? What did you mean?'

'Uh, that they always hung around together. All for one, that kind of shit. All the time, in each other's pockets. Didn't even have much to do with any other of the Asian students. Always whispering and looking at the rest of us like we were shit.'

'But there were three musketeers.'

'There were three of them.'

'What do you mean?'

'Aramis, Porthos—'

'No you idiot – Sadiq, Rahman – and who? Do you mean there was another one of them?'

'Umar Ali.'

'Who's that?'

'Another student.'

'Why didn't you say anything about him last time we talked?'

'You didn't ask.'

Henry's right hand bunched into a fist, but it was himself he wanted to punch. In his experience, anyone talking unwillingly to the cops, as Mark was, doesn't just blab unless they're unloading guilt. No one tells you anything, was what he'd learned over the years, unless you ask them. Henry kicked himself for not being on the ball.

'Do you know anything about Umar Ali?'

'Just a student. On the same course as the other two, politics, or something crap like that . . . But you're wrong,' Mark finished.

'About what?'

'There were four musketeers . . . well, sort of.'

'How do you mean?' Henry glanced at Donaldson. Still brooding.

'Aramis, Porthos, Athos . . . and d'Artagnan. Well, he's a sort of apprentice musketeer, but he's one of them. Seen the films.'

'How does that relate to Sadiq and Rahman?'

'Well, there was Umar Ali, making three . . . and Mr Haq, making four.'

'Who the fuck's Mr Haq?'

'College lecturer. He was always knocking around with them – and Natalie. She was always sniffing around them, too. If you ask me, Mr Haq was a bit too friendly with her – and them – and other girls. They were well into girls, cos they were good-looking lads and a bit mysterious.'

'In what way?'

'Always whispering, like I said.'

'Do you know anything about Umar Ali?'

Mark shrugged, rubbed his throat, eyed Donaldson warily. 'Not much . . . but there is one thing . . . I heard he was living with Mr Haq. Not arse-bandits, like. A lodger, I think.'

A feeling of dread washed through Henry. 'Shit,' he said. 'Do you know where Haq lives?'

Mark looked uncomfortable. 'Might do.'

'Just tell me.'

'Just off the town centre. I once followed Natalie to his place.'

'Street name?' Henry demanded.

'No idea.'

Henry turned to Donaldson. 'Shit,' he said again.

'What?' Donaldson grunted.

Henry took out his mobile phone, half-expecting there not to be a signal. There was. He dialled Rik Dean's number. 'Where are you?' he demanded curtly of the DI.

'MIR, why?'

'Natalie Philips? When we spoke to her mum, there was mention of a teacher at college, yeah? Hadn't her mum found something in a diary? Do you remember? I should fucking know this, but I don't,' Henry said, infuriated at himself.

'I remember. It got actioned. One of the teams went to see him, but there was no reply and, as far as I know, no revisit as yet. What's the rush? You sound stressed up again.'

'Find the guy's name and address.'

Henry heard Rik shuffling through papers. 'Here it is . . . yep, no reply, revisit to be allocated. I think things have moved on a bit since, though.'

'Name and address,' Henry said.

'Salim.'

'*Salim?*'

'Yeah . . . Salim Haq, or Haq Salim . . . interchangeable, I suppose.'

'Address?'

'It's . . . it's on Springfield Road, Blackpool . . . ooh,' Rik said, realizing. 'Which is where Driver picked up Natalie from . . .'

'What number Springfield Road?'

On receiving the information they moved quickly into position. Eight men, all dressed similarly in zip-up wind jammers, jeans and trainers. All were unshaven, their hair unkempt, their age ranging from twenty-six to forty-two. They travelled in four vehicles, a Range Rover, Ford Galaxy, BMW 320 and an Audi A4, two in each. They were at the address within minutes. They were not overly concerned about having next to no time for preparation. This was how they were used to operating. Prep time was a luxury; nice when it happened, but unusual.

That did not mean they were reckless. They were a close-knit unit, knew precisely how each other worked, were fitter than Olympic decathletes and they trained constantly using highly stressful scenarios that were as close to reality as could be. Sometimes they were allowed to plan, sometimes they just acted, ad-libbed and relied on their extreme professionalism and disregard for human life.

They had spent the previous night on the Lancashire Moors and the pre-dawn hitting their practice target, a disused hospital in which a hostage was being held. The place was booby-trapped throughout with tripwires, beams, alarms and people waiting to kill them. Their only briefing had been that this was a hot operation and that the hostage had to be freed. They did this at 5.05 a.m., successfully killing every terrorist and releasing the hostage. Then, before they could debrief, they had received the call from London ordering them to move to Blackpool and be ready for a real event. Training was over.

They had no time for anything other than a drive-by reconnaissance, their orders being that they had to act immediately. They discussed their tactics on the move, then went for it, all checking the mug shot they had received on their mobile phones and the names of the other two people suspected to be inside.

Gaining access to the building was easy. It was a terraced house, divided into two large flats, ground and first floor. They were in the hallway, outside flat number one, when they pulled on their full-face ski masks and drew their weapons out of their clothing.

The explosives expert fitted the plastic explosive to the front door of the flat in such a way that the hinges and lock would be blasted off and the door itself would be left standing, ready for the boot down and entry of the first two members of the team. The explosion was muffled, hardly loud enough to hear, and then they were in.

Once inside, they worked in pairs, moving through the lounge area, then into the two bedrooms.

Not one of the three occupants had been roused by their entry.

They found their first target in bedroom number one, the man whose face they'd just looked at on their phones. He stirred groggily, lifted himself on to his elbows and was dead before he'd even had a chance to rub his eyes. A silenced double-tap to the head.

The other bedroom contained the other two men, sleeping in camp beds. These men were woken, thrown out of their beds and their names demanded of them.

Then they too were shot dead.

And that was it. Job done. And away.

Karl Donaldson stood mutely over the body of Jamil Akram, still in his bed. He rubbed his tired face and shook his head. Henry came up behind him and laid a hand on his shoulder. Donaldson turned to look at him. His eyes were sunken, red and watery, his skin tight.

'They wanted him and they got him,' the American growled.

'This is what you wanted, isn't it?' Henry nodded his head at the dead man.

'I wanted him my way, but we gave him to them.'

'What do you mean?'

Donaldson brandished his mobile phone in front of Henry's nose. 'They were listening to everything, one step ahead.'

'That much is obvious.'

'And they had a team ready and waiting.'

'SAS?'

'Probably, who knows? Another thing for sure, this will get well buried.'

'Already happening,' Henry said.

Donaldson exhaled. Henry thought he looked much older now. The extraordinarily good-looking college-boy Yank had somehow gone and been replaced by a more weary, haggard, battle-scarred individual.

'At least they were stopped,' Henry said.

Explosives, detonators, time switches, power sources, fishing vests and maps of the Blackpool resort had all been found in the apartment. A quick scan of the maps and some tourist information leaflets had pinpointed the target and the mission. It all pointed to the third musketeer, Umar Ali, strapping explosives to his body and walking into Blackpool Pleasure Beach, the huge amusement and ride site in Blackpool south. He would have joined a queue for the most popular attraction therein. Then, when the queue snaked into the covered waiting area in which about two hundred people would be patiently waiting their turn, he would have detonated himself. The name of the attraction was the Big One, one of Europe's biggest roller coasters; making sense of the claim made by Rashid Rahman that this was just the start of a campaign and that the big one was yet to come.

'What's that?' Donaldson nodded down at a book in Henry's hand.

Henry held up the exercise book in a clear plastic evidence bag. Flowers and love hearts were inscribed on the front and back covers, brightly coloured by an immature artist. There were names in the love hearts . . . *Zahid* . . . *Rashid* . . . *Lewis* . . . *Mark*.

'One of Natalie's school books,' Henry said sadly. 'There're others. And this.' Henry lifted up a supermarket carrier bag which looked like it contained a hairy animal of some sort, but closer inspection revealed that it was human head and body hair. 'This is where they prepared themselves.'

Donaldson didn't seem to hear. He held Henry's gaze, his eyes watering over. 'They killed her, Henry,' he said. 'No, scratch that . . . I got Edina killed.'

Two weeks later. Henry's mobile phone rang, ringtone *Miss You*. It was 4.30 a.m. He rolled over with an annoyed curse, thinking, 'This cannot be right. I'm not even at home. I'm on leave.' His fingers found it. He tapped on the bedside light and rose on to his elbow and answered it.

'Henry – you awake?' It was Donaldson.

Henry slumped back on to the bed. 'Am now.'

'Where the hell are you? There's no reply at your house.'

'Away . . . posh hotel in the Cotswolds.'

'Got access to a TV?'

'Got a friggin' bubble bath thing in the bathroom,' he said, unable to remember the word 'jacuzzi'.

'Switch it on – find a news channel.'

The line went dead. Henry sat up and found the TV remote, pointed, pressed and the 42 inch TV affixed to the wall opposite the king size bed flickered to life. He found a news channel, then sat bolt upright, with a 'Jeez' on his lips. The American President Barack Obama was standing at a podium. He switched up the volume slightly, the figure in the bed next to him stirring and sitting up groggily. 'Sorry, love,' Henry said.

'What is it?'

'Look at this,' Henry said.

Alison Marsh sat up and draped an arm across Henry's shoulder and focused on the TV at the announcement that American Special Forces had tracked down and killed Osama Bin Laden, leader of al-Qaeda. Henry watched, stunned by the news. Alison was less impressed.

'Does this happen a lot?' she asked after the cameras cut away from the president and back to the studio. 'People ringing you up at strange times?'

'Unfortunately, yes.' He slid his arm around her naked body and pulled her to him.

'Know what I want?' she said dreamily. 'I want to be wined and dined. I want to be loved in public. I want us to say, "Hey, here we are – a real couple", then take the flack and move on. I also want you to change that ringtone!'

Henry pulled her to him, one eye still a little tiny bit on the TV, and said, 'Somehow, I think the world as I know it has just changed.'

She grabbed the remote control out of his hand, switched off the TV, threw it aside and forced him down on to the bed, then climbed on top of him.